US *in* RUINS

ALSO BY RACHEL MOORE

The Library of Shadows

RACHEL MOORE

US in RUINS

HARPER
An Imprint of HarperCollinsPublishers

Library of Congress Control Number: 2023944774
ISBN 978-0-06-328468-5

Typography by Molly Fehr
24 25 26 27 28 LBC 5 4 3 2 1

First Edition

For anyone whose emotions feel too big,
and for Mom and Dad, who always make room for mine.

"Omnia vincit Amor: et nos cedamus Amori."
"Love conquers all; let us, too, yield to Love."
—Virgil, "Eclogue X"

"His is the hand I want to be holding when we become ruins."
—Catherine Avery Hannigan, *Relics of the Heart*

ITALY, 1932

Statues watched as Van descended into what was left of the Temple of Venus.

June warmth had settled over the Gulf of Naples, sticky enough to raise beads of sweat against the back of Van's neck, but down here, the air was cool and still. Trapped almost. His boots crunched against the stone floors, dust stirring as he lit the oil in his lamp.

Behind him, Atlas fumbled down the last few steps with his eye pressed against his camera. "The papers are going to love this."

The camera flashed, and Van blinked. It was a newfangled thing, all black and chrome with a pop-up bulb. Atlas carted it around everywhere, snapping photographs of the excavation's progress. Atlas Exploration Company couldn't exist without the deep pockets of Atlas's family, founders of the Metropolitan Museum of Ancient Art, and those deep pockets required proof that their prodigal son wasn't merely gallivanting around Italy.

In the dark of the temple, the echo of the flashbulb stained Van's vision. The wrinkle between his brows dug itself deeper. Terse, he said, "Watch it."

"Relax, pal," Atlas said with an echoing laugh. "It's not like it's booby trapped."

It wasn't anymore. Because Van had disarmed all the traps the first time he followed the hidden staircase leading him deep beneath the earth.

"And we need a picture to go underneath the headline."

Van snorted. "What headline?"

"'Young Scholars Resurrect the Lost City of Pompeii,'" Atlas said in his best broadcaster voice.

"More like 'Van Keane Discovers the Treasure of the Vase of Venus Aurelia.'"

"Where's my name in that headline? You wouldn't be here without me."

With his white-blond hair greased, his collared shirt neatly pressed, and that Zeiss camera strapped around his neck, Atlas was better at funding and documenting excavations than he was at participating in them.

Van ignored him and trekked deeper into the temple, following the chipped tiles where they led to a marble altar, flanked by stone sentries. Five legionaries had been carved from white marble, etched with dark veins. They each perched on engraved pedestals that bore a Latin inscription. Instead of a gladius, bows strapped across their backs with full quivers of stone arrows. Venus's guardians.

Atlas circled the guardians, weaving between their pedestals. "*Aqua, Ignis, Terra, Aura*, and *Mors*."

One for each of the elements, and a fifth: death. Where the rest were depicted as broad-shouldered soldiers in greaves and paludamenta, the statue of death's skeletal frame had been pierced through the chest with a carved arrow, right into a heart bleeding red.

Somehow, it watched Van, just a skull with empty eye sockets. As if it could sense the shard in his pocket, that the treasure it had been sculpted to protect had returned home.

"The only one left standing in our way," Atlas said as he placed his hand on *Mors*'s bony shoulder. *Our way*, Van balked. "I wonder what his trial will be."

Does he know what I have done? Van could still feel the cobwebs clinging to his skin. Couldn't shake the catacomb cold from his limbs.

But then a wide, naive smile crept onto Atlas's face. "What are you waiting for?"

Van hovered over the altar. Three black porcelain shards had been arranged so that their jagged edges aligned. They'd fit together like puzzle pieces. Two more and the Vase of Venus Aurelia would be whole again.

"Drat. The shard. It's with my journal," Van said, rolling out his shoulders in agitation. He pressed a finger to his temple.

Forgetful. Believable. "I forgot it back at camp."

Atlas squinted. "That's unlike you."

"Is it?"

"You barely take your nose out of that diary of yours." Another one of his piercing laughs cuts Van right to the marrow.

"It's not a—"

Atlas clasped a hand on his shoulder. "I'll grab it. Left side under your pillow, right?"

Van frowned. "That's supposed to be a secret."

Glancing over his shoulder, Atlas was already running toward the entry staircase. "I thought we didn't keep secrets."

He was the closest thing Van had to a best friend, a brother.

"Don't do anything until I get back, okay?" Atlas called back. "Promise me."

"Promise," Van yelled after his receding footsteps.

And then he waited, still until the temple door slammed. His palms slicked with sweat. Could he really do this?

Steadying himself, he withdrew the fourth shard from his pocket. And then a fifth.

Gold danced across the surface of the Vase's pieces. Delicate brushstrokes depicting myrtle blooms and rolling waves were woven together by a string of Latin that could only be read when all five shards were reunited. If Van had been able to understand Latin at all.

Flat on the altar, he pressed the seams of two pieces together.

Aureus, amor aeternus et cor—

As soon as the last shard was fitted into place, the Vase

burned Van's fingertips. Hot. He staggered backward as the pottery began to float, light emanating from each shard. Gold dripped in the seams, fusing the shards back together.

Then, it stopped. The light dimmed. Van batted away the sudden darkness like he did after one of Atlas's poorly timed photo ops.

This was it.

Before he could step to the Vase, it shattered. Five shards clattered against the stone altar, but they didn't break. Van reached for them, and a shout died in his throat. Where his fingertips should have brushed porcelain, there was nothing. The shards had vanished.

They couldn't have *vanished*. That was absurd. The Vase of Venus Aurelia was myth, not magic. The key to a hidden treasure: vast piles of gold, undying fame, a way to finally be someone.

They'd fallen under the altar. That must have been it. There was always a logical explanation.

He moved to take a step, but his foot turned heavy. Stuck. Van strained, stretched. It did nothing. He couldn't move. He glanced down at his boot as the leather paled, faded, warm brown sapping to cool white. And like twining ivy, it climbed. Marble spread from his fingertips up his forearms, over his shoulders, down his chest.

Van struggled, fighting a scream for no one, until the very moment his heart turned to stone.

1

Margot loved nothing more than a good story. A call to action that couldn't be resisted and a sweeping adventure, a big reveal and a grand gesture. A kiss at the end, obviously. Windswept and sunlit and lipstick stained. The kind that made a girl believe in happily ever afters.

As she strode the paved streets of Pompeii, Margot flipped through a leather-bound journal, soaking up each slanted line like it was a *New York Times* bestseller. The pages had warped and wrinkled, yellowed at the edges from the last century. Dirt smudged over sharp-edged penmanship. At the front, written in heavy letters, ink pen dripping, it read: *Property of Van Keane.*

Each entry was dated back to the summer of 1932, starting on a June day not unlike this one. Van was only eighteen, but his team included some of the first archaeologists to dig their shovels into Pompeii's sunbaked earth. She paused toward the journal's middle, where the scribbled entries abruptly stopped. Nestled between the pages was a photo.

There were others, of course. Black-and-white snapshots capturing first glimpses of Pompeii as he dredged the city up—but this was her favorite. Van's hair was light, cropped on the bottom but longer on top, somehow both coiffed and careless. He had been sculpted in harsh lines and sharp relief. His mouth was pressed tight, eyebrows cinched. Hunky. Brooding. Totally her type.

It was the last photo of Van ever taken. He didn't know it back then, but later that night, while he scraped back the centuries by the light of an oil lamp, the ground would shake, shift. Unstable, the dig site collapsed. He'd gone too deep when the ceiling caved, crushed beneath the rubble with no chance at escape. It wasn't just Pompeians buried here. Somewhere below the earth were his bones, too.

He died making history.

In his last entry, he'd written, *Out here, there are only elements—sun, earth, a freesia breeze, and a sea so sparkling it isn't hard to believe Venus herself rose from the foam and chose this land as her own.*

Margot lifted her head to survey the city, letting the salt air thread through her chin-length curls. On a good day, they were unruly, but Italy's June-warm humidity had turned them outright unmanageable. She kept them out of her face with a satin scarf tied behind her ears. In this century, everything smelled like the teetering cypress trees and the oily faux-coconut of Banana Boat sunscreen. Still, Margot might have been walking exactly where Van had, surveying the same land.

Except she should have been watching her step. Too late to do anything but brace for impact, Margot barged straight into a classmate. She rebounded, scuttling backward and losing her footing, and plummeted directly into an ocean of plastic tarps.

Okay, *ouch*. That was definitely going to bruise. She blinked up at the frescoed ceiling, cherubs flying dizzy circles overhead.

None other than Astrid Ashby peered down at her. Her fair skin didn't stand a chance this summer beneath the harsh Italian sun, and her stark blonde hair had been pulled into a high pony, letting curtain bangs frame her face. Like the rest of the students at their excavation site, she wore a white T-shirt with Radcliffe Prep Archaeology stamped in the school's maroon on the breast pocket.

Astrid crossed her arms against her chest and barked, "Watch where you're going, Rhodes."

Another face appeared, one with wide-set brown eyes and a permanent wrinkle between her eyebrows. Radcliffe's head of classical studies was a suntanned white woman with deep brown hair that refused to stay coiled in a chignon at the base of her neck, turning a neat bun into little more than curly tendrils spraying out every direction. Dr. Hunt at least looked concerned for Margot's safety as she extended a hand. "This is not exactly what I meant when I said we'd get up close and personal with history, Miss Rhodes."

The entire class watched, snickering, as Margot hoisted herself out of the pit of doom. A whirlpool of embarrassment swam in her chest, a drowning tide. She took a breath and forced a smile. At least, she tried to. But Astrid's laser-beam glare threatened to disintegrate her at any moment.

"She's a threat to our whole excavation," Astrid said. Did she seriously just stomp? They were about to be high school seniors. Nobody stomped anymore. "She shouldn't be here."

Dr. Hunt placated Astrid with a *tsk*. "Every student chosen for this trip had to submit the same assignment. Margot's earned her spot here as much as anyone else."

Astrid fumed. "She's never even taken an archaeology class!"

"Good thing this is a summer class," Margot said. "For learning."

"Some of us are taking this seriously." Astrid tucked a strand of hair behind her ear, haughty. "And at least the rest of us actually *followed* the essay assignment and didn't write glorified self-insert fan fiction."

Margot's blood pressure rose so high her ears throbbed in time with her pulse. She pressed her fingertips into the soft of her palms until she was certain she'd leave permanent indentations. "Just because you won some dumb award—"

"The Pliny Junior Scholastic Award of Linguistic Achievement in Latin."

"—doesn't mean you're better than everyone!" Frustration swelled, tears welling in Margot's eyes, but she blinked them back. Exactly the kind of thing everyone expected from her. Too soft. Too emotional. Too loud. Too *much*.

Astrid grinned, a wicked slice of perfectly straight teeth. The poster child for orthodontia. "Not everyone. Just you."

When Margot squeezed her eyes shut, she saw Van's easy smile. God, the things she'd do to have the uninterrupted confidence of a white man. He'd probably just laugh. Astrid's comments wouldn't even make a dent in his armor.

Margot wasn't like that. The snide look on Astrid's face seared into the folds of her mind, branded her skin like a hot iron. She didn't know how, in the wise words of Taylor Swift, to shake it off.

She opened her mouth, a tart retort already forming, but before she could say anything else, Dr. Hunt stepped between them with palms spread wide. Every interaction Margot had with her, she had exuded Cool Aunt energy, but right now, her professor was all business. "I'm going to operate under the assumption that it's the jet lag talking and give you two a chance to work this out. Rhodes, Ashby, you're partners for the summer." She turned to the other eight students selected for the summer abroad and added, "The rest of you, pair up.

Rule number one, always use the buddy system."

A murmur coursed through the students, but Dr. Hunt fixed Margot with a stare.

"Put the notebook away for now," she said, lowering her voice, "and try not to destroy a UNESCO World Heritage site on the first day of our dig."

Margot nodded. It wasn't like she could argue around the lump in her throat.

In the last six years, Margot had tried on countless versions of herself. Ballet, watercolor painting, musical theater, six months of violin lessons—like a Barbie playing dress-up. Nothing ever stuck. And Astrid was right about one thing. As the class paired off, Margot recognized most of them from passing glances across campus and evenings spent organizing the school yearbook, but not from class. Because Margot had never stepped foot in an archaeology classroom.

She'd only decided to take a real stab at archaeology a few weeks ago after finding a flyer for Dr. Hunt's trip posted on the library's bulletin board. Six weeks in the south of Italy, soaking up the sun, discovering ancient artifacts, solving millennia-old mysteries. Plus, *helloooo*, Italian boys.

Three nights in a row, she curled over her laptop with an IV drip of caffeine, hammering away page after page on her application essay. A few hundred Google wormholes later, she'd basically taken a crash course on Roman antiquity. She triple-checked her margins, double-spaced it, and slid her essay into

Dr. Hunt's office with only an hour to spare.

But these students, they all knew each other, needling elbows into each other's sides and cracking jokes that went way over her head.

Astrid grabbed the only other girl on their trip by the arm. "Suki, partner with me."

Suki Takeda was tall and slim with light brown skin, and she fiddled absentmindedly with the ends of her deep brown braids. She'd wasted no time taking a pair of scissors to her class T-shirt, and instead of the brown boots everyone else wore, Suki opted for a chunky pair of Doc Martens. "Nice try. I'm working with Rex."

"He looks a little . . . preoccupied," Margot said. She pointed over Suki's shoulder, where Rex Yang sparred against Topher Kitsch, a Black boy with box braids, using shovels like gladiator swords.

Suki put two fingers in her mouth and whistled so loudly a bird crowed, fleeing the branches above them. Rex and Topher snapped to attention. Running over, they flanked Suki on either side. "Rex," she said, "you're with me."

Rex raised his eyebrows so high they disappeared beneath the harsh line of his black hair. Mostly limbs and sinewy muscle, Rex moved with easy grace Margot knew had to be from hours upon hours of cheerleading practice. He smiled. Easy, confident. "If you say so. Sorry, Toph, you're on your own."

Astrid, evidently desperate to escape Margot like she was Typhoid Mary, pivoted. She raised her eyebrows at Topher in a silent plea.

Topher raised his open palms and said, "No way. I'm going to see if Calvin still needs a partner." Then, as if realizing Margot was literally standing right there, added, "No offense, Margot, but you're not . . ."

"Archaeologist material?" Astrid offered. There was a lilt to her voice, mean-girl playful. "Who wears red lipstick to a dig site anyway?"

Astrid linked arms with Suki, and the boys trailed after them. Every remark died on Margot's tongue.

So, what? She wasn't the daughter of some bigwig west coast museum curator like Suki, and she didn't hail from a long line of archaeologists like Astrid, but what did it matter that Margot grew up in a blink-and-you'll-miss-it Georgia town, taking etiquette classes with Miss Penelope instead of memorizing the names for each layer of sediment? She wasn't embarrassed to try something new. And she *definitely* wasn't going to be embarrassed about her lipstick. The leading lady always had a calling card—a signature scent or a beauty mark. For Margot, it was a perfect shade of red lipstick.

Dr. Hunt led them deeper into the excavation site—a shell of stone walls with a labyrinthine floor plan and enough tarp-covered pits that they really should have had school-issued helmets. The first doorway opened into a wide foyer. Cracking frescoes caked the walls. Soft blues faded into pastel pinks. They must have been dazzling jewel tones when they were first painted, but everything lost its color with time.

"This summer, you and your partner will document all of your findings and write a report that touches on the meaning of these discoveries and why it was meaningful at its time of creation." Dr. Hunt steered the class around a bend, revealing a tent-covered courtyard and five roped off dig plots. Pines jutted out from the harsh soil, hedges encircled fountains that must have once drizzled streams of clear water, and ivy dripped down the walls like gelato on a hot day. "Collect your tools, and let's get started."

Margot scooped up two full sets of items—brushes, a picket, a fancy measurement device, some shovel-looking things. Rex and Suki knelt at Plot E, already digging into the hardened earth.

Astrid, on the other hand, sulked at the edge of Plot D. Apparently the *D* in Plot D stood for *Definitely going to lose her freaking mind*. Astrid's eyes were darts, and Margot was the target.

"Here," Margot said, holding out a second set of tools. "I grabbed some for you."

"I'm good," said Astrid.

Suki giggled into the palm of her hand. From a leather pouch, Astrid unsheathed a gilded shovel with a glossy wood handle, burnished with an insignia Margot couldn't quite make out. Astrid huffed onto the metal and polished it on the sleeve of her shirt.

The extra shovel thudded against the dirt, slipping out of Margot's fingers.

Astrid asked, her ice-blue eyes narrowed, "Why'd you steal a spot on this trip?"

Margot sagged. "I didn't steal anything from anyone. You heard Dr. Hunt—"

"Please, Pasha Manikas scored a ninety-nine percent on the Classical Archaeology final last quarter. We were going to be roommates." Astrid sniffed, puckered like she smelled knock-off perfume. "Your essay shouldn't have qualified. It was fiction, for god's sake."

"Dr. Hunt seems to disagree," Margot countered, but regret wormed into her stomach, burying itself in her gut.

The students who had been selected for the trip had their application essays posted on the school website.

There had been Suki's—"Charon's Obol: An Investigation of the Roman Afterlife."

Astrid had titled hers "Eternal Languages and the People Who Spoke Them."

Then, way, *way* at the bottom was Margot's: "All Rhodes Lead to Rome."

And maybe it was self-insert fan fiction in the literal definition of the phrase. Margot had written about finding the Vase of Venus Aurelia, pouring in details from Van's journal. The

Vase was Pompeii's greatest treasure, blessed by Venus herself to grant whoever pieced it back together unimaginable wealth and notoriety, the promise of being loved by all who encountered you. If Margot discovered it, she'd never be dismissed for being too girly, too indecisive, too irrational again—she'd be respected, understood, appreciated. Loved.

The only problem was that, according to legend, Venus shattered the Vase, deeming the power too much for mere mortals. If anyone was able to complete each of her five trials, they would be rewarded with a piece of the Vase. But that was the hiccup. It was just a myth.

There was no road map. No flashing arrow saying *Trial of Venus, due north!* No one had ever seen all five pieces. No one until Van.

"You're never going to find that stupid Vase," Astrid snapped. "People have been looking for it for the last two thousand years."

Margot shrugged, batting her lashes. "Maybe they just didn't know where to look."

"But you do? You don't know a trowel from a spade." Astrid laughed, cutting. "Forget it. I'm not letting you ruin my GPA because you think you're Lara Croft."

Margot held on to Van's journal like a buoy in a raging sea. Her heart slammed against her rib cage, emotion bubbling back up. Her dad always said she felt things too much. That she thought with her heart instead of her head. It wasn't her fault that her heart had a megaphone and her head had anxiety.

Before she could scream or cry or both, Margot bolted out of the tent and scaled the short stone wall, landing in an alleyway. The distant din of Astrid's laugh trailed after her, but Mount Vesuvius loomed in the distance. On a day like today, the skies blue and a gentle wind lifting Margot's hair off her neck, it was hard to imagine the mountain demolishing an entire civilization under ash and dirt. For centuries, this town, these roads, had been buried. Abandoned and forgotten.

Now, cobbled streets and colonnades had been pried from the earth's grip and exposed once again. Margot could almost imagine the faded ink lines of elevation maps the original explorers must have charted when they first arrived, like all the places Van had touched turned golden in the afternoon light.

Margot slid onto her butt, curling her knees to her chest, and wormed her arms out of the straps of her backpack. She pried open Van's journal and it fell back to the last entry. The spine had probably creased, she'd flipped to this page so many times. Her index finger trailed over his penmanship, feeling the grooves where his pen indented the paper.

Sitting here, she could almost imagine him next to her. His tawny hair, his knife-sharp jaw, the way his linen shirt stretched across his broad shoulders. The heroes in romance novels always smelled like sandalwood, and he probably did, too. Like sandalwood and salt, a trace of evergreen—that intangible scent of a day spent outside.

He'd searched for the Vase even though no one else believed it could exist. Like believing in soulmates or the Loch Ness Monster—both things Margot was happy to trust were out there somewhere. He would have understood Margot. She was sure of it.

Unzipping her mustard-yellow backpack, she dropped Van's notebook into its depths, right between a beaten-up paperback novel and a wad of linen she miraculously snuck through airport security. She didn't dare breathe as she unwrapped the artifact.

Red clay, painted black. Streaks of gold wove across the exterior, myrtle blooms and a fragment of Latin painted at the edge, the last word broken off. A piece of something spectacular, like glass before the mosaic.

A shard of the Vase of Venus Aurelia.

2

Technically, Margot hadn't been trespassing when she found the shard. Her school library's archives were strictly off-limits, unless you had written approval from the head librarian. Which she totally had.

Admittedly, she was supposed to be doing research for her final English paper, a thematic interrogation of her all-time favorite novel, *Relics of the Heart* by Catherine Avery Hannigan.

In the book, rival archaeologists Isla Farrow and Reed Silvan scoured the Mediterranean for an artifact believed to be nothing more than a story: the Vase of Venus Aurelia. Their adventure—long nights together, searching for the Vase, finding each other instead—had captivated her mom. The first time Margot read it after unearthing it from a box her mom left behind, she'd been spellbound, too.

Her copy had seen better days. The mass-market romance

was all roughened edges and curled corners from being read and read again. She could still remember her mom hunkering down with it on the hammock she'd string up in the backyard each June. Every time Margot fanned through the pages, they smelled like those summers: coconut-scented tanning lotion, heaping scoops of strawberry ice cream, and freshly washed cotton sheets, sun-dried.

So, really, it wasn't Margot's fault that her foot slipped on the library's rolling ladder in the section on Roman mythologies or that Van's journal happened to be right where she landed. Definitely not her fault that behind it, wrapped in faded muslin, was something curious. Something uncatalogued—and therefore unmissed when she'd slipped it into her pocket.

The library at Radcliffe Prep was filled to the brim with antiques—priceless artworks, one-of-a-kind prints, and first edition texts. How they filled that library wasn't something they advertised, and whatever kinds of questionable collection development tactics they used didn't really matter to Margot. But she had never expected to see a Vase shard, like she'd stepped inside the pages of *Relics of the Heart*.

Unfortunately, Isla and Reed's archaeological escapades conveniently underrepresented the dirt under her nails, the sweat clinging to the back of her neck, and the sunburn not even Supergoop! could keep at bay. And that wasn't even counting the trek over to Italy. By the time they made it back to their hotel, Margot's limbs had achieved the consistency of overcooked pasta. The jet lag and heat exhaustion combo punch was enough to KO somebody.

Yesterday, when they'd first arrived at Hotel Villa Minerva— which was so small it hardly counted as a hotel, let alone a villa—Dr. Hunt had doled out room assignments, but Margot already knew her fate. There were only three girls on the trip. There was a triplet bedroom with their names on it.

Sure enough, room 320 beckoned them. The third-floor suite was drenched in teal paisley wallpaper, and a lopsided chandelier clung to the ceiling for dear life. Bouquets of silk flowers and faux ivy had been draped over the tops of a cedar armoire. It was giving Grandma chic and smelled appropriately like mothballs and lemon cleaning spray.

There was one single bed and a set of bunk beds. Astrid had unceremoniously Neil Armstronged her suitcase onto the single bed like a flag on the moon, which left Suki and Margot to rock, paper, scissors for the bunks.

Margot had started saying, "I'd really like to—"

"I sleepwalk."

Margot blinked. "You sleepwalk?"

Suki batted Lancôme-long lashes. "I once walked all the way to In-N-Out in a dream. I bought a double-double with cheese, Margot. You've got to give me the bottom bunk."

And that was that. Better to squish than be squished, she reasoned.

Tonight, Margot landed on her bunk with an *oof.* All right, maybe she minded a little bit that her mattress was evidently a layer of bricks thinly disguised beneath a bedsheet. But the way the exhaustion hit her, she knew she wouldn't be awake long enough to care.

Suki and Astrid trailed in after saying good night to Rex, Calvin, and Topher across the hall.

"You know, I didn't think you were going to last the whole afternoon, Margot," Astrid said.

"Thanks for the concern," Margot huffed, muffled into her pillow.

"I'm serious." Palm to her heart, Astrid looked like she really thought Margot was going to fall for her fake sincerity. "I don't know how you're going to survive the entire summer."

Margot shuffled onto her elbows, irritation chafing every nerve. Suddenly sleep was entirely out of the question.

Astrid sighed. "God forbid you break a nail."

"Don't worry. I brought my gel kit."

Astrid's grin was anything but sweet. The kind of saccharine smile that accompanied a good, old-fashioned *bless your heart*. "I'm sure you did."

Suki leaned around the bedpost. "What colors did you bring?"

"Suki!" Astrid griped.

"What?" Suki asked. "Free mani."

Astrid rolled her eyes so far back, Margot was surprised she didn't strain a muscle. "The point is that you'd only pass this

23

class because we're partners. Without me, you'd be completely helpless."

There was no graceful way to flop over on a bed to come to your own defense. It was more fish-out-of-water than anything. When Margot finally righted herself, she said, "I know I'm not a pedigreed archaeologist, but I'm here."

"Please. You don't know an amphora from a krater. I bet you don't last the week," Astrid said.

Margot dropped down the ladder and squared her shoulders. Heat worked over her skin, her body temperature rising. "You don't know anything about me."

Astrid didn't back down. "I've seen enough. Everyone else has done fieldwork before. You aren't ruining my summer for me, one way or another—you'll either give up and crawl home, tail between your legs, or I'll get it through Dr. Hunt's head that you don't belong here, and she'll send you home."

Margot didn't bother excusing herself to the bathroom. When she felt that first prickle against the back of her throat, she knew the waterworks were coming. She slammed the door behind her, and there was a crash on the other side. Guilt twined around her ribs—her overreactions never came without a price—but she couldn't stop herself.

Her eyelashes clumped together, wet with tears. She ran her hands under cold water, letting the chill sink into the soft skin of her wrist. Her therapist said it helped soothe her central nervous system and deactivate fight-or-flight mode. Which was definitely needed at the moment. Red crept up the column of her neck like being around Astrid all afternoon had given her a bad rash.

As much as she hated to admit it, maybe Astrid was right. It was only day one. Her manicure *was* already wrecked. How was she going to survive six whole weeks?

An exhale shook Margot's lungs. She couldn't keep crying. Not right now. This was what she always did—she jumped headfirst into something, exhilarated and determined, but swam to shore when the waters were deeper than she imagined. Not this time.

Reaching into her pocket, Margot clutched the shard from the Vase. She traced her fingertips along the flecks of gold. It was a charm, warding off Astrid's evil energy. When Margot looked at it, the ground beneath her feet felt solid again.

She'd made it this far. And maybe, she could belong here.

Like a shot from a starting gun, the gazillion-year-old corded phone she'd seen on the side table rang with a vengeance. Margot nearly leaped out of her skin, and she poked her head through the bathroom doorway. Astrid crouched on the floor and swept up the fragments of a black coffee mug, broken into chunks of porcelain—it must have taken a nosedive when Margot slammed the door.

"Easy. Don't Hulk out on us again," Astrid said as she deposited the pieces on the dresser. Then, turning over her shoulder, she snapped, "Are you going to answer that or what?"

"Do I look like a receptionist to you?" Suki grabbed the screaming phone and answered with a gruff "What's up?" While whoever was on the other line spoke, her eyes zipped toward Margot. She pointed a finger at her and mouthed, *It's for you.*

But it couldn't be for Margot. Because no one knew she was here.

Suki nodded as if the caller could see her and then said, "You're looking for Margot? Margot Rhodes?"

Margot shook her head wildly. Eyes wide, pleading.

"How do I know you're not some creepy stalker?" A pause. "Oh, you're her dad?"

Doomed. She was absolutely doomed. Margot clasped her hands at her chest, namaste-style. She begged with a harsh whisper, "Please don't say I'm here. Don't say anything about me. Tell him you've never heard of me."

A few mental calculations placed it around one p.m. in Dogwood Hollow, Georgia. Lunchtime for her dad, breezing between meetings to grab balsamic and burrata paninis at Evelyn's corner café. Late enough for him to realize she wasn't answering his texts about whether or not she wanted potato salad on the side, which was a dead giveaway because Margot *always* wanted potato salad on the side. She'd masterminded the whole plan—it wasn't that hard to disappear for six weeks. How could this have happened?

Suki listened for a second. "Yeah, okay. She's right here."

Margot's whole body slumped. "Are you kidding me?"

"He said he was going to call the school back to unenroll you." Suki covered the receiver with the palm of her hand, shoulders shrugged up to her ears. "Also, your dad sounds like kind of a DILF."

"Suki," Margot hissed.

"Just saying."

The phone burned when Margot held it to her ear. Her voice sounded stiff, pinched. *"Hiiiiii."*

"Hey, Gogo," her dad said from the other end, and her heart squeezed at the nickname. Behind him, she could hear the bluebirds singing and the faint hum of the street quartet's string instruments—they always gathered in the town square on Friday afternoons. Rupert Rhodes could hardly walk ten steps without saying hello to someone because when you're the Deep South's small-town version of a real estate mogul, you basically know everybody. "Want to tell me what's going on?"

"What do you mean? You sound like you're running late for a new client meeting. Maybe I can catch you after work."

His sigh could be felt across the Atlantic. "You mean today or six weeks from now?"

Every brain cell in Margot's head shifted into overdrive. Last night, while he was showing a house over in Copper Springs, she'd left a note under his coffee mug, outlining the details of her flight. Except she'd said she'd be boarding a flight to New York City to spend the summer with her mom in Manhattan doing . . . whatever it was her mom did without her. It wasn't like her parents were on speaking terms. There was no way it could have backfired *this* badly this quickly.

But he'd called her. On a corded phone from the last millennia.

"Have you talked to Mom?" she asked, chewing on the inside of her cheek. Could he tell the way her voice hitched? The problem about being the human embodiment of a mood swing was that Margot couldn't hide her emotions to save her life. Lying to him was out of the question. She'd orchestrated this so that she wouldn't *have* to lie. At least, not to anyone's face.

"Sort of," her dad bristled. "I left her a voicemail and then got a text saying she had no idea you were coming for the summer, and if she had, she wouldn't have booked a two-month hiking trip down the Appalachian Trail."

"That's so weird because—"

"Tell me the truth, Gogo," he said. "Why did I get forwarded to a hotel concierge named Giuseppe when I called your school office?"

"Because I'm in Italy."

Even 4,300 miles away, she knew the way his eyebrows would worry together, creased down the middle in a wrinkle that never fully went away. "Little Italy?"

Margot picked at her bottom lip, flaking off bits of pigment. "No, uh, the big one."

Someone on the other end honked—probably at her dad for stopping, stunned, in the middle of the street, if she had to guess. It was like the cogs started spinning in his head again. "Dr. Hunt's excavation. You went to Pompeii even when I told you not to. I knew sending you to that boarding school was a huge mistake."

"Dad, I—"

"I can't believe you would do this, let alone how you managed to pull it off."

It was, Margot wagered, a rhetorical question. Her dad didn't really want to know that she'd forged his signature on the permission slip so that she could turn it in on time. Or that she'd signed up for a part-time job at the campus coffee shop, spending her evenings brewing vanilla lattes for tired-eyed seniors and saving every cent so that she could afford her plane ticket without asking him to help pay.

He was the whole reason she was here in the first place. If the Vase of Venus Aurelia could make everyone love Margot, that had to include Rupert Rhodes.

"I earned this spot, Dad." Much to the chagrin of the blonde-haired brownnoser conveniently eavesdropping on this conversation from the other side of the room. Margot dropped her voice, just for good measure. "It's not just a phase this time."

"It's always something with you. But this is too far, Gogo. I'm booking you a plane ticket home."

"You can't be serious."

"Of course I can. I can't be anything *but* serious right now. I wish you would try it. You're just like your mom sometimes."

Another agitated breath blew into the speaker, crackling on Margot's end of the line. "The second you're back on American soil, you're grounded for the next century."

Margot sank onto the windowsill. The phone's sticky beige cord wrapped around her as she leaned her chin into her hand. The last dregs of evening sun splashed everything in Aperol orange. Aperol she still wasn't legally allowed to drink until the end of summer (the drinking age in Italy was eighteen!), but she wouldn't be here by then if her dad had his way. There was a *whoosh* of air on his side, and Margot could practically feel the bite of the air-conditioning in his downtown office. She was running out of time to convince him.

Clutching the receiver so hard her fingers felt like they might snap off, Margot pleaded, "I'm working on this really important research project that will be completely life-changing. If you just let me stay. Two weeks, even. One week. Dad, I promise—I'll never leave my dishes in the sink ever again."

"What's that? Hold on." There was a rustle, the sound of him covering the phone with his hand, and a hushed back and forth. "Margot, I've got to run. Client emergency. I'm buying you a ticket. You're coming home. Not next week. Now. End of conversation."

It always was. Because nothing Margot did was ever enough for him.

For the last six years, it had only been the two of them. Her mom vanished after enough shouting matches to leave them all feeling battered and bruised, and her dad became the single father of an only daughter. He was the one person she could hold on to, but he'd retreated into his work, out of reach when she needed him most.

Before the divorce, he'd always known how to calm her down with two hands on her shoulders, their foreheads pressed together like maybe he could transfer some of his cool-tempered tendencies to her through osmosis. She couldn't help but laugh when his eyes blurred together up close.

But lately, it was like they were constantly speaking different languages. He was always running around town, busying his days with buyer calls and his nights with paperwork. These days, the only time he made for her was to tell her she was messing something up or overreacting.

Margot knew her dad better than anyone else—how he took his coffee, how he swore there was a left and right sock, how he refused to watch movies with sad endings—but it was like he didn't know her at all. Or, worse, he did, and still didn't love her.

The Vase of Venus Aurelia could fix that. *Would* fix that. It had to.

Suki and Astrid watched expectantly as Margot set the phone back on its receiver.

"So?" Suki prompted.

There was really only one thing to do. Margot forced a smile that definitely didn't reach her eyes. A pathetic excuse for a lie. "Looks like you're stuck with me."

3

Margot couldn't sleep, and it had nothing to do with Astrid snoring like a Weedwacker.

She had the covers pulled up over her head and her phone flashlight nestled between her chin and *Relics of the Heart*. The words faded in and out of focus as her dad's conversation replayed on a loop in her head, overtaking Isla and Reed's banter. Which was totally rude because Margot had just gotten to the part where Reed kissed Isla as a decoy midheist, and it was steamy with a capital *S*.

Her dad must have gotten busy with work. A plane ticket hadn't yet manifested itself in her inbox, but Margot didn't dare dream she was off the hook. Rupert Rhodes was always running from one meeting to the next, but even he wouldn't forget something like this. He was probably calling the airline support desk on his way to another open house at this very moment.

If he had actually listened to her, he'd understand that Margot hadn't come to Italy just for the gelato. Van had documented his journey that fateful summer. Every wrong turn, every last-ditch effort, every triumph. His journal wasn't just a historical text—it was a map. All Margot needed to do was retrace his steps, and she was certain she'd find the rest of the Vase shards.

There was no way she could be expected to lie here and listen to Astrid's obstructed sinus passages for the next eight hours, especially if her last moments in Italy were slipping away. It was nearly midnight, the only light coming from stars and streetlights. No one would know she'd been gone at all.

Margot threw off her scratchy sheets and descended from the top bunk. She timed her steps with Astrid's breathy inhales to cover up the ladder's ungodly squeaking. By the door, she slid her feet into her high-tops, wrapping the laces around her ankles to double knot them. There was no telling what she'd encounter in the ruins. Quicksand? Rolling boulders? A tall, dark, and handsome dreamboat she'd become enemies-to-allies-to-lovers with? She had to be prepared for anything.

Without warning, Astrid rolled over, arm flailing wildly. Margot froze, leg midair, but her roommate just reburied her face in the pillow, content to snore until morning.

Slinging her backpack over her shoulders, Margot pocketed the room key. She shoved it down into her denim jacket, right next to the Vase shard and Van's journal. She hadn't bothered to change out of her pajamas—a pair of multicolored striped shorts and a matching button-up top—but she stashed her red lipstick in her backpack's side pocket for good measure.

The elevator dinged when Margot reached the lobby. It obviously hadn't gotten the memo that this was a *covert* operation. She slinked around the base of a sturdy column, pressing her back against the pillar to run recon.

On one end of the (horribly carpeted) lobby was an arched front door. Standing between her and sweet, sweet freedom was the front desk where Giuseppe the concierge yawned, tapping absentmindedly at his phone. Giuseppe was a pinstripe of a man with a mustache just as thin and dark circles so severe, she wondered if he'd ever had a good night's sleep in his life.

She couldn't exactly ask him for a lift to the ruins. There was no way the hotel shuttle would take her because the gates of Pompeii closed hours ago. A taxi would get her there—or the driver might kidnap her and scrape her insides away from her bones like a vulture scavenging dinner. No, thanks. Walking would be one hell of a workout, but she'd rather not risk any kidnapping or the aforementioned maiming.

What she needed was a ride of her own.

Margot squared her shoulders and held her chin high as she approached Giuseppe. All she needed to do was lure him away from the desk. She'd snag a key from the valet and be halfway to Pompeii before he ever realized something was missing.

In etiquette class, Miss Penelope always said there were three steps to making a good first impression. Smile. Make eye contact. And speak confidently. So, Margot wore her best pageant grin, looked straight into Giuseppe's coffee-black eyes, and said, "I'd like another feather pillow."

Giuseppe glanced up from his phone, sloth-slow.

"Please," Margot added.

He laughed so hard, a little bit of spit flew out. Margot inched out of the splash zone.

"Is that a no?" she asked. Then, hopefully: "Or a maybe?"

Giuseppe looked down his nose. "Our pillows do not have *feathers*."

Of course they didn't. Hotel Villa Minerva wasn't exactly a luxury accommodation.

"Two pillows, then," Margot said. "My roommate, she snores like the dickens. An extra pillow would help all of us sleep better."

The concierge clicked off his phone and stood, only to tower over Margot. His lips pinched, eyes slitting. "You sleep in your jacket?"

Margot had to quit musical theater because she couldn't stop laughing when saying her lines. They felt like a lie on her tongue. Instead of saying anything, Margot shrugged, nodded, raised her eyebrows in quiet innocence.

Giuseppe caved. His heavy shoulders sagged even lower and he resigned himself to the linen closet. While he dragged out polyester pillows from beneath a pile of two-ply bedsheets, Margot skirted around the desk with one eye over her shoulder.

"Keys, where are you?" she whispered, digging through the drawers and rifling through cabinets. They had to be around here somewhere. Tape, three staplers, a handful of overly doodled pen pads. A cough drop supply, thirty-five ink pens, a stack of sticky notes. No keys. Anywhere.

The last drawer was labeled *Servizio di Parcheggio.*

Parking?

Margot tugged it open, and loose keys slid around the drawer, each wearing a diamond-shaped Hotel Villa Minerva tag. Jackpot. She grabbed one off the top and closed the drawer as quietly as humanly possible. Beggars really couldn't be choosers.

She hopped back onto the other side of the desk only seconds before Giuseppe reappeared, his arms loaded with pillows. His voice was laced with annoyance when he asked, "Anything else?"

"No, just . . ." A stack of brochures at the end of his desk caught her eye. Guidebooks to Pompeii, Naples, Pisa. Perfect. "A map."

"Where am I taking—"

"Room 320. Thank you!" Margot said, pacing backward. She waved—the hand with the key—but quickly pocketed it with a grin. If Giuseppe saw or managed to care in his obvious state of sleep deprivation, she didn't stick around to find out, high-tailing out the front doors.

Outside, the pastel evening had bled into nighttime navies. The air was still heavy with humidity, but a swirling breeze tossed her curls around, sticking to the oily layer of gloss on her lips. Yellow scooters lined the back wall of the hotel. When Margot clicked the key fob, one of them lit up.

Her chariot awaited.

Every mile down the road was a step backward in time. The full moon cast a silver lining over each clay shingle. She steered between peeling stucco buildings and iron balconies spilling with houseplants, past delicatessens and miniature orange groves, down quiet streets with modern Pompeians closing shops while Mount Vesuvius herself loomed in the distance, a smudge on the night-dark horizon.

When she swerved onto a side street near the ruins, Margot cut the headlights by way of trial and error, smacking every button and pulling every lever. Cramped buildings turned into sparse fields as she neared the back of the ancient metropolis. The road ended abruptly, but Margot didn't yield.

Kicking up dirt and dust, the scooter sputtered down the field, digging out grooves in the grasses. Her Vespa was lacking all major off-road qualifications. When the tires refused any forward motion, Margot yanked the key out of the ignition.

She huffed an errant curl out of her eyes. This was fine. All in the name of adventure.

Pulling the map of Pompeii from her pocket, Margot found a patch of moonlight and skimmed her finger along the printed alleyways, examining her options. Van's journal didn't say anything about nighttime security—but that was because nighttime security didn't exist last century. Honestly, each of the main gates were probably swarming with guards. She'd need a prayer just to get through without getting caught.

There had to be another route.

She pinpointed a spot near the Necropolis of Vesuvio Gate. It didn't look like the fifth region had any major excavations, largely untouched and smoothed over with greenery. Which meant that the guards didn't have anything to actually guard. If she was going to make it inside without getting caught—or subsequently arrested by Interpol and, like, deported—this was her best chance.

Chaparral clawed at her legs and snagged the satin threads of her shorts as she hiked across the hillsides. Pines and palms threaded together overhead, cloaking her in shadows as she paced toward the ruins. Each step along the dirt path clouded dust in her wake, and the tree line broke as she neared the necropolis.

Ahead, a flashlight beam halted her. Guards.

Any farther and she'd be destined for a life in handcuffs. (Or at least boredom, back home and totally grounded.) The only thing standing between Margot and Pompeii was a chicken-wire fence that lined the city limits. Going around clearly wasn't an option anymore, so the only way inside the ruins was . . . over.

Her hands clawed through the metal lacework. *At least,*

she thought sourly, *they don't have an electric fence*. When she got to the top, Margot couldn't hesitate, couldn't give herself the opportunity to second-guess. She leaped. Tucked, rolled. Sun-hardened soil rattled every bone, every joint, every cavity filling from too many Halloween sweets.

But when she lifted herself off the ground, there were no sirens blaring. No alarms rang. She hadn't tripped a secret infrared thermometer monitoring the perimeter.

Immortal Pompeii wrapped around her—past and present, all at once. If she closed her eyes, she could imagine the crackling fires extinguishing after a long day, the sound of sandaled feet slapping the earth as kids ran home, the smell of olive branches and lemon trees, of ash and earth not so different from now.

In the dark, Margot barely remembered the crooked paths Dr. Hunt had led them down that afternoon. The patchwork of cobbled buildings all looked the same. She might have been totally lost, but Van knew where to go. Margot fanned toward his first journal entries. He'd written:

> *Perhaps love truly isn't surface level. The temple where the Vase will be returned, a palace for a gilded goddess—it had been under my nose, hidden in plain sight the whole time. Everyone else underestimated this patch of dirt, despite the clear and obvious evidence we had to believe ceremonies had been performed here. I could nearly hear the ardent prayers on the wind. Even the myrtle blooms pointed this way.*

To enter Venus's temple, all I had to do was ask at the temple door.

Her heart thrummed at the sound of his words. If Van were here, he'd spearhead the way, surging bravely into the fray like any hero would. But he wasn't here. And Margot was stuck deciphering his very romantic but terribly complicated riddles.

Seriously, he couldn't have just said *X marks the spot?*

Margot scanned her surroundings, searching for anything even vaguely temple-y. The whole city was patches of dirt. She slipped Van's journal into her backpack as she wove through the narrow alleys. Everything looked the same. Brown. Nondescript. Half-deteriorated. Stone walls rose around her in every direction, but nothing that screamed Venus Was Here.

Except. The soft white blooms on a sparse few myrtle shrubs. They filled the air with fragrance, and she let herself follow it like a bloodhound hunting. Their boughs stretched toward the ribboning moonlight and guided her forward, forward, forward.

She took one step, then another, until she was full-out sprinting between the crumbling buildings. Her head swiveled back and forth, back and forth, until she worried she'd loosen the bolts so much it would fall right off. Adrenaline spilled through her veins, turning her exhilarated and nervous and acutely aware of how much trouble she would be in if any of the guards caught her trespassing after hours.

Margot ran until pain surged in her waist, until her lungs

burned. She slowed to a stop at a crossroads and slinked into the shadows as a guard whistled past. He didn't seem particularly invested in his patrol, tossing his flashlight into the air and catching it behind his back with one hand while swiping on his phone screen with the other, humming a melody Margot didn't recognize. Easy, practiced motions. Absolutely nothing out of the ordinary to see here.

Ahead, a big grassy knoll capped the hillside. Blooming myrtles encompassed its borders. It was as good of a chance as any. Suddenly, the guard swiveled left, and Margot jerked right, ducking behind another decaying structure.

If she could make it there.

Margot counted her breaths, waiting for the guard to round the next corner. At ten, she ran for it. Her feet pounded against the pavement. All she could do was pray the guard didn't turn around because when she reached the top of the hill, there was nothing there.

Nothing to hide behind. Definitely no temples. Just a few half-decayed columns and patches of wildflowers.

She propped herself up against one of the stone outcroppings, sucking air deep into her lungs. Too bad she'd never had a track-and-field phase.

Think, Margot, think. Van had criticized his fellow excavators for not seeing what was right in front of him. What was she missing? He'd said all he had to do was ask.

"Hey, Venus," Margot said, whisper quiet. "Any chance you

want to tell a girl where your temple is?"

Only the wind answered. So much for a voice-activated homing device.

There were a few other crooked stone structures jutting out of the earth—remnants of pillars, a patch of tiled floor, half walls and hearths. Margot snuck through the courtyard, investigating. If she were the goddess of love, where would she hide her temple?

Another flashlight beam appeared at the edge of the court-yard. Then, another. That was so not good. Up here, there was nowhere else for her to run except down. The guards patrolled the hill's base in a lazy arc—routine movements, but with every step, they inched closer.

Margot ducked down behind a wall of smooth, sunbaked stones. The center had been cut out. Almost like an oven or a fireplace. A hole not quite big enough for her to shove herself into, but definitely big enough to try.

Her head knocked against the ceiling as she curled into a ball. Something jammed into her spleen. Summering in Italy was supposed to be about a trillion times more glamorous than this.

By the time she dared to glance around the pillar, the guards had grouped together at the bottom of the hill, but it was too dark to tell if they were looking straight at her or something else entirely. Her heart thrummed like it knew the answer and was afraid of it. Prison orange was *not* her color.

Margot inched back into the shadows, but the stones jabbed her side again. Twisting, she realized one of the stones had pushed itself out. She knelt down to nudge it back into place, knees pressing into the alcove floor. The pressure shifted beneath her. The ground shook, moaned.

Uh . . .

Looking behind her, Margot gulped. The center of the meadow opened like a yawning mouth. Her head whipped between the stone pillar and what was evidently the doorway to the literal underworld.

Perhaps love truly isn't surface level, Van had written. She didn't know to take it so . . . literally. *I could nearly hear the ardent prayers on the wind. All I had to do was ask at the temple door.*

Margot hadn't said a peep. But she'd knelt. As if in prayer. The weight of her knees must have tripped a lever, which had Rube Goldberged the entrance.

She leaned over it now and peered into the unyielding black. A breath of stiff air blew her hair back from her face, laced with floral perfume and smoke. Below, there was a stairwell. Super creepy and foreboding.

But she'd come all this way. She couldn't turn back now.

4

The stairwell could have used some serious Swiffering. Dust swelled with every step. Margot pressed the satin sleeve of her pajama shirt over her nose and mouth, relying on the faint light of her phone's flashlight to lead the way forward. Her battery was at 7 percent.

Make that 6 percent.

With a totally-not-heart-attack-inducing thump, the door slammed closed behind her, suffocating any trace of moonlight. If Van were here right now, he would have lit a torch and speared down into the darkness, slashing through cobwebs with a flickering flame. Margot just kept that little LED bulb pointed forward, praying that all the spiders were dead and she wasn't going to join them.

"Okay, Margot," she said to herself, and the cold walls soaked up the sound. Silence pressed on her eardrums, heavy from the weight of nothingness. "This is what you came here for."

The stairwell led down and down in an endless chase, the walls grooved with timeworn etchings and flaking pigments from ancient frescoes. She imagined Van next to her, leading the way. He'd probably studied for years to become an archaeologist of his caliber at such a young age—fluent in all the classical languages, an encyclopedic knowledge of Roman iconography, a preternatural ability to sense the right places to dig.

As if she'd manifested it, a spiderweb snared Margot's legs, and a squeal erupted from her chest. She balanced against the wall, trying to extricate herself from the sticky gossamer. Van's exact words about the temple had been, *The darkness yielded only to heavier shadows until I was sure I would never see the light again*. And boy, he hadn't exaggerated.

"God, relax." She took a deep breath, shuddering. "If Van can do this, so can you."

Except that maybe that wasn't true. So much could change in a hundred years. For starters, a girl like Margot probably never would have been hired by Atlas Exploration Company. Or been able to wear pants without causing a tizzy, for that matter.

But more than that, tectonic plates could shift again—the same kind that buried Van. The walls could cave in. The rubble could block off exit routes. And her only way out had closed the moment she descended into the stairwell.

Each step downward plunged her deeper into her own thoughts. She could almost hear her dad's disdain across the Atlantic. *You're always getting in over your head, Gogo.*

And he was right.

She was a cannonball splash when everyone else was dipping in their toes. Most of the time, it meant that Margot had to work twice—no, three times—as hard just to go the same distance. It meant late-night study sessions in the library running on venti mocha frappé fumes because she spent all week deep-diving into research wormholes about unsolved mysteries that had nothing to do with passing pre-calculus or poetry.

This time, though, she genuinely was in over her head. A hundred feet of soil separated her from the surface.

Now, panic swirled through her chest, anxiety like a black tide beneath her rib bones. What had she been thinking, coming here alone? It was like one moment she felt mountaintop high, and the next? Low as Mariana Trench. A pendulum she couldn't anticipate or navigate.

The grip on her phone turned slippery. Why hadn't she remembered to charge it before she ditched the hotel? The last thing she needed was to get trapped under the ground *and* not be able to play Candy Crush as she slowly starved to death.

The stairwell flattened out, and Margot snapped back to her senses. The air was chilled, too cold despite the balmy evening above ground. When she looked up, she stood before Venus herself.

Or, at least, the fresco was life-size and almost completely intact. Periwinkle blues, pastel greens, and baby pinks swirled together to paint the goddess. Sea-foam clothed her, and she balanced a gilded vase in her palms. A Mona Lisa smile crooked her mouth up, and her eyes were closed, lashes skimming the tops of her cheeks.

When Margot turned, slivers of glass crunched beneath her step. An oil lamp. Her breath hitched in her chest. Had that been Van's? She tried to imagine his path, following his hidden footsteps. Her measly flashlight beam barely carved away the temple's darkness as Margot's soles *tap-tapped* against the stone floors, echoing in the empty chamber as she treaded deeper.

So, yeah. Astrid could absolutely eat shorts. Margot totally found a top secret ancient temple. That surely secured her membership card to the Very Serious Archaeologist club.

The pillars (Doric? Ionic? She had no idea.) stretched endlessly overhead. Even craning her neck back, she couldn't find the ceiling through the shadows. How deep had she gone? This temple was cavernous, devoid of any of the light and life it may have housed all those centuries ago. If she spoke at anything above a whisper, she felt certain her own voice would reply.

The farther she strode into the nave, the sweeter the air smelled. Like a department store perfume counter, the fragrance was inescapable—nectar and sea salt, incense and amber. It dragged her forward, feet moving down the hall as if of their own volition. At the other end of the temple, there was an empty marble pedestal protruding from a wall of sediment, not unlike museum displays or sacrificial altars.

Surrounding the altar in a semicircle stood five marble guardians. Chiseled and massive, the men towered over her. They clutched bows in their fists, fletches of arrows sheathed across their backs. Margot closed the space between her and the nearest statue. His face was expectedly stoic. Lips pinched into a flat line, a prominent Roman nose halving his features in perfect symmetry, hooded lids at half-mast, both scrutinizing and disinterested.

A shiver trailed down Margot's spine. A little too lifelike.

This close, the marble was flecked with deep red, spreading through the fingertips like veins. Margot followed the trail of maroon toward the statue's chest, where an orb of bloodstained red dripped, right where a heart would have been. The jet lag must have been getting to her because it almost looked like the crimson patch was churning like a tide, ebbing and flowing, pulsing, beating.

She rubbed her eyes. Totally imagining it.

This one's pedestal read *Ignis*, and he aimed an arrow, one eye winking closed to find an imaginary bull's-eye. Marble flames licked up his forearms. Next to him stood *Aura*, wind-swept and searching with a hand over his brow. Then, *Aqua*, surrounded by rising tides, and *Terra*, with climbing greenery carved in surprising detail twisting around the guardian's bare feet, twining up his armor-clad calves.

48

The last guardian, *Mors*, was enough to give Margot nightmares for the rest of her life. While the other guardians were men, *Mors* was just a skeleton, pierced through the chest with a marble arrow.

A shudder ran the length of her spine. "Yikes. That had to hurt."

Pacing back to the pedestal, she tried to ignore the way it felt like their empty stone eyes followed her. Margot couldn't shake the spear of cold fear that dug under her ribs. Her denim jacket wasn't nearly enough to keep it out.

She trailed her fingers along the altar. The smooth surface was cool beneath her hand, like everything down here, untouched by summer's heat. She wrapped a fist around the shard in her pocket, and the clay warmed in her fingers. Like it belonged here, and it knew it.

As she lifted it toward the altar, something creaked behind her.

"Holy—" A figure in the corner of Margot's vision made her soul try to leap from her body.

The shard slipped out of her fingers but she couldn't turn to see if it shattered, didn't even hear the impact. On instinct, Margot raised her arms to protect her face like she'd learned during her brief tae kwon do stint in middle school—yes, another phase. Right between telling everyone she wanted to become a veterinarian and learning to play electric bass guitar to join a punk band called Tight Jeans.

Adrenaline—hot, insistent—pounded through every inch of her body as she whirled around, eyes unsteady as she fought to find the shadow. Her flashlight beam did a ridiculously bad job of lighting up the temple.

Her pulse slowed when she realized the shape in her periphery was not a secret serial killer but just another statue. Because apparently five wasn't enough. Thanks for the heart palpitations, Venus.

Margot scooped up the shard, slipping it back into the inside pocket of her jacket, and followed a path of painted tiles toward where the statue posed, solitary and shadowed. On each stone, a flower had been rendered in breathtaking detail, a white myrtle bloom, wreathed in gold. They were too beautiful to walk on. Hopscotching would suffice.

The closer she got to the statue, the more the painted flowers wilted. First, the colors seeped from the blooms. Then, the petals shriveled. One fell, then another. The stems bowed their heads as if praying. The flowers had died by the time Margot reached the feet of the statue.

But this statue . . . wore boots.

There was no mistaking that the marble had been masterfully worked. Each fold of stone replicated cobbled leather. The stone shoelaces had aglets, for god's sake. She could trace the ridged cotton of socks where they vanished beneath the rough hem of well-worn trousers.

One hand was half-tucked inside a pocket, and the other

outstretched for something long gone. The statue even wore a watch. The sculptor had carved delicate numbers into the analog face, hands that pointed to 11:36.

It didn't make sense. Every bit of this was anachronistic. Sure, the Romans had invented loads of life-changing things. Indoor plumbing. Paved roads. Carbonara. But they definitely didn't have Rolexes.

Margot followed the trail of marble sleeves to the straps of suspenders, up a marble neck with a vein jutting out along the column, to a marble face that had her staggering backward. The sharp line of his chin, the crooked bridge of his nose, the way his mouth tilted like he knew a secret. Recognizable even in the nave-cold stone.

Van Keane?

It couldn't be. No one would have dragged a slab of marble into this forgotten temple just to chisel out a memorial to Van. But . . . every eyelash, every dimple had been lovingly carved. His mouth turned downward, lips parted just so. A crack in the stone split diagonally from his brow bone, over the bend in his nose, and down to his chin.

Margot propped her phone up so that her flashlight beamed onto the statue. Reaching into her backpack, she grabbed one of the brushes Dr. Hunt had handed out that afternoon. Getting a closer look, that was all.

She started at his hand. With fingers flexed, he'd been carved like he wanted something—needed it—but could never reach it. For a moment, she felt his agony as if it were her own.

The sleeves of his buttoned shirt had been pushed up his forearms, carelessly creased. A holster of excavating tools had been etched against his right hip. No detail had been spared.

He was so real. Exactly like he'd been in the photographs. A jolt of electricity coursed through Margot's veins.

She lifted onto her toes but barely reached the statue's chin. Her brush ran the length of his shoulder, dusting across his jaw. Then, gingerly, she swept the bristles along the marble's uncertain edge, right where the split had opened. Over his arched eyebrow, his nose, his cheeks. If she squinted, she would have sworn she saw freckles in the smooth white marble.

Her fingers trailed up his cool, stone arms, wrapping behind his neck, as she leveraged herself up to stare into his blank eyes. "Why are you here?" she asked the statue with little more than a breath.

And maybe it was the way her heart drummed in her chest, but she could almost feel his beating back.

With a fingertip, she traced the harsh lines of his face. Endless questions swam through her head, but there was no denying that this statue had been carved by *someone* to look just like him. Margot had half a mind to think it had been sculpted by Venus herself.

Beneath her hands, the marble quivered. A hairline fracture split off from the groove in his cheek. Margot flinched and swore. She staggered backward—had she caused that? Just like her, to touch a statue without thinking and destroy it with one breath.

Then another earthquake shuddered through the statue, slicing across the bridge of his stone nose. Fissures grew deeper, seams in the statue's foundation. Marble chipped off his cheekbone, his shoulders.

A thread of yellow light coursed over the statue, filling in every gap in the stone, burning bright as daylight as Margot squinted, then shielded her eyes with a hand.

Through the haze of light, Margot watched as the cracks multiplied. A thousand faint lines trailed over the statue's face, each spilling with gold. The whole thing would disintegrate. It'd be ruined. And it'd be her fault.

Now would have been a great time to find out this was all an elaborate practical joke. Something Astrid and the boys had planned to prove Margot didn't know what she was doing and didn't deserve to be here.

"No!" Margot gasped. Desperately, her hands grasped at the falling pieces. She pressed them back where they belonged, but the harder she tried, the more stone scattered.

The marble crumbled in a pool of molten light. Margot blinked away the spots in her vision as shadows reclaimed the space, and in the narrow beam of her phone flashlight, a set of too green eyes watched Margot right back.

Her heart thundered in her chest, drowning out every logical thought. But the stone shifted and shattered, revealing skin underneath.

With a groan of stone on stone, the statue shook off the last remnants of marble and stretched his arms out overhead, flexing them behind his head. A rattling breath shook out of lungs that apparently hadn't been used for, like, a hundred years.

It wasn't a statue of Van Keane.

It *was* Van Keane.

5

Margot screamed. Van screamed back.

And, look, it wasn't like Margot was a devout realist. Every decision she'd ever made had come from the heart, not the head. She believed in fairy tales, in happy endings. Signs from the universe, Santa Claus, soulmates. In basically everything she could. What was life without a little storybook magic in it?

But *this*? In what universe did statues become people? Certainly not hers. Margot's brain short-circuited. The longer she stared at him, the less she could believe it.

He looked exactly like he had in the photo—his tawny hair tousled like he couldn't care less, a jawline she could cut a steak with, and suspenders stretched over the broadest shoulders Margot had ever seen.

He also looked . . . mad. At her, specifically.

"Why are *you* screaming?" she asked, shrill. "I'm the one who's supposed to be screaming."

Van tried to say something, sucking in a deep breath, but it triggered a hacking cough. All the dust would do that. He glared at her, his face turning red. But that was probably just the lack of oxygen.

Margot felt like she'd chugged forty ounces of Mountain Dew. Blood rushed through her head, dizzying. It made her daring. She stepped closer. "You're really him, aren't you? Van Keane?"

Hard eyes cut up at her. "Who," he finally choked out, "even are you?"

"I'm Margot Rhodes." She smiled and stuck out her hand for him to shake.

"Margot Rhodes." He said her name like he'd just tried cilantro and discovered it tasted like soap. He glanced at her hand—only glanced, decidedly did not shake it. Heat prickled the back of Margot's neck at the rejection. "Mind telling me what you're doing in my temple . . . in your pajamas?"

"Your temple?" Margot asked. To her surprise, there was a lilt to her voice, playful, teasing. "You don't look like the goddess of love."

"Finders keepers." Van rolled his neck as if oiling the hinges, testing for creaks. Every action was laced with annoyance. Like he'd been terribly inconvenienced in that statue and was late to an appointment he couldn't miss. "So, what are you? A secretary? A reporter?"

"I'm an archaeologist," Margot said, squinting.

Van pivoted so fast that Margot nearly impaled herself on a sharpened marble bow, nocked by one of the guardians. She startled onto her heels as his gaze ran the length of her, a computational look in his eyes. "I know every archaeologist in southern Italy, and you're not one."

Margot bristled. "You couldn't possibly know that."

"Then, who are you working with? Speichler? Charles and deWolfe?" Van asked. Then, shaking his head like he was already three steps ahead of her side of the conversation, he added, "Doesn't matter. Atlas will be back soon, and you'll need to be long gone."

"No, he's . . ."

Van arched an eyebrow. When Margot trailed off, breathless at the weight of his look, he closed the space between them, looming over her. "No one knows how to find this place except me. Not even Atlas knows how to operate the temple door, I made sure of it. How did you get in here?"

The words froze in Margot's throat. Her cheeks flushed, reminding her pink was a verb. Because, well, how could she tell him that *he* was the only reason she'd found the temple?

Van leaned close enough that she could feel his breath, hot against her ear. "I'm going to ask one more time. What are you doing here?"

"The same thing you are," she said, a stubborn, determined edge to her voice. "Looking for the Vase of Venus Aurelia."

"Why would you be looking for——"

Van brushed past her, stalking toward the altar. His palms slammed against the polished stone. Head hanging toward his chest, he swallowed a groan of frustration. When he turned back to Margot, she suddenly wished she'd taken Master Park's tae kwon do lessons more seriously.

"What have you done with them?" Van's voice plateaued, unamused and impatient.

"I didn't do anything with anything," Margot said. An admittedly flimsy argument for an equally vague accusation.

A laugh cracked through Van's chest, hollow. "Please. The shards of the Vase, they were all right here moments ago. I don't need to *look* for them because I already found them."

Margot inched forward, slowly, the way you'd approach a wild, wounded animal. "Do you know what happened to you?"

How did you break it to someone that they'd missed the invention of the internet, the introduction of women to the workforce, and the rise, fall, and unfortunate comeback of low-rise jeans?

Van didn't back down. "I *was* fitting the Vase of Venus Aurelia together, but now it seems someone's stolen the shards."

"No. *No.* I didn't. They weren't there when I came down here, and they haven't been for a long, long time. But you . . . you have no idea." At Van's expression—a mixture of confusion and rising irritation—Margot sighed. "I mean, of course you don't. How could you know? Down here probably looks the same to you now as it did then."

Van cursed under his breath. He ran an agitated hand through his hair while the other searched his pockets. "Could you quit all your blabbering, kid? I've got a few more pressing issues than how the ruins look."

Kid. It wormed under Margot's skin. The polite placating she'd grown too used to hearing when people underestimated her. Not this time.

Her voice grew thorns. "The shards are gone."

"What aren't you telling me?" Van's fist fastened around the collar of her shirt.

This close, she could see the pale greens of his eyes, the contour of a nose broken at least once, and there, on his otherwise fair cheeks, a smattering of freckles from spending too much time in the sun.

Her traitor of a heart leaped. Not the time. When she'd imagined Van Keane, she thought he'd have been a noble explorer, someone curious and driven. Instead, he was just a jerk with something to prove.

"I haven't seen the shards," Margot said. Her voice softened. Even if he was a jerk, she couldn't deny the way his cheek twinged, the muscle clenching in frustration and disappointment. Everything he cared about: gone. She could feel his desperation as if it were her own. "No one's ever seen them all. Except you."

His knuckles grazed the skin of her neck, clutching her tighter. His lips pinched into a line. Steam could have poured out of his ears, and it wouldn't have surprised Margot.

"Take a look around. They're gone," Margot said. The bite found its way back into her voice as she placed a hand over his knuckles, attempting to extricate the collar of her jacket. It didn't matter how prestigious he was or how cute his lone cheek dimple was when he smiled. She was not some rag doll for him to throw around. "If you'd listen to me for two seconds, you'd know that when I walked in here, you were as stone as those statues, and you have been for the last century."

That was enough for him to loosen his grip entirely. "Elaborate."

"It's been ninety-six years since you walked into this temple for the first time, and you're the only person who's ever gotten even a little bit close to finding the Vase of Venus Aurelia, which is a huge deal, like congratulations, and everybody thought you died but apparently you were just turned into a statue, and your team split up after the accident, and then someone found your journal, and it ended up in my school library, and—" Margot gulped down a breath. "Now you're here. With me. And no Vase."

Which was just a teeny tiny lie, but Margot could still feel the curve of her lip, angling upward in a betraying smile. Hopefully Van couldn't read her like an open book. And-slash-or hadn't somehow developed supernatural X-ray vision during his tenure as a hunk of marble that would let him see the shard shoved deep, deep into her pocket.

Telling him about it now would sacrifice the only upper hand she had. She couldn't afford to do that.

Van finally let go of Margot's collar. Which was now completely wrinkled, but whatever. She hit the floor with a *thud*.

He thumbed at a divot between his eyebrows. "How?"

"How what?" Margot asked, picking herself up.

"How did I get turned into a statue? How did the Vase vanish? How did this all go wrong?" He'd slumped against the altar. With his head pressed between his palms, his shoulders sloped in on themselves. Before Margot could say anything, do anything, to console him, Van zipped upright. Composed, calm. Like maybe some of his memories all rushed back to him at once. "That's it."

"What's it?" Margot's eyebrows shot up. "You know where the shards went?"

The cogs in his head were spinning—she could see it in his eyes. He was focused on something hidden, puzzling it out. Not listening to her at all. To himself, he whispered, "They reset. They have to be earned again."

It only hardened Margot's resolve. "I'm going to find it. The rest of the Vase."

"No, you're not."

Okay, so he apparently had very selective hearing.

"Yes, I am." Margot pulled her shoulders back, ironing out the curve in her spine to look him straight in the eyes. "I have to. It's the whole reason I'm here, and you're going to help me do it."

Van laughed once, one monosyllabic bark. "I don't do partners. Not anymore. And I definitely don't work with you."

Margot squared her shoulders. "Why not?"

Van's calculated stare bore into her. In the dark centers of his eyes, all her insecurities reflected back at her. "You lack the qualifications."

"Like what?" Margot asked, crossing her arms to hold herself together.

"Like proper attire."

"I have other clothes back at my hotel," Margot huffed. "So, that's not even a good argument. Plus, you'll never find them all without me."

"I'll take my chances," Van said, a triumphant slant to his words.

Margot wished she could say she was above pleading, but she wasn't. "I'm telling you that you need me as much as I need you."

"Which is why you couldn't be bothered to put on proper clothes?"

"This is very cute, very respectable sleepwear!" Margot groaned, stepping closer. She pressed an accusing finger against his chest. "If I hadn't come down here, you'd still be a two-ton pile of stone. It wouldn't kill you to say thank you, you know. I'm not some—"

Margot's phone decided that was an incredible time for the battery to die.

A stifling darkness shrouded them, suffocatingly heavy. Then, with a strike, a globe of orange flared the end of a matchstick. Van returned a box of matches to his pocket and reached for a torch that hung against a nearby pillar. He doused it in flames. Stark shadows probed through the temple in contrast to the sudden light.

The nave illuminated—taller and wider than Margot could have possibly imagined. The ruins overhead were nothing in comparison to the grandeur of this buried temple.

Every wall was painted in brilliant colors, colors the sun hadn't been able to wash away. Rich, indulgent pigment stained every surface, painting visions of rolling fields with wildflower blooms and still seas. Twin staircases on either side led to railed balconies that wreathed the temple's walls. A palace suitable for a goddess.

Van barely noticed. This place was old news to him.

"I'll survive just fine without you," he said. Not cocky, just . . . certain.

Peering up at him, Margot wanted to shout. To tell him he was wrong about her—to prove herself to him and everyone else who thought she couldn't do this. In that precise moment, when Margot felt like she could 1,000 percent handle anything thrown her way, certain that she, too, could survive just fine on her own, an arrow zinged between their noses.

With a crack, the marble projectile embedded into the wall.

Margot paled. Slowly, she pivoted toward the statues standing sentry around the altar. *Ignis*'s bowstring still vibrated.

The guardians were alive.

6

The five guardians nocked new arrows, each aimed at Margot's chest. Every muscle in her body seized. Van, however, wasted no time transforming into an action movie hero. He slid between *Mors* and *Terra*, swiping an arrow from the quiver strapped to *Terra's* back. Wielding the sharp edge of the arrowhead like a knife, he sliced through *Ignis's* bowstring.

Margot was too busy last quarter taking astronomy and trying out for the rowing team to take Dr. Hunt's class, but she was pretty sure fighting living statues wasn't taught in Classical Archaeology.

"You should move," Van instructed.

Right. *Right.*

Margot ducked right as the bowmen released, dust filtering over her head as their arrows slammed together. Her hands and knees pressed against the chilled stone floors as she scuttled out of the cross fire.

The guardians swiveled on their stands, tracing her every stride. It was unnerving to watch a statue move, as they moved with a gravity, slower and heavier than humans, but they only twisted in place, their feet glued to the spot.

"At least they can't——" Margot began.

Aqua was the first off his pedestal. His cloak of waves moved with him as he took booming, marble-heavy steps.

She gulped. "Never mind."

The rest of the guardians followed, treading forward. Toward her. Their footsteps slammed into the ground. Each pounding movement rattled the temple's foundation, like the whole thing might just crumble.

Along the temple walls, Van touched the bulb of his torch to a ledge circling the first floor. A trail of fire snaked around the perimeter, blooming with orange firelight that sheared through the shadows.

Unfortunately, all the extra light only made it that much easier to see the guardians hunting Margot.

Fight and flight screamed equally loudly in her head. Flight: run toward the staircase at the far end and dig her way out if she had to, never looking back and never wondering what might have been. Fight: prove to Van that she wasn't some foolish girl in over her head and convince him to work with her to find the missing shards.

"You should have never come down here," Van called from across the hall. He swapped his torch for the chisel and trowel he had sheathed at his hip, wielding them like twin blades.

Fight, it was.

Maybe Van had the right idea. If she destroyed the guardians' weapons, they'd be, like, at least a little easier to escape. All she needed to do was what he'd done.

Everywhere Margot ran, the guardians shifted toward her. She jumped, stretching all her fingers, and snatched one of the fletchings in *Aura*'s quiver. The statue spun on its heels, slow for a human—but significantly faster than any statue should have ever moved, which, as far as Margot was concerned, was not at all. Unfortunately, their arrows didn't seem to be constrained by the same sluggishness.

The pale face, so close to her own, caught Margot off guard, and she fumbled, tripping over her heels. Her stolen arrow skittered over the ground, just out of reach. She crab-crawled away from *Aura* just as he reached for another arrow behind his head, sending her scooting backward until she was pressed flat against the wall. This was not going according to plan.

Aura took aim, his marble bowstring stretching with unnatural elasticity. Behind him, Van sprinted and slid, carving his chisel down the guardian's back. The dull blade wasn't enough to do any lasting damage, but just enough to make it so Margot wasn't tragically impaled.

"What are you doing?" Van asked her. He managed to somehow seem completely unflustered by the fact they were being *attacked* by *sentient statues*, like this was just a regular day's work for him.

"Trying to not get killed by these giant, evil Cupids," she said. The *duh* was silent.

Van shook his head, almost imperceptibly. Margot knew what disappointment looked like. He didn't offer her a hand up or anything. "Try harder."

He didn't wait for a response—he dashed toward the front of the nave and left Margot scrambling to catch up. Seriously, how long were his legs? Her feet slammed with every step, the stone jarring every joint.

Mors veered into her path, and Margot screeched to a halt. The skeleton's eyeless skull craned down at her, and bringing a hand to his chest, he pulled the arrow out of his pulsing red heart.

She had to do something, or she wasn't going to survive long enough to do anything ever again.

Come on, green belt. Don't let me down now.

Margot brought her knee to her chest, and when she kicked, foot impacting the statue's hand, the arrow dropped out of the guardian's fingers. It hit the floor with enough force to snap it in half. An elated laugh ripped out of her in surprise.

"Oh, my god, did you see that?" Margot asked, but Van had already hiked halfway up the stairwell.

No way was she getting left down here alone. She raced to catch up with him. Margot's breath burned in her lungs, searing a seam in her waist. A couple too-close-for-comfort arrows sliced past her ears as she took the stairs two at a time.

"There's no way out," she said when she met him halfway up. "It locked from the outside."

This time, he didn't even bother to shake his head. "There's always another way."

"I'm telling you, I didn't see——"

Van punched a brick in the wall three times. On the third, it slotted into place and the ground overhead shuddered. The ceiling sank closer, but as soon as Margot thought it was going to crush them, it scrolled sideways and inched into a compartment at the top of the wall. Perfectly engineered.

Margot had never been so relieved to see moonlight.

Aboveground, Van stomped on the base of the hollow pillar where Margot had knelt. As she hauled herself to join him (he didn't even offer his hand), she recognized it now—a niche for lit candles. This empty courtyard must have once been home to a sanctuary for Venus's followers, a sacred place to gather. A facade for the real temple below the earth. The pressure from Van's foot triggered the release of the door, and it slammed closed behind them.

Unfortunately, they'd traded stone guardians for security guards.

Flashlight beams bounced around the knoll. All aimed directly at Margot and Van. Beneath the bright lights, Margot could imagine what they looked like. Her in a pair of striped pajamas and a denim jacket, Van straight out of a 1930s L.L.Bean ad, and both of them covered head to toe in a layer of dust so thick, it would take Margot three Everything Showers to scrub it off her skin. There had to be some way for them to make it out of this alive and unhandcuffed.

Margot didn't think. She just grabbed Van's hand and pulled him left down the slope of the hill. They plunged into the darkness of the ruins, rubble rising up around them in every direction. At their backs, guards shouted, faint and fading as they raced farther away. What they said, Margot had no idea. Her Italian was limited to *Scusi!* and spaghetti—the necessities.

Van shook off her grip as soon as his feet hit the ancient pavement. He aimed toward the front entrance, but Margot jerked him by the suspenders—instead heading north toward the necropolis. The sudden change in momentum threw him off-balance, and his arms pinwheeled toward her, just as a flashlight beam cut across them.

Margot landed on top of his chest, squeezing him into the earth. His firm, muscular chest. This close, he smelled like rough leather and stone pine, like long afternoons in the sun. Exactly like she'd imagined.

"Get off of me," he ordered.

Well, he wasn't *exactly* like she'd imagined.

Heat rushed to Margot's face. She forced herself upright and blew a loose strand of hair out of her face. "Sorry. Just trying to make sure neither of us get arrested tonight."

Van stood, dusting himself off. "Why would we get arrested?"

"For starters, we're trespassing." Margot tucked the rogue curl behind her ear, listening for the guards' approach. "Pretty sure there's probably a destruction of property charge in there somewhere. Intention to commit larceny? I mean, we're basically treasure hunters."

That was the *Legally Blonde* era talking, when she'd shadowed a local judge for all of four days.

Evidently, Van wasn't convinced. He turned the corner toward the front entrance, and Margot rushed to cut him off.

"Don't," she said. "Trust me. There are guards everywhere. The Nola Gate is a no-go. Head north until you pass the creepy graveyard. I've got a getaway car."

Van's eyes nearly popped out of their sockets. "You can *drive*?"

"A bunch of statues just tried to kick our ass, and that's what you're shocked about?" Unbelievable. Margot shook her head. "I'll hold the guards off and meet you outside the gate when the coast is clear. I've left a yellow Vespa nearby, but wait for me."

Turning her back on him, Margot settled herself with an inhale. Not far off, she could hear the slap of the guards' feet against the pathways, the echo of their shouts. She could do this. All the best escapes had a decoy.

Cupping her hands around her mouth, Margot shouted, "I'm over here!"

Behind her, Van asked flatly, "That's your idea of holding them off?"

Whipping around, Margot's cheeks burned when she saw Van standing exactly where she'd left him, hands shoved in his pockets and those scrutinizing green eyes trained on her in the pale light. She asked, "Is now the right time to criticize my methods?"

Van crooked his head, appraising her. His expression was unreadable, like he'd buried whatever he might have felt deep beneath the surface and Margot would have to pry it out if she ever wanted to understand him. Then, wordlessly, he tugged a chained compass around his neck up from underneath his shirt and checked his position before turning and heading toward the necropolis.

Margot took another steadying breath, bracing for the moment when security spotted her. She'd lead them on a goose chase, buying Van enough time to get ahead, and then she'd lose them in the fifth region, hopping the fence just like she had when she got here. It was just like Isla and Reed escaping the Durham Crew under gunfire on Crete in chapter eighteen of *Relics of the Heart*. Divide and conquer. Easy.

"Looking for someone?" Margot hollered.

A lone beam rounded the corner at the far end of the alley. Margot held her ground. She had to wait until the exact right moment, giving Van as much time as possible to make it past the ruins' edge.

"*Signorina, fermati adesso!*" one of the guards replied. Not that Margot was in a position to dissect the sociopolitical hierarchy of the night-duty guards, but if she had to guess, he was the head honcho. He had a head full of dark hair and a face as wrinkled as a T-shirt you forgot in the dryer.

Except that Margot couldn't *fermati adesso*, whatever that meant.

"Sorry," she responded. "I haven't reached that Duolingo level yet!"

Three more flashlight beams appeared. Then, three more. No, five more. Margot quailed, pacing backward with her hands held palms-out next to her face. The guards spoke, overlapping each other with shouted demands Margot couldn't comprehend.

Around the next corner, another line of security guards materialized, fencing her in. Margot froze, staked to the ground with a spike of terror.

Okay. Maybe Van was right. This was a bad idea. Terrible.

The guards waded closer. She'd stalled between the buildings, closed in a dead end. What had Van said? *There's always another way.*

Scanning the ancient street, Margot searched for new escape routes. There had to be something, but the structures leaned into each other, one stone wall flush against the next. A window had been carved into the stone facade, and the tiled roof had been remarkably preserved, the clay faded into pale red.

Well, when one door closes, a window opens.

Margot bolted toward the window and hoisted herself through feetfirst. She landed in a lousy excuse for a somersault, tumbling over herself in a tangle of limbs. Recovering, she sprinted through the house, zipping around walls plastered with ruddy-faced cherubs who looked absolutely nothing like the guardians they'd left in the temple below.

At the back of the house, she launched herself over a half-decayed wall. Or, at least, tried to. With gravel biting into the soft of her palms, her hold slipped, sneakers skidding, and the skin of her knees scraped against the stone.

Okay, ow. That couldn't slow her down. She hooked a leg around the top of the wall, vaulting herself over, and scrambled down the backside.

The alleys were so narrow. If she stayed, the guards would corner her in three seconds flat. Using a window as a foothold, Margot stretched, grappling at the clay roofline. She heaved herself up with a groan.

From the rooftop, Margot spotted Van. He'd passed the graveyard and turned toward the city's yellow glow, a moth to a flame. Margot raced along the roofs, balancing with her arms out, ancient roof tiles tinkling to the ground as she cried out a belated "Sorry!" Beneath her, the guards and their flashlights followed her every step. Whatever they hollered was lost on her, but she imagined it sounded a lot like, *That's very much not allowed* and *Get off the roof.*

Fortunately for the guards but unfortunately for Margot, there wasn't much roof left. The shingles evaporated, chipping off at the edge of a courtyard. Throwing her arms out for balance, she walked the thin ledge of the retaining wall like a gymnast's beam as the guards barreled into the building below.

At the far side of the courtyard, Margot climbed down and made a fast break for the outskirts of the city, leaving the ruins strewn behind her. The fifth region's wide-open fields swayed in the lilting wind. She hopped the fence with so little grace, she was glad no one had been around to see it.

Wait . . . no one was around.

Ahead, silhouetted in the moonlight, Van hiked over the hillsides. What part of *wait for me* hadn't been clear?

Even running as fast as she could, Van felt impossibly far. "Slow down," Margot called.

Van didn't look over his shoulder. Margot had the lung capacity of a Choir Girl #7, not an Elphaba or an Eliza Schuyler, and her body screamed for air when she finally caught up with him. With her hands on her knees, her chest heaved, heart slowing back to a normal operating tempo.

"It's this way." She steered him toward the rut in the grass near the cul-de-sac with the flickering streetlight. Shaking the residual adrenaline out from her arms, Margot said, "That was incredible. I felt like a real Indiana Jones."

Van's forehead wrinkled. "Who?"

"He was . . . a little after your time." With her hands in her pockets, Margot ran her thumb over the shard's smooth side like a worry stone. "So, where to next?"

"I told you, no partners. I don't need someone to worry about saving."

"What are you talking about? You saved me, and then I saved you. We're even."

"Doesn't matter." Van's pace didn't slow. "I'm not associating with some troublemaking girl with a brain full of bad ideas."

"I told you. You need me," Margot said. And this time, she knew she had the upper hand. "You don't know anything about the twenty-first century. We have wireless internet and cat cafés and Uber Eats. What are you going to do without a credit card or an ID or an international data plan? You don't even have a car."

"Sure, I do." Van lifted his hand out of his pocket, dangling a diamond key ring stamped with the Hotel Villa Minerva logo. "Goodbye, Margot Rhodes."

Margot checked the side pocket of her backpack where she thought—no, *knew*—she'd stashed that key, but it was empty. "How did you—hey! Give that back! You can't just leave me!"

Van didn't stop walking. Didn't hesitate or turn back. Definitely didn't slow down as Margot sprinted toward him. He just stuck the key into the scooter's ignition and flashed the high beam on. Revving the whiny little engine, he shot off into the winding streets of citrus and stucco.

Without her.

7

Margot's blisters had blisters. Her bones ached in protest with every step back to Plot D.

She'd spent the entire five-mile walk back to the hotel last night wondering how Van could be so utterly un-Van-like. He'd written about Pompeii like it was a spectacular adventure, something spellbinding. He was supposed to be dashing and inquisitive, a regular Reed Silvan. And sure, he would have challenged her, but it would have been because he knew she was capable of something remarkable, not because he didn't believe in her.

Her Van would have never stranded her in the middle of the night in Italy with no phone.

Her Van didn't exist at all.

Margot's welcome to Plot D was as warm as she'd expected. Astrid and Suki had both been downstairs for breakfast by the time she'd pried herself out of the death trap that was the top bunk's sheets. She almost hadn't put on her lipstick. Almost.

In the daylight, the ruins were starker and more undeniable. There was no hint of magic threading through the streets like there had been last night. There was only stone, ancient and unforgiving, exhumed from its resting place for poking and prodding by curious minds.

Now, the class sat cross-legged in front of their excavation plots, and Dr. Hunt trekked back and forth as she lectured.

"Venus was the patron goddess of Pompeii, which meant she was viewed as the city's primary caretaker and worshiped by its residents. Of course, we know Venus as the goddess of love, but the city of Pompeii also quickly found its footing as a major trading post and a travel destination for Romans throughout the empire, thanks to her generosity." She pointed to the fresco on the courtyard's wall. The depiction of Venus here was scantily dressed, requiring a level of maturity that far exceeded anything Rex and Topher were capable of. "Gods and goddesses have many different names—we call these epithets—and Pompeii's Venus was known adoringly as Venus Felix, or Lucky Venus, and sometimes as Venus Aurelia."

"Golden Venus," Astrid said quickly, not waiting for Dr. Hunt to call on her despite her arm rod-straight in the air.

Margot glowered across the dig site. She didn't have to be a Latin scholar to know that one.

"Precisely," Dr. Hunt said, a soft smile gracing her lips.

Margot's hand shot up, and Dr. Hunt nodded, encouraging her to speak. "And what about the Vase of Venus Aurelia? Why do you think no one knows where its pieces are?"

Rex said, "Because any archaeologist worth their salt knows the Vase is mythological. You know, a make-believe story."

Dr. Hunt cocked her head. "Actually, Mr. Yang, many myths were formed on the foundations of truth. Achilles may not have truly fought in the Trojan War, but the Trojan War was fought. As for the shards, Venus was notoriously ruthless. Like Psyche descending into the underworld, I suspect the trials of the Vase are equally demanding. Impossible, even."

"If you completed them all," Suki asked, "would the Vase really make everyone fall in love with you?"

"No wonder Margot wants to hear all about it," Astrid sneered. "She definitely needs it."

Margot's shoulders fell. Trying to exist near Astrid was like trying to floss with barbed wire.

Dr. Hunt didn't acknowledge Astrid's comment, thank god. She breezed forward, saying, "The myth is, like many, unclear. Some researchers suggest the Vase was believed to bestow gold to whoever successfully completed the trials. Others say the hero would be *golden*, eternally beloved and bestowed with Venus's gift. It's a linguistic conundrum."

"Do you think it's really out there?" Margot asked, even if Astrid snickered behind her.

Considering, Dr. Hunt trapped her chin. "I think history always finds a way of surprising us. That's why we dig. Everybody, grab your spades and get started."

Margot's phone buzzed in her backpack. She waited until Dr. Hunt drifted toward Plot A to slip it from its pocket.

Her dad had texted. Margot's stomach hit rock bottom as she thumbed open the message.

Gogo, saw on the online itinerary the class was going to Rome tomorrow. Booked a nonstop flight from FCO to ATL that evening at 7 PM. Forwarding the details.

Another notification popped up at the top. An email. From American Airlines.

Her chest ached, right behind her sternum—the vagus nerve, her therapist had called it. She pressed two hands against the bone to try to calm the swirl of emotions before it became a storm she couldn't control.

How was she supposed to find four more shards in *thirty-six hours?* Talk about a Herculean task.

Margot's legs stood of their own accord. She was pulled by an invisible tether she couldn't fight and didn't want to. She'd come here for a reason. She wasn't giving up this time.

"Where are you going?" Astrid asked, snide.

"I . . . There's something I have to go do," Margot said half-heartedly. What she needed was to run. To get out of there. To find the rest of the Vase shards before it was too late.

* * *

Margot didn't have Van, but she did have Van's journal. And that boy was nothing if not meticulous. Entries had been dated and time-stamped, chronicles of each step on his quest for the Vase of Venus Aurelia.

Unfortunately, he also apparently wrote in little riddles.

Mysterious and intriguing? Admittedly, yes. Indicative of trust issues? Perhaps. Irritating and obnoxiously inconvenient? Definitely.

Start at the top of the forum and head due east for three cross-hatches.

Google Maps didn't accept crosshatches as a unit of measurement. Margot stood beneath a pine that stretched halfway to heaven, casting swaths of shade across the triangular forum, trying to make sense of her paper map. She blazed through the crowds of white-sneakered tourists down Via del Tempio d'Iside, which turned into Vicolo del Menandro, which turned into . . . a fork in the road.

Turn right for eighteen heartbeats.

At what bpm, Van?

Margot walked until the road split again, frantically deciphering his instructions. She followed Van's cryptic clues until she stood at the entrance, and the only thing separating the ruins of Pompeii from the bustling modern city of Pompei (with one *I*) was a silver turnstile. Trailing over Van's neat handwriting, she read and reread his words, triple-checking his directions.

Onward thirty-seven quarter-kilometers opposite the sea.

Somewhere behind her, the blue-green waves must have sparkled under the morning sun. This was the right path forward. She just hadn't expected to have to leave the grounds of the ancient city.

As soon as she pushed through the gate, the ruins gave way to awning-covered doorways and wrought-iron balconies, sidewalk seating with laminated menus and arched windows offering glimpses into pubs and pizzerias. The buildings were each painted in salmons and peaches, rich golds and paper whites. Margot rushed to cross the street, propelled by Van's words.

Right at the dripping myrtle, and an immediate left at the statue missing two limbs.

Follow the northern perimeter of the piazza along the avenue of trees.

Perpendicular to Mount Vesuvius for sixteen paces.

Margot slowed to a stop outside a sign that read Martines Cucine. It was a lopsided, goldenrod-painted restaurant with red shuttered windows and flower boxes spilling with wide orange blooms. Outside, couples clinked wine glasses and swirled creamy pasta around their forks, laughing and leaning into each other. It was picturesque: something out of an old movie, timeless and romantic.

Except for the shouting.

Tugged forward by the sound, Margot peered down a

cramped alleyway. Beside a stack of crates, a man in a striped apron and a massive white toque gestured wildly, hollering at someone hidden.

Another voice answered. A voice Margot recognized.

"I'm not trying to steal your bread," Van yelled. "I don't want your bread at all!"

"You can't come into my kitchen. This door is locked for guests." The man scratched his monster of a mustache. "How else can I say it? You are not welcome here. Go to the front."

Margot inched closer, her back pressed against the stucco exterior. Van's voice seemed to lift out of a carton of ripe lemons. "I don't need to go to the front. I need to go sixteen paces east. *This* is east."

Sixteen paces. That was Margot's next instruction. Of course Van would be searching for the shards, too.

Creeping around the crates, she got a good look at him. Van wore the same clothes as last night, woefully out of place with his suspenders and khaki pants on a sweltering summer day. He'd rolled down the sleeves of his shirt, and color gathered beneath his eyes, evidence of a sleepless night.

"Yes, eat. Out front. Luna will seat you."

"Not eat. *East.*" Van's agitation manifested in every inflection. He started like he was going to push past the chef through sheer force of will. "I don't have time for—"

"There you are!" Margot said, waving. She brushed a smile on her face, easy and eager. Maybe the key to not being caught in a lie was only telling the truth. "I've been wondering where you ran off to."

"You're here," Van said, a simmering heat radiating off him. "Dandy."

The chef glanced between them, his hat wobbling with the movement. "A table for two?"

Margot looped her arm around Van's, bringing her hand up to rest in the crook of his elbow. She leaned her head in sweetly like she'd done it hundreds of times before. Van's bicep tensed beneath her cheek. His whole body was tense, actually. She squeezed her fingers tighter in return.

"I think we just got a little lost," Margot said. She dialed her southern drawl up to a hundred and batted her lashes for good measure. "We're awfully sorry for any trouble, aren't we, *sweetheart?*"

When Van didn't say anything, Margot jabbed his kidney with an elbow. Through gritted teeth, he said, "Yes. Awfully."

"My boyfriend here, he's so bad with directions. Terrible, really." Margot nodded toward the kitchen door where sauces bubbled, filling the air with oregano and rosemary. "We wouldn't want to keep you from the lunch rush."

"*Grazie*," he said. Then, eyeing Van, he added, "Maybe keep your boyfriend on a leash."

As soon as the chef vanished behind the swinging door, Van whirled in front of Margot, extracting himself from her grip. He leaned close. Close enough for her to notice the speckles in his eyes—flecks of gold through the green, amber as a fossil. He seethed, "Boyfriend?"

Margot smiled. "Worked like a charm."

"How did you find me here?" His eyes drifted to her hand, wrapped around a very familiar leather-bound notebook. "You stole my journal?" he asked, cutting like a butcher knife.

Margot paced backward. Both hands clutched his journal. "I didn't steal anything. I borrowed it. From a library."

His mouth flattened, eyes creasing. "And you're here, which means you read it."

Paling, Margot stuttered, "Well, listen. I mean, yeah, but it's really . . . well-written?"

"Give it to me."

"It's not like I knew it was your diary. It's a historical text, okay!"

Van's expression somehow grew even more annoyed. "It's not a diary. It's a *journal*. My journal."

He held his hand out, expectant.

"No. No!" Margot shucked off her backpack and flung the journal to the very bottom before zipping it tight. No way was he taking it away from her. "You can't have it back. If the librarian finds out I took it and I don't return it, I'm toast."

"So, you did steal it?"

"Not the point."

"Give it back to me."

Margot took another step, but she rammed into the fruit crates. "I can't do that."

Van placed a hand on the box behind her head, cornering her. Every move he made was stiff, like he'd slept on the hard ground. "Because you think you're going to use it to find the Vase of Venus Aurelia."

Margot tipped her chin upward so she could look him dead in the eye and asked, "Is that so hard to believe?"

"Yes," he said, like it was obvious. "You don't stand a chance. This isn't amateur hour."

"I'm not an amateur—"

Van's eyebrows threaded together. "Really? Because you're acting like one."

Margot tugged her arms against her chest. "Am not."

"Are, too."

"Am not—okay *now* who's acting like an amateur?"

Van retreated. He flexed the muscles in his hand, shaking out his fingers like he'd clenched them so hard they'd cramped. "This is why I don't work with partners."

"I get it. I'm stuck with a partner I don't want to work with either, but haven't I proved myself useful already?" Margot asked.

Scrubbing a hand over his face, Van sighed. His glare didn't exactly fade so much as wear away, his resolve like silt in a riverbed, eroding. "Could you keep it down? I'm thinking."

"You know, trying to silence women might have been cool in the thirties, but it's such a faux pas these days."

"I'm not trying to *silence women*," Van scoffed. "I'm trying to silence you."

"I didn't see this restaurant in your diary, that's all I'm saying."

His fingertips dug into his temples—she had no doubt he blamed her for that migraine. No, it couldn't have anything to do with the fact that he'd spent the better part of the last century entombed in stone and now he was in way over his head.

Then, it clicked. "Your instructions are wrong."

Van straightened, defensive. "Certainly not."

A smug grin washed over Margot's face. "They might have been right a hundred years ago, but not anymore. Some of these buildings are new, aren't they? And now you don't know where to go."

"You're wrong." His mouth twitched. "I know exactly where I'm going."

Margot peered both ways down the alley. A dead end. "But you can't get there."

A metaphorical light bulb flashed behind Van's eyes. His gaze darted from the top of Martines Cucine to the bottom, scanning left to right. She could practically see him downloading information, analyzing his options.

His attention snagged on the tower of wooden boxes.

Wordlessly, he picked up the lemon crate and repositioned it against the restaurant's wall. Retracing his steps, he stacked a carton of tomatoes on top of it. A tower. He couldn't go through the buildings, so he'd go over them. Even if she kind of hated him, Margot had to admit it was a good idea.

She heaved the next crate into her arms.

"What are you doing?" Van snapped.

The weight nearly toppled her over, but she managed to drop her carton on top of the one he'd just moved. "I'm helping you."

"No, you aren't." He grabbed two crates next. Like he was trying to make a point.

Margot's shoulders sagged, flustered. "Are you kidding? I just saved you from Italian Gordon Ramsay. Don't I get a little bit of credit?" She scooted the last crate out of the way with her legs. "You don't think I can handle a little parkour? I took three months of gymnastics. I was made for this. I'm coming with you, and there's nothing you can do to stop me."

Van's face scrunched up, caught somewhere between annoyance and amusement. He didn't climb the crate tower they'd built. Instead, he stayed quiet as he pried up a metal sewer cover that had been buried beneath the boxes and dropped it against the ground with a crash.

Sinking down the first rung of a ladder descending beneath the city, he finally said, "We'll see about that."

8

Margot severely underestimated the extreme yuckiness of the sewer system.

The stench clogged her nose, so rotten she was certain she would never smell anything nice ever again. Not her favorite cinnamon vanilla perfume, not a fresh bouquet of peonies, not gooey chocolate chip cookies hot out of the oven. Just rotten eggs for the rest of her days.

But she wasn't going to let Van prove her wrong just because of a little biohazard situation.

Van peered over his shoulder, checking to see if she was still there, and she wiped a Colgate smile across her face. She didn't get braces for nothing. But the second he turned forward again, trudging through the soupy brown muck, Margot's face screwed up in disgust.

This was not her preferred way to spend an afternoon, that was for sure.

Down here, the walls curved overhead. Van had to walk through the deepest waters in the center of the tunnel so his scalp didn't scrape against the ceiling. Every few feet, streams of pale light filtered down from above, striped through the storm drains. A relieving detail. That meant they weren't in a *wastewater* sewer, just a stormwater one. Still, Margot kept to the sidewall where a step had been carved into the channel, so only her socks got soaked.

She groused, "I don't recall your diary mentioning this part."

Van breathed out of his nose. "Like I said. It's a journal, and I didn't ask you to come. In fact, I explicitly told you not to."

She stuck her tongue out at him and retracted it when he glared at her again. "I just saved you. Again. That makes the score two-one."

"We're keeping score?" Van asked.

"Only because you refuse to admit I'd make a great partner in crime."

Street names had been carved into the stone walls, and Van followed them like a breadcrumb trail. The tunnels cut a hard right, just like Van's journal had said—*turn clockwise at the next junction.* At least they were on the right path. The thought of adding another shard to her collection made the whole *needing a noseplug* thing a little more worth it.

As Van led the way, Margot slung her backpack off one shoulder and opened the main compartment. Wrapped up in linen, the first shard had been tucked safely inside a zippered pocket, but Van's journal . . . Van's journal *had* been right there.

"What did you—"

"Looking for this?" Van asked. He waved his journal in one hand and then slid it into his back pocket. But his head craned downward, reading something.

Not just something. Margot riffled through her backpack—pawing through makeup bags and spare maxi pads and an emergency supply of Biscoff cookies she'd snatched from the airplane—but she didn't see it.

He hadn't just stolen back his journal. He'd grabbed *Relics of the Heart*.

"How do you keep doing that?" Margot asked, shocked.

Van declined to answer. He may have been turned to stone before SCOTUS established the Miranda rights, but he was a pro at remaining silent.

Margot stretched for her book, almost toppling off her pathway, but Van held it out of reach, turning to another chapter. Curse him and his long arms. He flipped through the pages, and Margot braced for impact. She'd heard it all. *Romance novels aren't real literature. Why don't you read something useful? What a waste of paper.* As if the book that made Margot believe in hope after her parents' happily ever after had shattered wasn't worth its weight in gold.

After what felt like eons of him examining page after page, he said, "You seriously dog-ear your books?"

Margot's mouth hung open.

"What kind of Neanderthal doesn't use a bookmark?" he prodded.

"That's hardly a criminal offense."

Van's eyes widened theatrically. "And you wrote in the margins?"

"That's none of your business!" she said.

He lifted an eyebrow. "Like how reading my journal is none of yours?"

She gave him a withering look, but it did nothing to stop his finger from skimming the pages.

"*Love a golden hour first kiss,*" he read, tilting the book sideways to read her scribbled notes. "Here, you underlined *brooding love interest* thrice."

Margot reached for the book again, and this time, her fingers grazed the curled edge of the cover. But it wasn't enough. Her grasp slipped, and Van's didn't hold.

Relics of the Heart splashed into the stormwater.

"You're such a jerk!" Margot said, more a gasp than a sentence. She plucked the book from the sewage sludge and shook it off, praying it was just damp and not destroyed. "You did that on purpose."

Van hesitated. He stretched his fingers back, popping the bones. "I . . . didn't."

"Yeah, right," she said with a groan.

"I spent the last ninety-six years as a statue. Give me a break." His voice was so taut, she almost wanted to believe him.

The chapters stuck together as Margot flipped through them, trying to make sure they didn't dry like that. If they did, the book would never recover. Her eyes stung with tears when she saw the black ink running, dripping from one page to the next.

Relics of the Heart wasn't just a love story. It was the only piece of her mom that her dad hadn't kept from her. And if he'd known she'd taken it, he certainly would have tried.

When her mom left, she'd packed up only what she could fit into a carry-on suitcase and a tote bag. Everything else had been shoved in the spare bedroom and sat dormant until the paperwork had been finalized. While the ink was still drying, her dad had piled it into the back of the car to take to the donation center—erasing her from their lives like she was a wine stain on a white tablecloth and he had a gallon of bleach.

Relics of the Heart had been the one thing she had stolen out of those boxes. Margot couldn't let it go.

She knew she should be mad at her mom for leaving. And for a long time, she had been. But Parker Rhodes didn't have a secret boyfriend or leave to start another family. She'd left for an adventure, a life bigger than anything Dogwood Hollow, Georgia, could have ever offered.

That much, Margot understood.

Now, she shoved *Relics of the Heart* back into her backpack and slowed to a stop next to Van when the tunnels split. To the right, the stones had dried, and to the left, shadows clung to the curve of the sewers, the waters darker, deeper.

Margot's gaze darted between them. Creepy tunnel of doom or a nice, light, *dry* tunnel. She knew which one she chose. "Let's go this way."

"Head south until the double palm, and then look below the last column." Margot recognized the last line of Van's directions immediately. Matter-of-factly, he added, "This way is south."

Margot pouted. "Why can't this way be south?"

Van reached under his shirt for his chained compass. An emblem Margot couldn't quite see had been engraved on the yellow gold face, and when he flipped it open like a locket, the little white arrow pointed due south. He tapped the glass with his forefinger. "Because it's not."

"Well, the vibes are way better over here." Margot trekked into the dry tunnel, relishing the solid floors beneath her feet.

Van didn't budge. "The vibes?"

Margot nodded. "You know, like how that way looks cursed, and this way doesn't."

"Thankfully, the poles are not beholden to your so-called *vibes*, and neither am I," he said before plunging down the darkened corridor.

Swearing under her breath, Margot trailed after him. Here, the darkness was cloying, the smell thicker. Van blurred into an outline ahead of her. Her palms slicked with nerves.

The channel filled, and while Van was only up to his hips, Margot waded through chest-high tides. She hiked her back-pack as far up as she could, then hefted it over her head, trying to protect it. "When you found the shards before," she asked, "how did you do it?"

Van's response came quick, defensive. "I completed the trials."

"Sure." Margot stepped on something squishy but unseen in the murky water—ew. She wouldn't let herself imagine the myriad wretched things it might have been. "But I mean, no one else had ever done it. How did you even know where to look?"

He turned right, and Margot followed on his heels. She could tell in the way the corner of his mouth lifted and sank again that he was measuring how much to trust her with. Van Keane probably never did anything without thinking it through from six different directions.

"It's like the old myths—the gods needed everything to be proven. So, heroes were given tasks." He zapped the magic straight out of it with his cold analysis. Margot found it hard to believe that somebody this gruff, this unyielding, had managed to outwit the goddess of love. "They were instructions, and I followed them."

"Are they dangerous?" Margot asked.

Van rolled his eyes. "If I say yes, will you give up and leave me alone?"

"No," Margot said with a shrug.

He sighed, a whole-body movement that came with the sloshing sound of the water all around his waist. "They are dangerous, but I'm not the type to be able to afford to walk away from a fight."

"There's a reward for finding all of the shards, right?" Margot asked as they trudged farther into the shadows. The waterline receded as they turned another corner, stepping back onto dry ground. "Did you . . . get it?"

Her real question went unsaid: Why didn't it work? Because obviously it didn't work. He'd been hocus pocused into a statue, the Vase had disappeared, and Van was only about as likable as escargot. Hardly *eternally beloved*. Maybe he was simply too callous for Venus's magic to work on him.

Van leaned over his shoulder, peering down at her. "You seem to know a lot about the Vase."

She hurried to say, "I've studied it in class, that's all."

"I thought you said no one but me had ever seen the shards." A caustic tang lifted the corners of his words.

Margot swallowed. If she said anything, her feeble attempt at a lie would just make it more obvious she'd stashed a sliver of the shard as far down in her backpack as physically possible. She didn't trust Van any farther than she could throw him, and she had skipped arm day for the last forever. So, it was her turn for the silent treatment.

"Yes, there's a reward. There's an inscription on the Vase, a Latin phrase," Van said, conceding. "It means that gold awaits whoever pieces the shards back together."

Margot raised an eyebrow. "You mean, whoever pieces it

together will be golden. You know, like, adored."

Van laughed. A sound so unthinkable coming from him that Margot actually startled backward. "You can't be serious." At Margot's flat-lipped expression, Van sobered. "You're serious."

"Venus was the goddess of love," she said, like it explained everything.

"So, she's going to give that power to just anybody? The treasure is gold. It's the only logical solution." Van's words were measured. Less like he was arguing and more like he was informing. It sparked something desperate and defiant in Margot.

"Just admit it. You obviously didn't get it because Venus knew her power would be wasted on you. You know, you really ought to give me more credit—"

Van halted abruptly. "What's that noise?"

Margot listened: the slow trickle of water shifting beneath the city, the reverb of cars racing across the streets overhead, and then, on top of it, a pitter-patter, close and growing closer.

It almost sounded like . . .

A fat, gray rat skittered down the sewer. A shriek tore out of Van at deafening decibels. He flung himself toward Margot, and instinctively, her arms wrapped around him. The rat scampered up the tunnel, completely unfazed by the ruckus.

Van's chest and shoulders heaved with frantic breaths. They stood like that, chest to chest, until his breathing matched the rhythm of hers. Then, like Van woke from a trance, he lurched out of her grasp. Clearing his throat with a cough, he said, "Vermin carry diseases."

"Whatever you say, tough guy." A laugh spilled out of Margot. It was easier to be brave when the person you wanted to impress just squealed at the sight of a rodent. "Admit it," she said, not bothering to hide her smug smile, "you need me."

"I'll admit nothing of the sort."

Margot crossed her arms against her chest. "We're both searching for the same thing. Why can't we search together?"

"I can think of a few reasons," Van said, continuing forward.

Margot didn't budge. "Tell me."

"You're impulsive and unpredictable. Emotional. Untrained. You don't know north from south, and you've clearly never used a set of spades in your life. I have no interest in working with someone who will jeopardize my chances for success."

The words struck Margot like a blow to the chest. Van's features didn't falter, didn't flinch. He delivered every line item in her list of inadequacies with clinical precision. And Margot's heart stung like he'd cut open all the deepest parts of her and left them there to bleed.

Her lip quivered, and she hated it. Hated that she couldn't squash down her feelings into neat little boxes. Hated that he was right about her. About everything.

She wanted to run, hide, lick her wounds in private. Some incessantly loud part of her wanted to give in, give up. To quit like she always did when things got hard or monotonous and run off to try something she hadn't failed at yet.

But she couldn't. Not this time.

"You're wrong about me." Her voice cracked, caked with emotion. "I need you because you know where to find all the trials, but I've been trying to tell you that you also need *me*."

Digging into the depths of her backpack, Margot pulled out her secret weapon. The shard weighed heavy in her palm. Van grasped at it, almost like his hand had a mind of its own. "The shard from the trial of *Ignis*. How did you—"

Margot swiped the shard out of his reach. She folded it back into its linen cloth and returned it to the inside pocket not even Van could pick. "I know you don't understand, but if I don't find this Vase before my dad drags me back to America, my life is *over*."

Van still stared at her backpack, a puzzled look on his face.

"Let me help. I'll do anything."

His lips thinned, a look Margot had quickly learned to recognize as his thinking face—certain that an analytical whirring could be heard coming from his robot brain if she listened hard enough. Margot wasn't sure what it said about her that in less than twenty-four hours she'd started picking up on his mannerisms. (That she was observant? That she couldn't stop herself from noticing him, whether she liked it or not?)

Finally, he asked, "Anything?"

"You name it," she said.

Van stalled next to a decrepit ladder, one hand on the middle rung. "I want the treasure. You can keep the Vase."

Margot squinted. "What if there's no treasure?"

"There's treasure. There's always treasure."

"But what if it's—"

"The power of love?" Van asked, his voice lightly mocking. He rolled his eyes. "You can have it. But every ounce of gold is mine."

"Deal. Yes. Absolutely." The words spilled out of her.

Because Van might be wrong about the gold, but he was right about her. Without Venus's magic, Margot would always be too impulsive, too unpredictable, too emotional. Only the Vase could change all that. She'd stop being a problem her dad wanted to solve and start being the daughter he always wanted.

Without another word, Van climbed the rusted rungs and punched open a hatch. Margot followed after him, knowing he would not hesitate to leave her behind again if given the chance, gritting her teeth and vowing to keep up.

But the second she stepped off the ladder, Margot's jaw unhinged, gaping. "What is this place?"

"This," Van said, "is the Nymphaeum."

9

The Nymphaeum stretched what seemed like miles above them, culminating in a domed ceiling that had been painted sky blue and dotted with feathered clouds. Lining the walls were a hundred niches, each wreathed with sprawling vines and blooming flowers all handcrafted from stone. The room was dominated by a paved basin. Inside it, columns jutted upward, holding up intricately carved statues of beautiful women—or, Margot supposed, nymphs.

The statues seemed to dance, each midtwirl with skirts billowing around their lithe frames on an invisible breeze. Their hands clasped together, a daisy chain. At the highest point, a nymph with angled features raised her hand toward the heavens.

Van closed the hatch they came through and, as if reading her mind, said, "It used to be a reservoir. A sanctuary. A place they would worship the nymphs, goddesses of the springs. There would have been all kinds of plants—trees, flowers, you name it. The fountain fills from a redirected spring. Surprisingly advanced for the first century."

Margot tried to imagine it. A chill radiated off the stones, seeping through her skin and demanding to be felt. What used to be a sparkling grotto of blue waters had long since dried up, but Margot trailed her fingers along the stones and felt the indentations where pouring water had worn it away. Fresh vines of too-green ivy crept down the walls, thirsty and searching.

It would have been so romantic if it weren't for the skeletons.

Mismatched piles of dried-out bones were scattered across the floor. An empty rib cage in a heap by the statues, a skull in front of a staircase that wound up and around the walls of the Nymphaeum. Margot's stomach rolled at the sight, but no way in hell was she going to let Van see her squirm. He already thought she had no merit as an archaeologist—the last thing she wanted to do was prove him right.

"So, the shard's in here somewhere?" Margot asked. It felt wrong to walk across the mosaic floors. Chipped glass had been pressed into ornate patterns, not that different from the floor in the temple, the color faded from the years. Too beautiful for a place so haunted—and, if the skeletons warned of anything, dangerous.

Van, however, didn't take such a delicate approach. He

slammed the side of his fist against the wall, testing it. Dust scattered in the wake. The stone he'd punched bore the image of a gold-plated shell, now fractured. "Used to be, at least."

"Did you ever consider *not* destroying this place in the process?" Margot asked. She could hear it in her memory, the way Dr. Hunt has chastised her. *Try not to destroy a UNESCO World Heritage site.* Getting blamed for Van's heavy-handed approach was not something she was interested in.

He didn't answer. Typical. But he did sucker punch another stamped stone. Margot cringed, imagining the bruises forming on his fist. The structural integrity of this build seemed pretty solid based on the way he wrung out his aching fingers after the second hit.

"Where did you find it last time?" Margot asked.

Van smacked another brick, and this time, the stone budged. He cocked an eyebrow and said, "Here."

Nothing happened. Margot watched Van, waiting, but he was undeterred by the anticlimactic moment. *Okay, hot shot. Now what?*

He climbed up the staircase, shoulders squared and taking them two at a time. Halfway up, he wavered, dragged back as if something had tugged on his shirtsleeves. Like, maybe his conscience.

"You can swim, right?"

"Um. Yes?" Margot jogged up the staircase, careful not to slip on the crumbling edges. Swimming hardly seemed of relevance. This place was as dry as the bones strewn across the floor.

A noise behind her had Margot spinning on her heels. Thankfully, the statues of the nymphs stayed blessedly still. The noise happened again, and this time, Margot recognized it.

A drip.

"Is that . . . ?" her voice trailed off as she listened. Another drip, and then another.

Water poured out of shells that dotted the limestone facade. It spilled against the stones, washing away the layer of dust on the mosaic basin and rendering everything in stunning, sparkling clarity.

"The trial of *Aqua*," she said, thunderstruck.

"Nice of you to catch on," Van said. He'd rounded the corner, fifteen or twenty steps ahead of her.

"So, the nymphs are the trial," Margot said. She scoured her brain for the remnants of research she'd done while writing her application essay. "In the legend, Venus wanted to prove that anyone searching for her Vase had eyes for only her, right? Nymphs were beautiful deities, and Venus was notoriously jealous. We just have to not get distracted by the nymphs. Easy enough, right?"

A gruff noise released from Van's chest. "Not exactly."

Real comforting.

As the waves rose, lights gleamed beneath the surface, illuminating the grotto. Bioluminescent shells? It was hard to believe Margot arrived here by way of a literal sewer. This was something straight out of a storybook. With the water creeping higher in the basin, the underground sanctuary buzzed with an ancient energy. The same kind that had hummed through the temple. Something that felt an awful lot like magic.

Van halted inside one of the niches. They were roughly eye level with the highest nymph but on the opposite side of the Nymphaeum. He scanned the sanctuary, and as much as Margot tried, she couldn't read his mind.

"What's the plan?" she asked.

"Retrieve the shard."

"Obviously," Margot said. Although she didn't see how that was possible, given the shard was nowhere to be found. "What can I do to help?"

The sea of clear water climbed up Margot's calves, past her knees, to her thighs, but Van didn't move an inch. He waited. And only when Margot's ribs squeezed beneath the cold tide did he say, "You? Stay."

"Stay?" Margot balked. She wasn't a dog. How was that her one task? Just *stay*.

Code for *don't touch anything, don't mess anything up*. Margot stretched onto her tiptoes, breathing as deep and as wide as physically possible. When she couldn't last any longer, and when the rising tide kept rising, she kicked her feet off the ledge and let the water carry her upward. Unfortunately, it was hard to sound authoritative while doggy paddling.

She never said how *well* she could swim. She hadn't thought it would matter.

Van could still stand, but even he wouldn't last for much longer. The water was rising too quickly. He scrutinized Margot like she was a relic beneath a magnifying glass.

"What?" she asked, surprised by how vulnerable she felt beneath his gaze. Suddenly, she was hyperaware of the way her T-shirt pillowed beneath the surface, lifting up past her belly button.

Van shook his head, rubbing his jaw. "Don't make me regret bringing you here."

Margot's face lit up, and she could all but feel the glow radiating off her. "You won't. Like I said. I'll do anything."

Van tapped a painted stone with a forefinger. "This stone doesn't leave your sight. Understood? I'll meet you back here once I have the shard."

"But," Margot started, her words muffled by a rising wave. She spat out a mouthful of water. "One problem. There is no shard."

"Look again." He pointed toward the nymphs.

In the center, the tallest nymph with her ringlets of stone hair and her outstretched arm stared at them, almost like she was alive. She unfurled her fingers when the water rose past her hand.

Margot rubbed at her eyes. No, not imagining things.

In the statue's upright palm sat a familiar slice of black-and-gold pottery.

Margot's mouth hung open in shock. "That's——"

"Don't do anything rash," was Van's parting line before sinking beneath the tide. Like she was nothing more than a skin condition.

The water had lifted them nearly to the top of the domed ceiling, only a few feet left. Margot gulped down as much air as her lungs could hold and slipped beneath the surface. She grabbed for purchase on the ledge of the niche, holding in one place. Her eyes stung when she opened them beneath the water—probably contaminated with about a trillion germs. But she didn't exactly have another choice.

Van swam farther and farther away. As the water churned, he anchored himself with the hands of the nymphs, using their linked arms as a rope to guide him toward the highest and that glint of gold in her palm. If she tried really, *really* hard, Margot could almost pretend she was in the overly chlorinated pool at the Nassau resort they used to vacation at when she was a kid, and Van was diving for rubber torpedoes on the bottom. Even though Margot had quit swimming lessons when they asked her to dive in without plugging her nose and preferred the shallow end, playing for hours like she was a sunbathing mermaid.

All she had to do was stay right here. Perfectly doable.

A steady stream of bubbles floated up from Van's nose as he reached the nymph. A sigh of relief nearly spilled out of Margot's mouth, but she couldn't sacrifice that precious oxygen.

He'd grab the shard, and her lungs would quit burning soon enough.

Van glanced back at her, and Margot gave a big thumbs-up. Something indecipherable crossed his face, his eyebrows drawing together and an unspoken sentence on his lips. But he turned again before Margot could understand it.

As soon as Van lifted the shard off the nymph's palm, the currents shifted. Wild as a riptide, a jet stream shot out of the niche and jerked Margot into the center of the sanctuary. Her arms struggled against the current. The harder she pushed, the stronger the pull.

Margot tumbled upside down, completely losing her sense of gravity. The pearlescent shells shimmered and streaked through her vision. Panic slithered between Margot's ribs, squeezing, squeezing. Begging for her to find air.

A hand—Van's, of course—grabbed Margot by the arm and hauled her out of the whirling tide. He kicked them upward, and Margot clung tightly to his grip, afraid to let go, to sink and never be seen again.

They broke the surface, heads ramming against the ceiling. Margot had never tasted air sweeter. Flattening her palms on Van's shoulders and wrapping her legs around his waist, she fought to hold herself above the waterline.

Bubbles streamed out of Van's mouth. He kicked furiously beneath the water to keep them afloat. Finally, he managed to say, "Watch it. Your knee's in my spleen."

"Did you get it?" Margot asked. "The shard, is it safe?"

He lifted the shard, and momentary relief flooded Margot. Emphasis on the momentary. As the jet pushed gallons of water into the Nymphaeum, their already measly oxygen levels were quickly depleting.

"What do we do?" she asked.

Van bobbed below the surface. When he pushed back up, he said, "That stone I showed you. It's the shutoff. We have to release it."

Stretching for the last drops of air, Margot's hand slipped, limbs all knotted with Van's. His grip faltered. Waves wrenched the shard from his hand.

The sound of Margot's shriek was muffled as the undertow jerked her beneath the surface. A current wove through the nymphs, and a riptide wound around Margot's legs, begging her to join their dance.

No, no, no.

Van dove after the shard, but Margot zeroed in on the jet stream and the stone trigger behind it that engaged the drain valve. With hands clawing at the carved facade, Margot climbed downward. The tide fought every inch, but her focus was solitary. She wouldn't screw this up.

She slammed her palm against the stones until one sank into the wall. The niche slid open like a door, and a rush of water dragged Margot and Van inward, their arms and legs pretzeling together.

A flash of gold shot past them. The shard.

Van swam after it with renewed energy. Margot, on the other hand, didn't move with quite as much control.

The chute whipped her around sharp corners like some kind of hellish amusement park waterslide. She kicked harder, trying desperately to catch up with Van as he sped toward the shard. One tunnel turned into two, and she was pretty sure Van propelled down the left side. Margot placed her bet, heading left with heavy arms and legs.

Here, the light from the shells had faded, leaving only darkness. Margot could barely see her hands in front of her face, let alone the fragment of the Vase.

For a terrifying, heart-stopping moment, she was certain she was alone, that Van had left her, and she was going to be sucked into this whirlpool forever. The panic lasted until she rammed into Van, propelled by the blasting current. There was nowhere else she could be. The walls curled around them, too close, and the water hadn't relented. They'd reached a dead end. Trapped.

Margot banged fists against the walls, panicked. She'd lost the shard, and now she was going to drown, all for nothing.

There had to be another hidden valve around here somewhere. There just had to be. The grit of unpolished stones tore at her skin with every impact. Van joined, each slam of their fists resulting in a dull thud.

Until. A gloriously un-thuddy noise followed as Margot

smacked the ceiling again and again. Her hands searched the round grooves, the bumps of words she couldn't parse by touch alone. It felt like a metal plate, similar to the one that covered the manhole.

Margot's lungs were going to burst if she didn't do something. She braced herself against the wall and kicked upward. The plate shot off, and water spewed toward the opening. Margot clawed her way out onto solid ground. A wet cough rattled her chest as Nymphaeum water expelled from her mouth onto beige linoleum tiles. She flopped onto her back, eyes stinging against fluorescent lights.

Van hoisted himself out of the watery depths and lay next to Margot, breathing equally ragged. Sour, he said, "Nice work sticking to the plan."

"You knew," Margot sputtered. Each breath was a wet wheeze. She couldn't convince her lungs to work in the right rhythm again.

"I gave you one task. One." Van wrung out his shirt, annoyance dripping off every word. *"Yes, Van, I can swim. No, Van, I won't nearly drown us both and make you drop the shard."*

Margot wasn't sure if she gasped in outrage or just gasped because her body was dying. "You knew!" she spat. "You knew"—another gasp cut through her—"that was going to happen. And—and you didn't warn me!" Her lungs interrupted again, faster now, like the air was slippery and they couldn't get traction. "All you said was stay. *Stay.* We almost drowned. I could have, I could have—"

"Hey," Van said. Then, firmer: "*Hey*. You're hyperventilating."

She heard him, but his words didn't sink in. Her hands, feet, face tingled, like every nerve ending was deep-fried and sizzling. Margot was vaguely aware that her chest was rising and falling—fast, too fast—but the edges of her vision blurred, blackened.

Van's hands grasped her shoulders, leaning so close that Margot stopped breathing entirely. Her central nervous system zapped back to reality. It was like the world came into twenty-twenty vision, the saturation rising and clarity all coming back into focus at once. All she saw, all she cared about, was the green and gold webbing of his irises, the constellation of freckles on his cheeks, and the strong tenor of his voice saying, "Margot, count backwards from one hundred."

"Ninety-nine, ninety-eight, ninety-seven—"

"I said from one hundred. You skipped it."

Trance broken. Margot flung Van's hands off her shoulders. She huffed, "What's it matter if I skipped it?"

His mouth turned downward. "You can't start at ninety-nine if you're counting down from one hundred. That's illogical."

Then, someone cleared their throat behind them. "Can I take your order?"

Only then did Margot register the chill of the tile floor they sprawled on, the way everything smelled like grease and salt. Stone walls that probably dated back to the Flavian dynasty gave way to red and yellow booths. Linoleum tables, curious onlookers, a giant menu boasting Big Macs and large fries.

They'd surfaced in a freaking McDonald's.

Margot turned to the employee. "Yeah, a McFlurry. He's paying."

10

Margot's shoes squeaked the whole way back to the ruins. Her clothes stuck to her in all the wrong places, her curls reeked of sewer water, and mascara stained beneath her eyes no matter how many times she swiped at it. Waterproof? As if.

She ditched her empty McFlurry cup (Oreo, obviously) in a trash can as they joined the line at the Nocera Gate. Their walk back had been silent. If Margot tried to talk to him, she was just going to cry or yell and let her too-big, too-much feelings take over. So, instead, she said nothing. Did nothing. Tried her absolute best to feel nothing, even if it ate her alive.

A horrible concoction of emotions swirled behind her sternum—leftover fear from the ache in her lungs, anger that Van would withhold crucial information about the trial that cost them the shard, and frustration at herself for agreeing to do *anything* to get the Vase without even wondering what *anything* would entail. She was just as naive and foolish as everyone expected her to be.

Naming her feelings helped ease the tar-black stickiness in her chest, just a little bit.

As the line inched closed to the city's entrance, Van's head swiveled around on his shoulders, clearly on edge. Every step they were about to take was one he had taken nearly a hundred years ago. The city unfurled in front of them like one of Van's maps, charted in faded lines. Margot didn't miss the faraway look in his eyes, like seeing a dream come to life. When he'd been left underground, trapped in that marble shell, most of this city had still been buried. As if realizing the same thing, his hands had curled into fists by his sides, nervous.

Despite everything else, Margot felt a pang of sympathy. "Different, huh?"

"I hadn't noticed it last night, but, yes, very." He ran a hand through his damp hair, lifting the threads of gold out of his eyes.

"I've never seen this many people here. And everybody has those . . . flashlights."

"Flashlights?" Margot's face scrunched up in confusion until she followed Van's gaze. "Oh, those are phones."

"You can make calls from your flashlights?"

Margot laughed, light. Some of her resentment chipped away. "You can do just about anything from those flashlights."

Van shoved his hand in his pocket, jaw tightening as the line inched toward the gate.

Something about his stature—his rounded shoulders, his uneasy posture—made Margot want to smooth the tension out between them. "I don't really feel like I fit in here either, you know. Everyone else on the trip, they earned their spot, but I'm still trying to prove I did, too."

"I know what that's like." A knowing look, a flash of memory, crossed his face. "I came from nothing, but Atlas had everything."

The line scooted forward until they were back inside the ancient city limits, and Margot steered them toward the dig site. Dr. Hunt's white tent loomed ahead. Dread pooled in Margot's knees, refusing to carry her forward. She could already hear the familiar refrain of lectures about how she was too hasty, too emotional, too much.

"And now we aren't any closer to remaking the Vase," Margot sulked. "My hair is going to smell like sewer sludge for the next eternity, Dr. Hunt is probably going to ship me home for insubordination, and we didn't even get the next shard."

Her feet decided to move again, but it felt a little too much like walking the plank.

"Margot, wait." Van halted in the middle of the road, and streams of tourists forked around him. Taking his hand out of his pocket, he held open a flat palm and a fragment of clay.

"*Oh, my god,*" she said, just a wisp of breath, a whisper only they would hear. Van had managed to grab hold of the second shard after all. "You couldn't have mentioned this an hour ago?"

"I just . . ."

"Didn't want me to mess it up again?" Margot finished.

His fingers coiled back around the shard. Even if he didn't say it, she knew it was the truth. But there was something in the way he held the shard like a peace offering that softened the sting.

He dropped his gaze toward her backpack, the other shard still safely inside. "Turn around," he said. When she twisted, he opened her backpack and slid the shard into the zippered compartment, right next to the first fragment. "Whatever you do, don't lose them."

"I won't," she said, turning back toward him and sticking out her littlest finger. "We're partners, remember? Pinky swear."

He examined her finger, all the while keeping his hand at his side. "That won't be necessary."

Margot's mouth sank into a frustrated scowl. Just when she thought they were making progress.

As they approached the courtyard, all eyes turned to them. Dr. Hunt lurched upright, pacing away from where she'd been helping Suki classify something at her foldable desk.

Margot imagined how she must have looked—disheveled and waterlogged. She'd been gone for hours with no warning, only to return looking like she'd lost a fistfight with Davy Jones himself.

"Margot," Dr. Hunt said, little more than a hiss. "Where have you been?"

"And who have you been there with?" Suki asked, butting in.

Margot stuttered, all her words gathering in her mouth but refusing to form coherent sentences. She needed an excuse, and she needed it fast, but her brain still sloshed with Nymphaeum water. "I didn't mean to, um. I—"

"She was with me," Van said behind her. "I just arrived. Margot came to get me from the train station."

Something stirred in Margot's chest. Sticking his neck out for her . . . it was sweet in an I-nearly-got-you-killed kind of way. "You know, because of the buddy system."

Dr. Hunt's attention shifted to Van. She blinked up at him as if trying to place him in her mind. "And you're?"

"Van . . ."

"Vanderson," Margot flubbed. "Last name. First name, uh, Chad. You know Chad. He transferred to Radcliffe during winter break and joined the archaeology club."

"Chad Vanderson?" Dr. Hunt asked, eyeing Van suspiciously. "Did I read your application essay?"

"Yes," the syrupy lie dripped easily off Van's tongue.

Dr. Hunt nodded half-heartedly. "There must have been a misunderstanding. Our trip is fully booked."

Margot gaped, unable to hide the shock on her face. No way did she unearth the key to finding the Vase only to get thwarted by academic logistics. "He can stay, though. Right?"

"I'm so sorry," Dr. Hunt said. "Without a co-chaperone, I can't supervise any additional students. I hate that you came all this way."

Suddenly, Van's posture shifted. His shoulders straightened, chin tilting at a haughty angle. Even the tenor of his voice lilted, cool and unaffected. "Surely you can find a way to accommodate me after everything my father has contributed to the school. I am a Vanderson, after all."

"He is a Vanderson, after all," Margot echoed. She plucked one of the tools from the holster at his waistband. "And look, he even brought his own trowel!"

"That's a spade, Margot," Van said, under his breath.

Margot swallowed hard. She scratched nervously at the skin on her neck. "Point is, he's totally ready for the class."

Dr. Hunt sighed. A sound Margot knew all too well. It sounded like every time her dad had to let her down easy. "There's just no—"

"He can be my partner," Suki offered quickly. Moon-wide eyes roved over Van, head to toe.

"That's okay, Suki. He can join Topher and Calvin at Plot C," Dr. Hunt said. To Van she added, "You'll room with them and Rex at the hotel. I'll make sure we get an extra bed for you. At least until I can get in touch with Radcliffe and see if we can straighten out this . . . misunderstanding."

Across the courtyard, Topher waved half-heartedly. The movement was laced with suspicion. Calvin, a redheaded boy who seriously needed to re-up on his SPF, crooked his head next to him, confused. No one, obviously, recognized Van from the archaeology club. Margot just hoped they wouldn't realize she'd Mandela effected them. At least until she got her hands on the Vase.

"Your father's money?" Margot asked as they neared their dig plots.

"The only thing deeper than the Vandersons' coffers is our confidence," he said, still even-keeled although Margot swore the corner of his lip tilted upward. With that act, Van deserved a daytime Emmy.

The rest of the students had definitely started to stare. Margot couldn't exactly blame them. Van was practically twice Margot's height and strong enough to carry her fireman-style in case of emergencies. But the sun had bleached the color from his hair, leaving streaks of pale yellow in a bed of rich blond, and freckles scattered across the high points of his cheeks— making him look far more approachable than Margot knew him to be.

Astrid's narrowed gaze settled on Van as he introduced himself to his new classmates with a few terse words. She asked, "What are you wearing?"

"Clothes," Van deadpanned. He unsheathed his tools from their holster and spread them out meticulously at the roped edge of his plot.

Margot dug inside her soggy backpack for *Relics of the Heart*. Her fingertips grazed the wrinkled cover, where Isla and Reed held each other, lips only a breath apart. The pages warped, still dripping. It was probably useless, but Margot fanned out the pages and placed them into a pool of sunlight, praying they somehow dried.

Van nudged his notebook next to it. Equally soaked, the leather cover had puffed up twice its size. Margot winced at the thought of losing such a precious historical document, the way the photographs would bleed.

Topher laughed, bringing Margot back to the conversation. It was a good-natured sound but still grating. "Yeah, buddy, those are some pretty sick suspenders."

Margot cut in. "His flight got delayed and he got rerouted through Morocco, and the airline left his luggage in Casablanca. Can you believe it?"

Astrid's forehead fully wrinkled like perhaps she could not, in fact, believe it. She sniffed the way you would after a whiff of bad fish. Which. Given their recent surroundings, maybe she had. "You know, he kind of reminds me of that guy you wrote your application essay about, Margot."

Her whole body froze. A thin laugh peeled out. She didn't dare sneak a glance at Van, observing on the sidelines. "What? No way."

"Actually, I totally see it," Suki chimed. "He's got that Rick O'Connell thing going for him."

Rex scoffed. "No one but you watches those old movies, Suki."

"We have *The Mummy* to thank for my bisexual awakening," Suki said, smiling. She tugged a strand of hair behind her ear, letting Rex's words slide right off her with an easygoing self-assuredness that made Margot's stomach clench with envy.

"Have you read Margot's essay, Chad?" Astrid hardly waited for him to shake his head yes or no before dragging out her phone. She'd probably bookmarked the page just to ridicule Margot with it. "Oh, you have to. Margot's the only student on our trip with no prior archaeology experience, so she really wowed Dr. Hunt with her . . . creativity."

To his credit, Van ignored Astrid remarkably well. He etched his chisel into the earth, scoring the dirt so that it was easier to shovel.

Margot, unfortunately, felt her cheeks turn redder than Georgia's red clay. "That's really not necessary. Let's not—"

"No, let's." Astrid beamed, her smile like a scythe. *"Sunlight spilled down the rolling hills and puddled at the feet of a fearless young explorer with Pompeii at his fingertips. Blond haired, green eyed, and every bit as dashing as the rumors said."*

Van's head whipped up. His eyes searched Margot, a silent question she wished she didn't have to answer. Of course she'd written about him. When she found his journal and the sliver of the Vase in the library, she couldn't get him out of her head. Every time she closed her eyes, he was there—as real and whole as if he'd stepped out of the pages himself. Writing his story for her application essay had felt like an extension of her own.

He was the whole reason she was here.

Astrid kept reading, much to Margot's dismay. *"The explorer stepped into the Temple of Venus and never looked back. The five missing shards had returned, and he was seconds from completing his destiny when the door swung open behind him. 'What are you doing here, Keane?' the woman asked."*

Van snapped a pencil from clutching it too hard. Great. She excavated the Incredible Hulk.

But beyond his affinity for crushing things, Van was . . . just a boy. A boy who never asked to be resurrected a century too late, who, if he hadn't been dressed like a Milo Thatch wannabe, could have easily passed as one of Radcliffe's rugby players or, like, a super buff quiz bowl member.

They wouldn't know he was the same boy Margot wrote about. They couldn't.

"This is my favorite part." Astrid scrolled down. Margot pinched her eyes closed, bracing for impact. *"When Van searched for the Vase, he hadn't expected to find love. But there she was. As undeniable as the sun."*

Shame slithered up Margot's spine. She knew what came next. A heroine who looked strikingly similar to her except with none of her flaws—Marlow Rhodes was decisive and even-tempered. The kind of girl with a magnetic core, the world orbiting around her.

"That's enough," Van said. There was something final in his tone. Knife sharp and dangerous. "I don't need to hear any more."

* * *

They scraped away the years of history, pitching into the earth until the sun followed. Margot's skin felt too tight—she couldn't tell if her cheeks were sunburned red or stained that way from continuous mortification. When they arrived back at Hotel Villa Minerva, Dr. Hunt gathered everyone in the lobby, rapping on her clipboard with her knuckles.

"Great work today, everyone." Was Margot imagining it, or did Dr. Hunt's eyes linger a little too long on her? "You have some free time tonight, but remember, tomorrow we're leaving bright and early for our overnight trip to Rome. On our agenda: a tour of the Roman Museum of Antiquities and Roman Archives. We'll be there one night, and I will not have spare toothbrushes, so double-check your toiletries bags."

She dismissed them, and the class dispersed toward the elevators. Rex clapped Van on the shoulder, and Van stiffened beneath his grasp. "We're in room three-eighteen."

Suki hung back. "We're all going out to find some pizza. You should join us."

"No," Van said. A single, solitary syllable.

"He's kidding," Margot interjected. She elbowed him in his side, and when he looked at her, she flashed an exaggerated grin.

He reciprocated, forced. "We'll be there."

Suki glanced between them, something like hope and hurt dashing across her face. "Okay, meet back here in twenty minutes."

Van nodded but didn't budge. He waited until Rex and Suki trailed off to pivot toward Margot, those green eyes smoldering like a forest fire. "You could have warned me I'd be going back to high school."

Margot barely batted an eye. "If I had, would you have said yes?"

He groaned, an obvious *no*. "Your friends are buffoons."

She peered ahead at the girls, Suki leaning her head against Astrid's shoulder as they walked, arms linked. Topher, Rex, and Calvin laughed, rowdy and chasing each other through the lobby as if they were in a game of flag football. Her fingernails dug into her palms when she remembered how they'd laughed this afternoon—decidedly *at* her, not *with*. "I don't know if they're really my friends."

"But you want them to be?" he asked.

His words pressed against a yellowed bruise from their earlier conversation, faded but still painful. She'd been a chameleon for as long as she could remember—trying desperately to become what everyone needed her to be, to find the place she belonged. She shrugged, noncommittal, because she didn't trust her words to come out evenly.

"They're still buffoons." He fiddled with the sleeves of his shirt, cuffing and uncuffing them. "They talked about me like I wasn't even there."

"Well, you're not supposed to be here. Or, at least, you're supposed to be a million years old."

His mouth pinched tight. "Do I look a million years old to you?"

"You look cranky." Margot's voice softened, then, as they slowed to the back of the pack. She could barely stand to look at him as she said, "Listen, I'm sorry I wrote my essay about you."

"Don't be."

Margot froze. She'd expected an earful about how she didn't deserve to be here based on the merit of her essay (or lack thereof). At best, some kind of lecture about how she was too busy living in her daydreams and needed to focus on reality. "Don't be?"

He examined her, his features incomprehensible. She'd grown used to feeling unmoored around him. But when he looked at her, Van's green-eyed stare pierced right through her, like Margot wasn't muscle and bone, marrow and blood, but a puzzle he could solve. "It's an invasion of privacy to read someone's personal writings without their permission."

Margot sagged. She remembered the rough edge to his voice when he'd said *I don't need to hear any more.* "I know, I really do. And you're right, I shouldn't have read your journal, but I—"

"I meant *them* reading your essay." Van slowed, stilled. The elevator went up without them. His head tilted, considering. "Although. How much of my journal *did* you read?"

"Enough," Margot said, her throat constricting.

Enough to know that he'd been orphaned, that he'd left New York City that summer with no one waiting for him to return, that he hated sharing a tent with Atlas even though he was his best friend because he still didn't trust him, that he wasn't really sure he'd ever trusted anyone. Enough to find the temple, to find him. To know him better than anyone ever had.

And that, she wouldn't apologize for.

11

That night, Margot sat in the window bay with the shutters wide open. The moon had risen high in the velvet sky, but the city hadn't quieted yet. The breeze carried soprano laughter, the rumble of an engine, the chime of a shop doorbell. Lingering in every sound was a sweetness, steeped in the balmy summer evening.

And tomorrow, she'd have to leave it all behind to board Flight AA 9372.

She leaned her head back, letting the faint scent of salt and citrus wash over her. The day after her parents finalized their divorce, her dad took her to a pier in a tiny seaside town where he bought her a cotton candy spear, three times the size of her head. (She later puked that cotton candy off the side of the carousel, but that was beside the point.)

He spent the whole day distracting her with carnival lights

and game booths and the smell of buttered popcorn so thick, she had to wash her cardigan three times to get it out. Every spin down that boardwalk kept the bad feelings at bay, at least in the moment.

Those reprieves never lasted forever. For each heightened feeling of molten joy in the good times, every dark was so much deeper. In the quiet hours of the night, when all she had to keep her mind busy were the spinning blades of a ceiling fan and her own spiraling thoughts, a restlessness thick as a quilt would sometimes blanket her, smothering.

The only thing that ever eased the ache in her chest was running from it. Not in the literal, track team sense. But throwing herself into something new. Ballet or bread making or backpacking through Europe—anything to outrun the weight of not being good enough. Just like she had on the pier when salt water and spun sugar had held back her tears. If she filled her days with sunshine and coastline breezes, maybe she didn't have to feel anything except the rush of adrenaline, the thrill of an adventure.

But if she found the rest of the Vase of Venus Aurelia, she'd be spared the weight of her dad's disappointment every time she decided to reinvent herself, trying to find a version of the daughter he'd know what to do with.

Suki wafted in from the bathroom, startling Margot out of her thoughts. The steam was heavy with the scent of the hotel's rosemary-and-lemon soap. A terry cloth towel bobbled on top of her head as she sank onto the foot of her bed, eyes trained on Margot. "So, tell me everything."

Margot stuttered, "Everything about what?"

Suki threw herself back onto the bed, arms spread starfish wide. "Why you blew off pizza night for your date with Chad, obviously."

Excuse me? Margot could have died right then, right there. "My what with *who?* I didn't go on a date with anyone. Definitely not Chad."

Astrid finished brushing out her white-blonde hair in the closet's full-length mirror. "Please. You're clearly obsessed with him."

"Me?" Margot asked. "Suki hasn't stopped drooling over him in the twelve hours since she met him."

Suki raised an eyebrow, completely unfazed. "Guilty as charged."

"I thought you had a thing for Rex," Margot said.

"That was before I knew Chad Vanderson existed. The heart wants what the heart wants." Suki rolled over and propped her chin up on her hands, her feet kicking in the air. "Seriously, how did I not see him at all last year? I totally would have remembered a face like his."

"That's what I want to know," Astrid said. She sat down on the floor next to Suki's bunk, and Suki weaved her fingers into her hair, threading the silk strands into braids. "By the way, thanks a lot for ditching me this afternoon just to go pick him up. You know how much I *love* doing your work for you."

Suki added, "And you guys bailed on dinner, sooooo . . . I demand deets!"

While the rest of the group scarfed down pizzas, Margot and Van slipped inside a vintage consignment shop filled with patched leather jackets and well-worn cotton blends. Astrid had been right about one thing: Van stuck out like a sore thumb in his suspenders.

Margot had piled her arms full of clothes and shoved Van into the dressing room. He'd grumbled with every quick change. There were spaghetti western cowboy hats and feathered boas and plaid bell-bottoms. His frown lines grew as deep as the Adriatic when he donned a shirt that barely stretched across his shoulders and did nothing to cover the flat planes of his abdomen.

Heat had flared against Margot's cheeks. "Crop tops are a fashion statement."

"Not one I plan on making." Van glowered. Absolutely no joy reached his eyes.

"Here," Margot had said as she slid a pair of outrageously pink sunglasses on his face. "To complete the Ken doll look."

His scowl had deepened. He ripped the shades off and plucked another option from the pile of shirts and vanished back into the dressing room.

The memory warmed Margot's cheeks as she hopped down from the windowsill. Goose bumps had risen on her arms despite the evening's humidity, and she tried not to obviously shuck them from her arms as the girls stared. "I told you. His luggage got lost, so we went to buy him some new clothes. Hardly scandalous."

A light flashed in Suki's eyes. "So, you're just friends?"

Margot gave a tight-lipped nod. *Friends.* Was that the word for what she and Van were? They were acquaintances. Reluctant allies, maybe. He did cover for her with Dr. Hunt, even if he nearly drowned her within the same hour. But anything more than that? It would take a pretty hefty suspension of disbelief. After all, he didn't do partners. She knew better than to think that he could do friends.

Margot went to shut the window but paused halfway. Below, the hotel's back door slammed, and Margot leaned out for a better view. Whatever she expected to see, it wasn't a very familiar set of shoulders in a daffodil-yellow T-shirt with the tag still flopping out of the back collar, wandering the parking lot.

"Oh, my god," Margot said, lurching upright. If it weren't for the wrought iron window guard, she would have tumbled out onto the pavement.

What was Van doing out there? And, more importantly, why was he doing it without her?

She slammed the glass panes shut with such force that Astrid startled backward and banged her head against the bed frame.

"What is it?" Suki asked. "You look like you saw a ghost."

Margot couldn't get her sneakers on fast enough. "Not a

ghost. Just, um . . . I just remembered that Chad forgot to pay me for the thrift shop. Thanks for reminding me."

She whipped out the door and bypassed the elevator entirely. Instead, she sped so quickly down the rickety set of carpeted stairs that her feet tangled underneath her. Everything spun until she crash-landed into the lobby with a spectacular finish.

"I'm fine!" she called out to Giuseppe, who may or may not have bothered to look up from his computer.

With a huff, Margot peeled herself off the floor and raced to the parking lot. She braced her hands against her knees and caught her breath as she scanned for Van.

There.

He beelined toward the back of the lot. Inhaling, Margot marched up behind him.

"Are you trying to leave me?" she asked.

Van didn't even glance in her direction. "At this moment? Yes."

"We had a deal."

"We still have a deal." Van shrugged, nonchalant. "You get the Vase, and I get the treasure."

Margot had to jog to match his fast clip. "Then where are you going?"

"To get the Vase."

Margot grabbed his shirtsleeve, halting him. "Seriously?"

Van stared down at her. "You barely survived the Nymphaeum. You'll just slow me down." His tone was horrifically even. Calculated and cold. He said it like it was obvious.

Margot only dug her heels in. "No, I won't. I swear."

Releasing himself from her grasp, he said, "You are quite literally slowing me down as we speak."

Van turned and yanked the handle of a mint green Fiat about the size of a sweet pea to no avail. The door didn't budge.

Margot clicked her tongue.

He pulled again, harder this time. Both hands gripped the handle, white-knuckled, as he put all his weight behind it. Van huffed. He wiped his hands off on his pants and tried again.

"You have to click the unlock button on the key fob," Margot said, taking pity on him. "And should you really be driving? Hasn't your license expired?"

The Fiat beeped and lights flashed unpredictably as Van smashed every button on the fob. Finally, he clicked the right one and pulled the door open. "I don't have one."

"You don't have a *driver's license?*" Margot halted, a realization settling. "You stole my Vespa, and you can't even drive?"

"I can drive fine," he bristled.

"Your complete lack of paperwork licensing you to operate motor vehicles totally disagrees."

"I lived in Manhattan, and a Cadillac wasn't exactly in the budget. I just walked everywhere." He clutched the keys tighter in his fist. "You don't have to be a genius to drive. Trust me, I've seen Atlas do it countless times."

"No way. Give me the keys," Margot said, palm outstretched.

"You're not coming with me." Van closed the driver's side door behind him.

Groaning, Margot marched to the other side and slumped into the passenger seat. The seat belt fastened with a click. "Yes. I am."

Van wrestled with his. He pulled as much of the belt out as physically possible. If he wasn't careful, he was going to manage to strangle himself. "What is this heinous contraption?"

His grip slipped, and the belt snapped backward.

"It's called a seat belt," she said. Van tried to mimic her movement but pulled too hard too fast and the seat belt seized. Margot reached around and gently guided his hand, the latch fitting into the buckle. "You wouldn't know because they hadn't been invented yet last time you were conscious. Which is why you shouldn't be driving."

Van twisted the key into the ignition. Headstrong as ever. He shifted the car into gear and leaned one hand against Margot's headrest to look through the back window.

Except instead of reversing, the car lurched forward.

"Van!" Margot screeched.

He slammed on the brake, millimeters from ramming into the building next door.

"Hold on," he said. "I've got this."

He twisted every knob, pulled every lever. The sunroof slid open, the headlights flashed, wipers skidded across the windshield, cleaning solution shot through the now-open sunroof.

Margot wiped the droplets off her face with the back of her hand.

She was going to die.

"Let me drive."

"I can do it," he said, his mouth pinched, forehead etched with deep grooves. Astonishingly, he navigated the car out of the parking spot without hitting anything. The only casualty was the death grip Margot had on the *oh-shit* handlebar. He wagged an eyebrow as if to say, *See?*

Until he tried to drive forward, and his lead foot nearly ran them straight into oncoming traffic.

Margot yanked the emergency brake. The tires screeched. Her skull slammed against the headrest, and Van turned to her, eyes wide as a passing car laid on their horn.

She unfastened her seat belt and Van's. "Get out. Now."

This time, Van obliged. They crossed paths in the headlights beam, and Margot shook the tension out of her shoulders as she situated herself in the driver's seat. She scooted her seat up as far as it would go and adjusted her mirrors.

"Are you sure you want to—"

Margot clicked a button on the center console, and an LED illuminated, shifting the car into Sport Mode. "If I can survive Atlanta traffic, anything's possible."

"You're a regular Alice Ramsey," Van grumbled.

She drifted onto the main road, exhaust clouding in their wake.

12

Pompeii disappeared in the rearview mirror. As she drove, Margot tried to focus on the road's dotted lines and not the way Van's knees banged against the dashboard, entirely too big for a car this small.

Yesterday, he'd been a boy she only knew in her daydreams. She could hardly reconcile the grumpy version in the passenger seat with the soft-hearted author of the journal he cradled in his lap.

He gingerly thumbed through the pages—the water had warped it, the paper all clumped together and dried that way, brittle and deformed. "Almost there. Left, I think."

"You think?" Margot asked as she twisted the volume knob down on the radio.

How far were they going to go? All the city lights had faded into a glow on the horizon. Ahead were miles of coastline in a desolate patch between Herculaneum and Pompeii, a volcanic wasteland that hadn't recovered. Van's directions sent them onto a gravel path riddled with potholes that rattled the car more with every mile they ventured off the main road.

Margot finally shifted into park, half-hidden beneath the canopy of a tree with gnarled roots. "Here? You're telling me Venus hid the shard in the middle of a field? And whatever that big blobby thing is?"

"It used to be an olive grove." Van stepped out of the car, and his shoes scuffed the hardened earth, kicking up dirt—or maybe ash. "And that blobby thing is the House of Olea. Home to some of this region's wealthiest merchants, allegedly blessed by Venus herself. Their oil was used in rituals in her temple, so they say she granted them favor, and provided them with bountiful harvests and ensured all of their daughters would be happily married. If you believe that kind of thing."

"Which you don't," Margot said.

"Not particularly." He started toward the building without any further instruction. "Keep up, kid. Wouldn't want anyone to think you're slowing me down."

Margot wrinkled her nose but rushed to keep his breakneck pace. "Why don't you?"

"Don't I what?"

"Believe in magic or happily ever afters?" Margot kept her eyes trained forward, afraid of what her face would convey without her permission.

"A guy like me doesn't believe in magic. It's impractical."

"Where's the fun in that?"

Van peered down his nose at her. "I'm not here for fun."

They halted in front of a string of caution tape. Well, technically *attenzione* tape. She might not be fluent in Italian, but the context clues were pretty obvious here. Whatever this place was, it had been off-limits for a long time.

"The House of Olea." Van bent beneath the barrier. "It was still an active dig site last time I was here."

House was a loose term. It was practically an outlet mall, with different wings fanning out from a central hub.

"Why would they just . . . stop excavating?" Margot followed him inside.

The structure jutted out of the earth, towering ten, maybe twelve, feet high. The roof had seen better days—patches of it gaped open, the clay shingles discarded in the dirt. In its heyday, it must have been a sight to behold. Even now, it left her breathless.

Although that might have been her dust allergy.

Van turned the corner, guiding them into a corridor with as many twists as turns. Here, the walls met at odd angles, creating sharp corners and unexpected crossroads. The deeper they dared, the darker the ruins grew as a cloud blotted out the silver moon. Black soot stained the walls, a reminder of the wrath of Vesuvius.

Something ivory slid beneath Margot's foot, and she fumbled

forward. Her goat-cheese pizza curdled in her stomach when she recognized it—a bone. Definitely human. Big enough to be a tibia, maybe a fibula? She hadn't taken an anatomy class yet, but she didn't need a PhD to know it once belonged to someone a lot like her.

"Why'd they stop?" Van kicked the bone out of the way, over toward the rest of the skeleton it must have belonged to. "Whoever was in here last either got what they came for or realized they never would."

Margot gulped. Not exactly the vote of confidence she'd hoped for. "Do you think the shard's still here?"

Van plunged into the halls. "Only one way to find out."

The way the walls wove together, it was hard to tell left from right in the beam from Van's borrowed flashlight. Margot couldn't pinpoint a surefire way through—and besides, through to what?

"Whose trial is this?" she asked as they strode down the abandoned corridors.

"*Aura,*" Van answered. "The guardian of air."

"I'm not sure I'd describe this house as airy," Margot said. "Hadn't they ever heard of an open-concept floor plan?"

The farther they strayed into the house, the closer the walls cinched together. Van's shoulders brushed on either side ahead, and he shoved his hands in his pockets, making himself as small as possible. Which, admittedly, wasn't very.

Cobwebs choked the narrow passages, tangling in Margot's

hair. No matter how much she swiped at them, she couldn't unravel herself. Death by spider silk mummification sounded like a horrible way to go.

A thick one snared her leg, and Margot was pretty sure the spider was still attached.

She groaned. "This place would seriously flunk a home inspection."

Somewhere in the House of Olea, something slammed into the earth. The impact rattled the ground, and Margot braced against the wall for support. She could feel her heartbeat in her stomach, her throat, her skull, like it was lurching around in her body, trying to fight its way out.

"What do you think that—" Margot started asking, but Van pressed a finger against his mouth, shushing her.

He cupped a hand against his ear. Margot listened, pinching her eyes closed to focus on the sound of . . .

Nothing. The house was still. No rival band of treasure-hunting looters attacking them from behind, no volcanic eruption promising imminent demise, no giant, evil spider building its web in preparation to eat them for dinner.

"I don't hear anything," Margot whispered.

"It's this thing called silence," Van said. Jaw rigid. "It happens when you quit complaining about everything."

What a jerk. Margot rolled her eyes. Still, she kept her lips zipped.

They paused at a crossroads. Out of the corner of her eye,

Margot saw something lurch in the shadows. Another heavy *thunk* shook the foundations of the home. Fear speared through her chest but was quickly replaced with a rush of excitement. They must have been getting close.

"Let's go this way . . ."

But Van had other ideas. He'd vanished around the next corner.

"Are you sure this is the right direction?" she asked, sprinting after him.

A muscle in Van's jaw twinged. "Yes."

She glanced over her shoulder, but this time, nothing moved in her periphery. "I thought I saw something back there."

"Margot, please," Van said. Tension rippled down his shoulders. "One of us is an expert, and one of us is here on a glorified vacation. Let me lead the way."

Margot gritted her teeth. Her nails pressed into the softs of her palms. She had to bite her tongue from saying something she regretted—he was her ticket to the rest of the Vase shards. With his journal destroyed, she'd have no idea where to look on her own.

But as soon as she had all five pieces of the Vase in her hand? Then, Van Keane was getting an earful of how she really felt.

Margot lost track of how many turns they took before their path ended abruptly, an unyielding slab of stone cutting them off. Van exhaled, stiff, and Margot miraculously refrained from using a pointed *I told you so.*

"This way," he grunted, retracing his steps.

Margot's irritation bubbled to the surface. She was tired of playing second fiddle to someone who clearly barely even knew how to play fiddle. "Just admit you don't know where you're going."

"It was just a detour," he grumbled.

Something thudded again on the other side of the house, and Margot brushed past Van. She sprinted ahead, breezing through the halls toward the sound.

The ceilings lifted cathedral-high in this wing. A gust of wind whipped through the house and blasted Margot's curls away from her face.

She'd never seen anything like this. A series of five pendulums lacerated the sanctuary. Massive feats of ancient engineering, the pendulums had been carved out of marble with bases as big as wrecking balls. They swung in a syncopated rhythm, each off-kilter just enough to make it impossible to cross the arched threshold at the end. A doorway Margot was willing to bet life and limb led to the Vase shard.

Van sidled up next to her. "And this would be the trial part."

"So," Margot said, "how do we do it? Without, you know, getting sliced and diced."

Van's face was all frown. His eyes traced zigzagged paths through the atrium. Scanning, searching. As if taking it in for the first time.

"You do know how to do it, don't you?" Margot prompted.

"Atlas insisted he complete this trial himself while I stood guard outside." He said the words under his breath, ashamed almost. "I never should have trusted him to do it alone. But I'll figure it out."

Van exhaled once and darted into the maze before Margot could say anything else. He ducked beneath the first pendulum and rolled into the lane of the second. Margot gasped and watched between her fingers.

The ground beneath him shifted. With his arms outstretched for balance, he took quick steps, but each pendulum swung faster than the one behind it. He bobbed, trying to nail the timing. Because if not . . .

Van hopped backward, seconds behind getting bulldozed by the pendulum.

Margot traced their dangerous arcs, the curve of their swings—all but one.

At first glance, it was as if the hinge on the first pendulum had gotten stuck at the top. But Margot looked closer. On a track below the pendulum's blade rolled a soccer-ball-sized rock so polished, Margot wondered if she'd be able to see the future if she looked closely enough. It depressed a clay tile directly under the pendulum's blade at its apex.

When the tile shifted, tilting, the ball rolled off. It tumbled between rows of columns, and when it reached the other side, it lodged in an identical tile. *Thunk*. The first pendulum released, swinging, and the second one stopped.

Margot counted her heartbeats. One and two and three and—tilt.

"Oh, my god." It all made sense. "It's like the Cave of Delphi!"

Van ducked beneath the pendulum. "The *what?*"

In chapter eight of *Relics of the Heart*, Isla and Reed arrived at the Cave of Delphi separately. They were still just rivals (not yet -to-lovers) that early in the book, working separately before they committed to teaming up. When they entered the cave, a gate trapped them inside, and to escape, they had to work together to trigger a series of chain reactions, placing stones in the correct order. That was the only way to lift the bronze gate before they were locked underground with a metric ton of pythons.

This boulder was like the Cave of Delphi's stones. It was a counterweight that triggered the pendulums.

She raced to the edge of the first lane, timing it so that she entered the danger zone right as the pendulum swung past.

"Don't move!" she shouted suddenly. "I'll grab the rock when it rolls to me."

The pendulum sank back over Margot, so close it might have trimmed a few of her hairs, but the rock rolled back to her, just like she knew it would. When it landed at her feet, she wrapped her arms around it. Or, tried to. It was heavier than it looked.

"Watch out for—"

The pendulum slammed into Margot's stomach. She let out a

surprised *oof* and dropped the stone as the pendulum lifted her into the air. She wrapped her arms around its base, desperate for purchase.

Van watched, a preposterously accusing look on his face. "This was your big idea?"

"Sorry, this is only my second rodeo!" Margot hollered. "Grab the boulder!"

The pendulum rose higher and higher until she was certain she'd get flattened against the ceiling. She squeezed her arms as tightly as humanly possible, curving her spine against the pendulum's blade, and pinched her eyes closed as she drew millimeters from the carved ceiling. Surely she was only seconds from being splattered like a bug on a windshield when Van hoisted the rock into his arms. The tile released, brakes churning overhead. Her back scraped the surface, but the pendulum froze.

Margot let out a relieved breath, but it didn't last. One boulder wasn't enough. They needed two or they didn't stand a chance. Her gaze combed through the nave. There had to be something else they could use to offset the timing. Then, maybe, they'd be able to make it through without getting bludgeoned to death.

But there was nothing. Just columns dividing the pendulums, each one with two sets of clay tiles that triggered each swing.

Except. Van.

Maybe they didn't need two boulders. They just needed two people.

Van returned the stone to the checkpoint, allowing Margot to swing back toward the ground. She hopped off the pendulum as it lowered. Rushing forward, she ran to the clay tile at the far end, and the second pendulum stopped midswing, creating a path for Van. His head whipped around, awestruck.

"The tiles control the pendulums," she said. "We have to work together. One by one, we'll pause the pendulums for each other until we get to the other side."

The polished counterweight rolled back to Margot's feet. She let it take her place on the tile while she jogged ahead. Like a relay race, Van rushed forward while his pendulum was frozen, and Margot darted off the tile seconds before the pendulum would have knocked her out.

Once, twice, three times, until Margot leaped past the last pendulum.

Van laughed, bright as a clarion bell. "That was . . ."

"I know," Margot said, cutting him off. "Reckless, careless, dangerous."

A slanted smile graced his lips. "Actually, I was going to say brilliant."

Fizz spread through Margot's veins like her blood was carbonated. When she inhaled, it was like she was breathing for the first time. She clasped her hands under her chin, nodding, pink and warm. "Then, thanks. Actually."

She and Van speared through the doorway, which was less *treasure trove of your wildest dreams* and more *forgotten storage closet*. Shelves had been carved into the chipped walls, and only a few clay amphorae remained. If they uncapped them, Margot wondered if they'd find two-thousand-year-old olive oil.

There was really only one place for the Vase shard to be.

Van approached a stone chest, carved with delicate details. Dust wafted out as he pried off the lid. The movement triggered a clanging sound behind them as the pendulums halted in their tracks.

Margot peered inside the chest, but instead of a fragment of clay, hand-painted by Venus herself, there was absolutely nothing.

It wasn't there.

Why wasn't it there?

Margot deflated. Every bone in her body went limp, sagging in disbelief. "I don't reckon there's a secret, second treasure chest we can open maybe?"

Van worked a hand through his golden hair and chewed on his lip, thinking. He kept at it until his hair rivaled Einstein. And he walked. Walked back through the pendulum's labyrinth, their blades all stilled. Walked through the hallways, backtracking through their winding turns until hazy light poured through the exterior door.

"Van. *Van*." She stopped him with a hand on his shirtsleeve. "What's going on in there?"

"In where?" he asked, surveying his surroundings like he was so deep in his thoughts that he hadn't registered them walking.

Margot tapped him on the forehead. "In there, dummy."

Van sighed, a full-body movement. He rolled his neck, shook out his shoulders, slumped his spine, and shoved his hands into his pockets, all in one go. Like he'd rebooted his system. "The shard's missing."

"Obviously. Could your notes be mistaken?"

"I don't make mistakes," he said, tugging his journal out of his pocket and waving it like a white flag. "This journal is meticulous."

Margot winced. "Well, that journal is also so water damaged, it's practically unreadable. You probably just misread something."

Darkness shifted in Van's stare. If he could breathe fire, she for sure would have been incinerated. He spoke slowly, carefully. "We found the first shard right where I'd found it last time. When the pieces disappeared from the temple, they must have all returned right where they'd been found."

"Except for this one, maybe."

Van shook his head, defeated, and ducked beneath the caution tape, back outside into the quiet evening. "This one, too. Someone must have found it."

This time it was Margot's turn to pinch her face up in pointed disagreement. "You think someone did what we just did? With the boulders and the screaming and all those dead bodies on the way in?"

Another sigh raked through Van's body. He tilted his chin toward the clouds. "If they hadn't, it would still be in there."

They left the House of Olea, no closer to finishing the Vase than they had been before.

13

Margot barely had time to sleep last night between schlepping back to the hotel empty-handed and Dr. Hunt's ungodly early wake-up call. A quick snooze on the train ride was all she had time to squeeze in before a miles-long trek through the waking city landed her outside the Roman Museum of Antiquities.

A breathtaking structure rose before her—taking up at least two city blocks. All stone, the facade was sculpted with hand-carved engravings, depicting armor-clad soldiers, willowy women, and wreaths of laurel. Lemon trees flanked the entrance, summer ripe and sweet smelling. Massive limestone columns jutted out of the earth, supporting a clay-tile roof and, beyond that, a domed ceiling.

When they strode inside, soft yellowed light swirled through the foyer, streaking through a window high overhead, and tendrils of morning light cast floating dust motes in high relief. Dr.

Hunt kicked off their lecture. She led the class beneath a stone arch to a marble room where glass cases with gold plaques housed artifacts from bygone civilizations.

As her classmates took notes, Margot caught a glimpse of their reflection in the glass. Not spending all day slumped over Plot D meant Margot broke out her cap-sleeved yellow polka-dot dress. It buttoned up the front and belled out around her hips, cutting off midthigh. Next to her, Van managed to look like a teenager from this century—layering his linen shirt over a thrifted tee.

The relics beneath the reflections shifted, stone tablets turning into papyrus, spears into swords.

"Maybe the shard ended up in a museum," Margot said to Van, hushed as they paced the quiet halls.

Van's mouth fell into that familiar unamused slope. "And maybe cars can drive themselves."

"Well, actually—"

Suki leaned over, tapping Van's shoulder from the other side of Margot. "Chad, do you have a pen I could borrow? I *totally* forgot mine."

Van stared at the exhibits unflinchingly. In one ear and out the other.

Suki smiled harder. She shot a frenzied look toward Margot. Clearly Suki wasn't used to not commanding the attention of anyone she set her sights on.

"*Chad*," Margot urged, wedging an elbow between his rib bones.

He jolted to attention. "What? A pen?" He patted his pockets uselessly. "No, sorry."

Which was a total lie because Margot knew for a fact there was a black ink pen tucked inside his journal, wrinkling all the pages in a way that would have sent Astrid into cataleptic shock. As his mouth flattened back into a rigid line, Margot watched his face for any tells. Either he was a very good bluff or feigning complete disinterest *was* his tell.

As Suki fell back to whisper something to Astrid, Van narrowed his eyes, turning to Margot. "Do I have jam on my face or something?"

"No," Margot said, too fast. Her belly warmed at the memory of Van swiping layers and layers of strawberry compote onto his toast this morning in the cramped, wallpapered dining room.

"Then, why are you staring?" Van asked.

"I'm not." She about-faced about as fast as humanly possible. Which only made Van cock his head, that much more curious. Margot whispered, "Are you okay with this?"

"The staring?"

"The museum. The history of it all. Doesn't it make you feel . . ." *Homesick? Unmoored? Forgotten?*

"—No."

"Right, I forgot. Robots don't feel anything."

Van's eyebrows did something wiggly—somehow rising and lowering at the same time in a squiggly scrunch.

Oh, yeah. Robots probably weren't big in the 1930s. Margot rattled her head. "Never mind."

Dr. Hunt stopped the class in front of a glass case filled with ancient weaponry, and all the hushed chatter dried up. She tapped her fingers against her clipboard, scanning the group. "Rome may be the City Eternal, but even it had its beginnings. Today, your job is to analyze its foundations and developments leading up to the days of Pompeii. You and your partner should use this to learn about the kinds of items you may find during your excavations."

Margot glanced toward Astrid, who was saying something behind her palm to Topher, but her icy gaze aimed straight at Margot. It made a slimy feeling slosh around in Margot's stomach.

Growing up in a town where everyone knew each other meant that everyone knew you right back. Margot had tried to become a hundred different girls just to stop being the girl whose parents divorced, whose mom skipped town and left her behind.

Transferring to Radcliffe was supposed to be her chance to find herself. To study new things—archaeology, cryptology, so many ologies to try!—and discover what she loved without being a spectacle to a bunch of kids who had watched her reinvent herself over and over and over again without ever getting closer to figuring out who she was.

Astrid, however, seemed hell-bent on making sure that didn't happen.

Dr. Hunt added, "I'll be passing around a worksheet for you to hand in at the end of the afternoon."

A unanimous groan rose up from the class. Margot included. There was no time for busywork.

She pinched her eyes closed, pretending that when she opened them, she would be a different version of herself. A version who wasn't going to bash her head through the glass if she had to listen to Astrid brag about her father's father's father for the rest of the afternoon.

"Let's go," Astrid said as she dragged Margot away from Van and shoved a worksheet in her hands. It was stapled. Not just a worksheet. A whole exercise. "I'm not letting you bomb this assignment for me."

Margot recoiled. "What's that supposed to mean?"

"Don't be cute," Astrid snarked. "You've barely put in any effort this whole weekend. I knew I was right."

"Right about *what*, Astrid?" Tension knotted in Margot's shoulders.

"You being here is ruining everything."

"What's your problem with me?" Margot snapped. She could feel it under her skin, her emotions slipping out of her reach. Even if she wanted to spool them back in, they'd still be a tangled, awful mess. "I don't think I've committed any serious crimes against you. I didn't copy your physics project or TP your dorm room or accuse you of stacking the votes so that you could win homecoming princess last winter."

The look in Astrid's eyes was so fiery, it could have melted steel. The jury was still out on *how* exactly Astrid had won the crown. But that was beside the point.

Margot threw her hands up, innocent. "Like I said. Not accusing. So, I'd love to know why every time you talk to me, you act like somebody just put a frog down your pants."

Astrid tucked her bangs behind her ear. "Oh, I don't know. Maybe because every time we're supposed to work together, you suddenly have an emergency that makes it impossible for you to do your fair share of the work."

Margot bit back, "I've done plenty——"

"I had this whole summer planned out so that I could get ahead on my college apps. Pasha Manikas and I were going to——"

"Shut up about Pasha Manikas!" Margot said a little too fast and a little too loud. "I'm sorry I'm not her, and I'm sorry you're stuck with me."

"You should be." Astrid leaped at the chance to gloat. "If you weren't so busy looking for that stupid Vase, maybe you'd actually learn a thing or two about archaeology."

"It's not *stupid*," Margot seethed. Her hands tightened around the cloth straps of her backpack like it was a parachute, a lifeline. She'd known enough to find Van, to secure the first two fragments of the Vase. "People have been searching for it for centuries."

"Exactly. My great-grandfather was one of those explorers.

Don't you think one of *them* would have found it if it were real?"

"I knew you couldn't go two seconds without bringing up your family." Margot's throat ached against the words she knew she shouldn't say but couldn't stop. "Are you ever embarrassed that you've accomplished nothing for yourself?"

Astrid's nostrils flared. She'd hit a nerve. "As if *you've* done any better. You cheated your way onto an excavation and want to act like *I'm* the one who hasn't earned my spot here? Please."

Margot's teeth clenched so hard, she thought they might shatter. "I didn't cheat at anything."

Whipping her phone out of her pocket, Astrid said, "Hey, Siri. Define cheating."

Siri's stilted AI voice responded, "Cheating. A verb that means to gain an unjust advantage by skirting the rules."

Astrid flicked an eyebrow, triumphant. "Say what you want about me, but you'll never be half the archaeologist I am."

Tears welled, hot and heavy, in Margot's eyes. Astrid's face blurred. Margot opened her mouth to speak, but it wasn't her voice she heard.

"That's a lot of hot air from someone with nothing to show for themselves," Van said as he suddenly stepped beside Margot. He must have heard them fighting halfway across the hall. "But what else would we expect from an Ashby? Your family legacy can only get you so far."

Red poured into Astrid's cheeks. "I'll have you know, I'm a Pliny Junior Scholastic Award winner."

"Congrats on your studies." Every word was level, precise. The only thing that betrayed Van's fraying temper was a glint in his eye. "Let's see how that helps you find something worth being remembered for."

"At least I have actually studied," Astrid said. Her eyes sliced toward Margot. "That's more than some of us can say."

Margot wiped the back of her hand across her cheek. It came back wet. She wasn't going to stick around just to get ridiculed. She raced out of the exhibit hall.

Astrid's voice trailed after her, saying, "Of course. Run away like you always do!"

She did. She slumped onto the first stiff stone bench she found, tucking her head against her knees and wrapping her arms around her head like a shield. Vaguely, she registered Van sinking down next to her. The threads of his too-big T-shirt from the thrift shop brushed against her skin.

Once the tears came, they didn't stop. There was no way to swallow them down or hold them in. They raked through her, tsunami tides against the shore.

Van didn't say anything while she wept. But he also didn't move. Didn't shy away from the storm front.

The back of his hand was so close to hers that she froze, scared he'd feel the tremble under her skin—the anxious adren- aline, the fear of never being enough. There was an uncertain pull to him, like he was a current in an endless ocean that could either guide her to high ground or cast her to sea. She wasn't sure which, but the memory of his words called to her, a lighthouse in the mist. *Actually, I was going to say brilliant.*

A bitter laugh rattled out of her. "Sometimes, I swear I don't even know why I came here if everyone hates me so much for doing it."

Van rested his elbows on his thighs, twining his fingers together. He stared at the polished floors rather than at her. "You know exactly why you came here, and no one hates you."

Had he participated in a completely different conversation back there?

A garbled noise erupted from Margot's throat in protest. "Astrid would sooner throw me in the snake pit than ever have to work on a project with me again. Dr. Hunt almost assuredly regrets bringing me here in the first place. My dad—"

She hadn't said actual words to him since their call. Just a thumbs-up emoji when he asked if she'd received her flight itinerary. What was there to say?

Van picked at the cuticle of his thumb. "Far fewer people hate you than hate me. Trust me. I'm not . . . always the most agreeable. Or so I've been told."

"Well, everyone who hated you is dead."

"Thanks for the reminder."

Margot winced. "That's not—sorry."

"It's fine." He peeked at her out of the corner of his eye. "It's true. Probably hated me until they took their last breaths."

"Doesn't that, I don't know, bother you?" she asked.

Van nodded, a noncommittal bob. "There are worse things in life than not being liked. People are going to come to their own conclusions," he said. "What people think usually says more about them than it does about me."

She wanted to agree, but she couldn't bring herself to do it. *Maybe*, she thought, biting into her cheek to keep from saying anything out loud, *I just want* him *to like me*. Because she wanted everyone to like her.

Van didn't need other people's approval, and somehow he still managed to get it. He had that whole broody and irritable thing going for him. He was Van Keane, after all.

Margot peeled her gaze away from him, ashamed of what he'd find if he looked too closely back into the blues of her eyes. She finally noticed where she'd run to, and suddenly she was rendered speechless.

Every inch of the walls had been lined with scrolls, delicate parchments handled with steady hands, next to stone tablets and chipped granite, stained with ink. Sconces protected lit candles, dotting the shelves with orbs of orange light.

Statues in varying states of disarray had been perched on smooth pedestals like Mr. Potato Head pieces—washboard abs with no head attached, the bald pate of some stoic emperor, a woman sliced in half down the middle: half a smile, half a dress, half a heart. At the far end of the hall, a Roman legionary stood with his hand on a blade and his head bowed beneath a helmet. Not an exact replica of the guardians but close enough to chill Margot to the bone.

"This room gives me the creeps," she said, shivering.

"Nothing here can hurt us," Van replied, his voice calm.

She shuddered again. "Don't you think that statue looks too much like—"

"It's not. Margot, we're perfectly safe."

And then, the soldier's head lifted. Stone scraped as he unsheathed his sword.

14

"Is this one of the trials?" Margot asked, her mouth wicked dry.

"No, definitely not." Van blanched next to her. "I swear to you, that isn't even one of the guardians."

Something told Margot this was the statue's first time sentient, and she hoped it would be his last. The legionary tested his legs with hesitant steps, each anvil heavy. Every movement the legionary made carved fissures into the tiled floor. A few quick flicks of his wrist and he mastered his parry.

Margot gulped. If her Girl Scouts stint taught her anything, it was not to make any sudden movements in the vicinity of a predator. "But you do know how to stop him, don't you?"

"Not yet." Van stood preternaturally still. Except for his eyes. Margot knew he must have been appraising their options—exit routes and risk factors, the probability of imminent death and dismemberment. She wished she could see what he saw, think how he thought.

All she saw was a room brimming with breakable relics and irreplaceable artifacts. All she could think about was how much trouble she'd be in if she wrecked this museum and the tang of panic that clogged her throat.

"Van—"

"I'm thinking."

Unfortunately, the soldier wasn't the only statue that decided to gain sentience. The headless torso tumbled from its pedestal, and the lone head blinked, a scowl carving into his marble features.

"Think faster," Margot said as the soldier marched forward. The tip of his blade tested the space between them, ready to strike.

The torso rolled itself to Van's feet, and he kicked it between its stone ribs. "I'm trying."

The left-handed woman waved her only hand, motioning for them to run.

Margot didn't need to be told twice. She launched herself through the doorway. The soldier's head whipped in her direction. She could feel its unnatural stare boring into her back. Van raced after her, and the legionary wasn't far behind, steps they could feel as much as hear.

"Why is he alive?" Margot asked as the exhibits bled together. Friezes and clay amphorae, gold-framed paintings and patterned textiles. The museum wrapped around them, a maze of shelves housing fragments of history, each carefully preserved. "And why is he so mad at us?"

Van spared a look over his shoulder. "When you came into the temple, you woke me out of my statue. Maybe I wasn't the only one."

"So, this is my fault?" Margot barked.

"All I'm saying is I didn't make it a habit of getting chased by statues that wanted to kill me before I met you." Van skidded around the next corner, where the exhibits narrowed, glass cases on either side shrinking closer.

Naked incandescent bulbs hung from the ceiling. One of them dared to flicker. Like it was trying to skyrocket Margot's pulse on purpose. She lost track of the turns they took—left, right, right again, left three times. So many zigs and zags, her head spun.

The statue tracked them like a hungry Tyrannosaurus rex. Booming steps rattled right through Margot, shaking every bone. Her head was still craned over her shoulder when she rammed into Van's back. Every frustratingly muscly inch of it.

"Why aren't we moving?" she asked.

"Dead end."

Her heart threatened to stop altogether. "Please tell me you've suddenly developed a sense of humor. A terrible, unfunny sense of humor."

She peered around his shoulder. Not joking. A little yellow sign hung in the center of a grated metal door. Margot was willing to bet it said something like Employees Only or No Margots Allowed.

A white woman with salt-and-pepper hair pulled into a

frizzy braid down her spine closed the rattling gate behind her, the sound jarring in the silence. One arm was burdened with the weight of what looked like months of research—lopsided papers and journals all stacked on top of a tome as thick as Margot's forearm—and she used the other to lock the gate with an iron key.

"Excuse me!" Margot called.

She took one look at Van and Margot and *tsked*. "Access to this department is reserved for curators and researchers only."

"We're researchers," Margot offered, keeping her tone light.

The woman peered down her nose. "Is that so?"

"We're researching the Vase of—"

Van unceremoniously knocked the stack of papers in the woman's arms to the ground. They spilled, scattering against the floorboards. A shrill sound came out of the woman's mouth, but Van used her distraction as an opportunity to snake the key out of her palm, wriggle it into the lock, and peel open the door.

"He's sorry," Margot said on Van's behalf.

Van said flatly, "No, I'm not."

He slammed the gate shut.

The archivist opened her mouth as if to call for security when the legionary barreled down the hallway. All that came out instead was a shriek.

In three massive strides, the statue closed the distance to the restricted section. The woman crawled out of his way, but he only had eyes for Margot and Van. It wasn't a comforting thought, as the soldier wrenched the door straight off its hinges.

Margot backed into Van's chest, her feet tangling in his. "We've got to go."

Van grabbed her arm and dragged her with him. He was running now, and Margot's legs did everything they could to keep up. This part of the museum housed looming pine shelves overflowing with patinated bronze and clothbound books. Records.

"Try not to tell strangers that we're searching for one of the world's most sought-after relics, could you?" Van snarked, still thinking about Margot's unfinished sentence.

Still, his hand lingered on Margot's arm, and her skin grew hot beneath his touch. It was purely for efficiency, that hand. He kept jerking her unexpectedly down different stretches of shelves, so there was nothing tender in the feel of his fingers against her forearm. Which made her even more glad he was too busy plunging down narrow corridors to notice the flushed pink on her face.

"What if there's something in here?" she said suddenly, loosening the hold he had on her arm. "Something about the Vase. Like why it wasn't at the House of Olea."

Now was really not the time to be slowing down, and Van knew it. "And what do you expect to find? A treasure map?"

"Anything is better than the whopping nothing we have to work with now." The floor shook with every step the statue grew nearer.

Margot grabbed Van by the sleeve and hauled him through the nearest door, locking it behind them. That would throw the legionary off their tracks. Hopefully.

Here, the bookshelves were denser, the texts thicker. In the narrow crevice between shelves, where shadows filled every space and the scent of yellowed pages was so strong Margot could taste it, Van's shoulders curled in on themselves like the edge of a well-read paperback to avoid knocking books off their shelves.

"Think, Van." Margot placed her hands on his arms, lifting onto her tiptoes. "There has to be something that could help us trace that shard down. There are about a million documents in this place. One of them could be a . . . a certificate or a ledger, or, I don't know, a . . ."

Van huffed a breath through his nose. If he wasn't so irritable, Margot almost would have thought it was a laugh. "Treasure hunters aren't really big sticklers for paperwork. We aren't going to find—Actually. Wait."

Margot waited as the cogs in Van's head whirred.

"Acquisition ledgers," he whispered, each word barely a breath. "Earlier, you said maybe the shard ended up in a museum. If it had, it'd be documented somewhere."

"Where would we find those?"

Van lifted his hands around them. Archived texts and artifacts filled every inch of this section. The shelves around them held books, sure, but practically none of them were labeled.

She raised an eyebrow. "My question still stands."

"That way," he said. "We're looking for records, not relics."

Navigating the corridors was a feat of bumping elbows, but Margot managed to twist around without knocking anything off the tightly packed shelves. Van, behind her, swiveled, too. Now, his breath was so close, she could feel the heat of it on the side of her neck.

Margot yanked down a random book wrapped in plastic. Someone had written indecipherable code on the packaging—or, maybe that was a call number. Distantly, she wished she'd taken that library cataloging elective last quarter when she'd had the chance.

Sliding out the book, it was more delicate than she'd even imagined. The binding frayed, and the spine split. Inside, plastic pages protected tattered parchment streaked with penned Latin phrases.

Craning over her shoulder, Van said, "Too old. We're looking for something from the last century."

They wove between the stacks, deeper and deeper into the archives. Something crashed behind them, the sound of a locked door splintering, and Margot pinched her eyes closed. The legionary. They didn't have much time.

Van reached into the shelf below and wiggled out an armful of books with deckle edges and white linen covers. "Look for any trades out of Pompeii."

Handing a few to Margot, they wasted no time flipping

through the records—tidy, dark black lines of text that Margot had to squint to read. Each time she discarded a book, Van handed her another.

Thumbing through the pages, Margot caught glimpses of the past—a few handfuls of expeditions dating back to Van's era, a couple of German archaeologists, someone British, a pair of Swedish names. Each one of them scraping at the earth, trying to reap what it had sown.

One cropped up a few times. Atlas Exploration Company.

"Atlas had his own company?" Margot asked.

Van made a noise caught halfway between a sigh and a snort. "And he never let anyone forget it."

Margot skimmed her index finger down the page. There were too many trades to count. Atlas Exploration Company sent shipments to the Museo Storico Navale di Venezia, Galleria dell'Accademia di Firenze, and about a thousand other museums across Italy. Dread congealed in her stomach. They'd never have time to hunt through them.

"These stop the same year you disappeared," she said, resting her painted nail on the last transaction.

Van nodded. "I guess it's bad press to have a crew member die on your watch. His family probably pulled his funding and forced him to go home."

But Margot tapped that last trade, something tugging at her thoughts like a loose thread. "You said Atlas had been the one to complete the trial of *Aura*, right? So, he would have known where to look for the shard after it reset."

"He wouldn't have traded it," Van said. Quick, tense. "I know Atlas. He wouldn't have wanted anyone else to find the Vase."

"Maybe it was an act of protection." Margot's thoughts were spinning so quickly, she could hardly keep up. "Think about it. The only way to put together the Vase is to have all five shards. Alone, it looks like any other piece of pottery. He couldn't get the rest of the shards, but as long as this one was missing, no one else could either."

A few stacks over, an entire shelf of documents collapsed. Reverberations shuddered through Margot's joints. The legionary stomped into view, striking against the cases with the hilt of his sword. Each pulverized bookshelf brought him closer.

Margot held her breath, didn't dare to blink, in case any of those movements would give away their admittedly lackluster hiding spot. Suddenly she understood every deer in every headlight. Terror coursed down her spine, zinging through her central nervous system and inching toward a full-blown panic attack.

Van tore the page from the ledger and folded it into his pocket. The noise drew the attention of the legionary. "Time to run."

Immediately, Van's hand found Margot's. This time, his fingers laced with hers, and he hauled her between the stacks. The soldier tore after them. One massive hand gripped the side of a mahogany shelf and tugged, toppling it as if it were weightless. Books spilled, hardcovers splaying and pages tearing, as it slammed into the next shelf. That one knocked into the next and the next, falling like dominoes.

The force of each downed bookcase jolted through Margot's bones. Propelling her forward, she gripped tighter to Van's hand. Books cascaded around them as shelves on each side staggered.

Margot and Van ran until they couldn't, until the museum spat them out through a doorway and they landed in a heap on the floors of an exhibit hall, all glossy marble and pristine glass cases like there wasn't a living, breathing statue trying to kill them.

Van hurtled upright, but Margot moved too slowly. The legionary's path of destruction had gotten him too close too fast. Now, his stone hand wrapped around her throat and hoisted her into the air. She didn't even have time to scream.

His hold tightened, and Margot pried at his grip. But she wasn't strong enough to break marble with her bare hands, so all her thrashing did nothing to slow the steady squeeze of its knuckles around her windpipe. If anything, it made him clench harder. Like he was annoyed. Could statues be annoyed?

Her vision blurred. Through the fog, she watched Van analyzing the situation. His gaze fell on her backpack, and the shards he knew it held, and then on her, caught as she was, in an unwinnable scenario. She would have yelled in rage if she had the breath—Van, weighing his options, like maybe *she* was optional.

Then, as if prodded, he lurched into motion.

For a second, he vanished past her periphery. There was a shatter—a glass case, maybe—and then the blare of an alarm. Red lights flared through the room, and an automated Italian voice warbled over invisible speakers.

Not good. Incredibly not good. Bad times a thousand.

Amid the black spots crowding her vision, Van reappeared holding a medieval lance with a rusted blade. Raising it overhead, he lunged it into the statue's bicep, piercing the stone. The legionary's grip slackened. Margot slammed against the floor and gasped for air, eyes stinging and throat chafed.

While Margot sputtered, Van sparred the soldier. His swordsmanship needed polishing, but he managed to disarm the statue, the marble sword clanging down to the tiles. It did little to dissuade him. The legionary landed jabs against the planes of Van—his ribs, his shoulders. He stumbled back, gasping as each blow fell.

Margot lifted onto her hands and knees, wobbly. She didn't want to see Van beaten to a pulp any more than she wanted to be arrested for destruction of property. Even if that property had a serious bone to pick with her.

In the corners of her vision, a legion of uniformed guards—flesh and blood ones, thankfully, but only by a small margin—aimed down the hallway. *Oh no.* Maybe it was the lack of oxygen going to her brain, but they seemed to be multiplying.

"Hurry!" she yelled at Van despite the way her throat scratched against every syllable. "I'll hold off security!"

Margot scooped up her backpack and scrambled across the floor, her lungs groaning in protest, and peeled up the statue's sword. She carried it with two hands, the tip scraping along the tiles. It must have weighed half as much as her.

Down the hall, the guards yelled something, but it didn't matter what they said to Margot. There was no way she was letting them in here right now.

The arched double doors had been wedged wide open with a doorstop, and Margot kicked it out from underneath the left side. She did the same on the right, and when both doors closed, she jammed the sword between their handles. That ought to hold them for a little bit.

She spun on her heels just in time to see Van's lance slice through the statue's neck. Halfway. It got sort of lodged there in the middle. He shifted his weight, and the blade finished the job. The soldier's head separated from its shoulders. It almost crashed against the tile, but Van slid, catching it in his arms like a basketball.

"Oh, my god," Margot said. Elated and jittery from adrenaline. Horrified at the consequences of their actions. The headless statue stared back, once again just unmoving stone. "Oh, my *god*. Who sculpted this?"

Van peeked at the gold plaque marking the statue. "Uh, Michelangelo."

"We're doomed. *Doomed.* What do we do?"

Security pounded, fists against the locked doors. The hinges rattled like hissing snakes.

"Here," Van said and pushed himself upright. "Help me get this back where it belongs."

Margot's arms quaked, steadying the statue's head on its broad neck while Van bolstered its torso. It looked totally believable. As long as no one looked too closely. Or wondered why a half-naked legionary statue was in the middle of a medieval weapons gallery.

The guards burst through the door, shouting a stream of frenzied Italian. Margot flashed a nervous grin, too big, and with the motion her hand slipped. The statue's head lolled to the floor.

15

Astrid wore a smug grin when security escorted Margot and Van back to the rest of the class. "Nice work, Rhodes. You put the entire museum on lockdown."

"Not now," Margot said, firm. Van must have been rubbing off on her.

While the guards argued with Dr. Hunt in rapid Italian, presumably about which jail they'd cart them off to, she and Van hunched over the page from the ledger. Their cheeks were so close, she could feel warmth radiating off him. Her heart pounded loudly in her chest, but she blamed it on the leftover adrenaline.

Margot yanked a yellow highlighter from the depths of her backpack—they'd already destroyed museum property, so a little color-coordination wouldn't kill anybody. She painted neon streaks across every instance of Atlas Exploration Company. Seven total.

"You know you were in the completely wrong wing of the museum to find worksheet answers," Astrid said, poking her nose back in their space.

"I said not now, Astrid. Obviously we're busy with something," Margot said stiffly. She shifted away from Astrid's prying gaze.

Astrid clenched her fists by her side. "Unless what you're busy with is the worksheet we're supposed to be finishing, it can wait."

Margot ignored her. She skimmed her finger down the date column. The first trade happened at the start of July, just weeks after Van's disappearance, and the last one at the end of September. Three months post-Van for Atlas to track down the Vase shard and trade it away. Her finger rested on the first museum.

"What kind of exhibits do they have here?" Margot asked Van.

"What do I look like, an encyclopedia?" He huffed a frustrated breath out through his nose. "Can't you ask your flashlight or something?"

"My—?" Oh. Margot tugged her phone out of her back pocket. She googled Museo Storico Navale di Venezia, and the website pulled up a digitized record of their collections, but when Margot scanned their pottery, nothing resembled one of the shards. It was mostly naval instruments and shipwreck findings.

Suki hurried over. When she saw Van, her eyes went as wide

as one of Miss Penelope's teacup saucers. The legionary had split his lip, red running through the creases. "Are you okay, Chad?"

"Fine," he grunted without making eye contact. His focus was solely reserved for the ledger, soaking in every line like there must be some secret code he could crack.

"I'm not clueless. None of this looks fine," Suki said.

Margot's blood ran cold as she watched Dr. Hunt chat with the security guards and a man in the most expensive-looking suit Margot had ever seen. The curator, maybe. She only had a few hours left before her flight, and getting arrested wasn't exactly on her summer bucket list. She focused, trying to read Dr. Hunt's lips, but unless she was *actually* talking about naked mole rats eating guacamole, Margot was clueless.

Dr. Hunt bade the security guards farewell and shuffled toward them. A stray curl draped over her eyes, and she smoothed it back behind her ear. Her expression wasn't angry. She almost looked . . . concerned.

"Margot, Chad," she said as she sidled up next to them. "The museum extends its apologies."

That couldn't be right.

The quicksand pit in Margot's stomach, which was threatening to swallow her whole, begged to differ. She was supposed to be lectured about how foolish it was for her to run off or how irresponsible it was to let her emotions carry her away.

Astrid's jaw sank halfway to the floor. "You're joking."

"Why would I be joking?" Dr. Hunt asked. Every drop of levity in her voice ran dry. "Margot and Chad could have been seriously injured with that statue in such a state of disrepair. They'll be investigating the structural integrity of all the statues in the gallery so that no one gets hurt."

Dr. Hunt turned to leave, but Astrid stopped her. "That's it? Margot *broke* a Michelangelo."

"No," Dr. Hunt said. "The head curator assured me that the statue of *Felix* was in line for refurbishment and shouldn't have been on display."

A thrill ran through Margot. She tried to imagine it from an outsider's perspective—the head had toppled off the soldier's head, courtesy of an unnoticed split in the marble, and crashed into the glass case holding the lance on the way down. She hadn't noticed any security cameras, and no one was going to believe the sole account of the scared-to-death researcher who witnessed the statue's spree.

For all anyone else knew, Margot and Van had simply been in the wrong place at the wrong time.

"Thank you, Dr. Hunt," Margot said. "A few scratches, but we're fine."

"She shouldn't have been there in the first place." Astrid's voice pitched higher. Her arms tugged across her chest in a defensive shield. "She was supposed to be helping me with our assignment. I'd like to request a new partner."

Suki perched on her toes, leaning around Van's shoulder.

"Ooh, if we're getting new partners, then maybe I could—"

Dr. Hunt cut her off. Her words were a sickle, slicing and definitive. "Okay, Astrid. You want a new partner? You'll join Mr. Vanderson for the duration of the afternoon."

Astrid's face fell into a shade of despair Margot previously believed had been reserved for souls carted across the Styx. "No."

"Yes." Dr. Hunt nodded. She rapped a nail against her trusty clipboard. What did she even have clipped to it? "Margot, you can work with Suki. I'll adjust everyone's partners, but only for today. Tomorrow, I want the two of you to figure out how to work together. Understood, Miss Ashby?"

"Understood," Astrid said, but the word came out thin.

Dr. Hunt and her clipboard clapped once and said, "Back to work!"

Van's hand grazed the skin of Margot's arm as he slipped something into her palm. Every nerve in her body went on code red. She gulped down the butterflies and unfurled her fingers. The ledger.

He nodded, just once, and Margot knew it meant *keep searching*.

The audience of prying eyes they'd gathered turned back to their worksheets. Except for Suki, whose forlorn stare followed Van to the other side of the exhibit. It bordered on creepy.

"Snap out of it," Margot said, waving her hand in front of Suki's eyes.

"Okay, okay." Suki had braided her hair in one long stripe, and she toyed with the end of it now. "I just don't understand why Chad wouldn't want to be partners with me."

Margot said, "He prefers to work alone, that's all."

In Suki's defense, Van had a gravitational pull to him, like he was the sun, and everything orbited him. As they paced through the exhibits, with Suki jotting down answers on her worksheet and Margot frantically looking up museums, Margot couldn't help but register Van's proximity.

She swore she was trying to focus, but her cell service was painstakingly slow.

And, yeah, maybe there was a twinge of jealousy in her chest when Astrid faced him and whispered something only he could hear. Van stared down at his new partner, hard and long, wearing an expression Margot had never seen on him before.

He pushed his hand through his hair, the gold streaks glinting in the museum's soft light. Margot's stomach twisted into knots like a soft pretzel. His eyes cut across the gallery to hers, and she one-eightied so fast, she nearly flattened Suki against the glass.

"Sorry," she said, flushed and distracted.

Suki glanced down at Margot's phone. "What have you been working on? Reading more *Relics of the Heart* fan fiction?"

Like a porcupine, Margot's spikes went up. "I'm not—"

Suki smiled, and Margot believed it. "It's cool. My mom loves that book. I'm pretty sure she owns everything Catherine Avery Hannigan has, like, ever written."

Margot softened. "Mine, too. This was always her favorite. But no, I'm—well, I'm trying to find this museum gallery, but Google apparently doesn't think it exists."

Suki's eyebrows perked up. "A secret museum? Let me see, let me see."

Margot smoothed the torn page over the glass and pointed to the last name on the list, La Galleria Bianchi. Her search finally loaded, but it was populated with spam sites and a boutique in Tokyo. Absolutely zero Italian museums.

"I've been to this place," Suki said.

"You *have?*"

Suki threw her head back. "Yes, it's unreal. You won't find it online. It's this underground antique market, basically. My mom and I came to Rome last summer for this big trade show, and I met this girl, Fernanda. She got me in."

"Can I meet her?" Margot asked. Then, "Not to date. Although I'm sure she's lovely. I need to go to that museum."

"Well, it's not exactly—"

"Please, please please." Margot was not above begging. Not now. She'd do whatever it took. "I'd seriously owe you."

Suki nodded, a devious smile glazing her lips. "Okay. So, here's what you're going to do."

While the rest of the class finished up their worksheets, Margot and Van stood inside the world's pinkest lingerie store. Van's face matched the fuchsia bra the mannequin wore. Everything was lace and satin, thongs and bustiers.

"Are you sure we're in the right place?" Van's voice was pinched. He scratched uncomfortably at his shirt's neckline, leaving a red patch against his collarbone.

"This is it."

Suki's instructions had been clear. Once they made it to the striped pink-and-red awnings at Mia Bella's, they'd go to the front desk and ask for Fernanda. What Margot hadn't expected was Van's instant mortification by a few frills and ribbons. He fidgeted with the gold-chained compass he kept perpetually around his neck, clicking it open, checking their orientation, tucking it back under his shirt. A nervous habit.

Behind his back, Van held a bouquet of fresh violets and calla lilies. Suki swore they were Fernanda's favorites, and a little buttering up couldn't hurt since apparently Suki never called her back. ("Long distance," she'd said, "you know how it is." Even though Margot definitely did not.)

"Let me do the talking," Margot said, weaving her arm through Van's and dragging him through the store. Van kept his head trained toward his feet like glimpsing an undergarment would result in instant incineration.

A man stood at the desk, nearly buried behind three dozen black glass perfume bottles. He cradled a corded phone shaped like a pair of pursed hot-pink lips between his bearded chin and a bedazzled shoulder pad. Acknowledging them, he offered a knowing nod and pointed across the showroom. Margot pivoted, following the line of his arm to a display of matching his-and-hers sets.

"Not that," Margot said, pointedly ignoring the heady blush creeping up her own cheeks. Van tensed beside her in complete and utter mortification. Margot was half certain that if it weren't for her brace on his arm, he'd have fainted on the spot. "We're looking for Fernanda."

The clerk pushed his palm against the receiver and shouted her name toward the back.

Fernanda appeared around the corner. Her bright blue hair had been braided around her head and patterned with clip-in butterflies. With her wide-set brown eyes, deeply tanned skin, and upturned nose, she could have been plucked right out of the Nymphaeum. *"Ciao, come va?"*

"Hi," Margot said, "We're looking for La Galleria Bianchi—"

Fernanda nearly shoved a pair of thigh-high socks into Margot's mouth just to smother her words. She leaned over the countertop, eyes slicing toward her colleague, who was now in a heated argument regarding *biancheria intima*. With a harsh whisper, she said, "Do not say it out loud."

Margot spat out the socks and lowered her voice. "Suki Takeda sent us."

"Ah, Suki." Fernanda dragged out the last syllable.

In response, Margot dug her elbow into the soft spot beneath Van's ribs.

He thrust the bouquet between them. "And these."

For a moment, Fernanda did nothing. Just stared at the bouquet clutched too hard in Van's fist. Finally, she took the flowers and lifted them under her nose. Then, her features hardened. "Tell her I say thank you."

"That's it?" Margot gasped. "What about the"—Fernanda glared, dagger sharp—"the other thing?"

"I don't know who you are or why you're here." Fernanda sniffed the bouquet again. "What exactly are you looking for?"

Oh, right. Okay, Suki had prepared her for this.

Margot cleared her throat. "We need two pairs of knee-high stockings in alabaster white, monogrammed with *AOA*."

Fernanda donned a sparkling smile. "Fabulous! This way!"

She came around the counter and guided them through the storeroom. Van glanced at Margot, disbelief written all over his face, and Margot could only hope she didn't *actually* end up with two pairs of socks out of this. Fernanda led them through a sheer gauze tapestry at the back of the shop to a cozy hallway made of exposed stones. A door was on either side—one labeled, one not.

"Enzo!" Fernanda said, hitting the side of her hand against the unmarked door three times. She didn't stick around for someone to open it. Offering Margot and Van a salute with the hand holding her bouquet, she neatly vanished between the racks of negligees.

"I can't believe that worked," Van said. His face slowly returned to its usual shade, his eyebrows finding their typical irritated furrow. "Do girls even like that sort of thing?"

"Flowers?" Margot asked. "Yeah, usually."

Van made a sort of unimpressed snort. "Why? They just die."

"It's thoughtful," she said. "Who doesn't like to be thought about?"

Van's feet scuffed the ground as they waited. "What else do they like?"

Margot shrugged, trying desperately to look nonchalant despite the way her pulse skipped very chalantfully. "You know, picnics, little gifts, handwritten letters. Romantic gestures."

"Sto arrivando!" called a voice from behind the thick door.

It swung open, and Margot jumped back to avoid getting smacked.

Whoever Margot had expected to round the corner, it wasn't a boy Van's height and about his age—eighteen-ish, not a-hundred-something. His skin had the bronze glow of someone who spent their afternoons in the sun, but his hair was so black, it almost looked blue. The boy wore a black hoodie, stamped on the front with a globe, tilted on its axis, with a ribbon encircling it, and he crossed his arms over his chest.

Was Margot imagining it, or did Van tense next to her? Almost protective.

A string of Italian words ran out of Enzo's mouth. Knowing him, Van probably understood them perfectly, but Margot could only blink like she was trying to solve a complicated math problem.

"Americans," Enzo said, finally, as if it explained everything. "Let me ask again: If you want to know love, how will you look for him?"

This was where Suki's instructions had ended. Every day, the bouncer had a new riddle. Get the answer right, and it was instant access to the world's most exclusive gallery of antiques. Wrong? They'd be on the curb quicker than Margot could say marinara.

"Um . . ." Margot faltered. She really should have taken one of Dr. Hunt's classes last year. Every intelligent thought she'd ever had suddenly decided to take a sabbatical.

Beside her, Van said, "You don't."

Margot whipped toward him, hands clammy. They only had one shot at this. He hadn't even considered consulting her?

At her antagonizing stare, he shifted his weight between his feet. "He said look for *him*. Not it. I can only assume that references Cupid, the Roman god of love. He'd been betrothed to Psyche but hid in the darkness each night because he didn't want to be loved because of his appearance or his reputation. He didn't want to be seen—only known."

Something unnameable twinged in Margot's chest.

Van refocused on Enzo. "So, how do you look for love? You don't. Love comes to you."

There was about a trillion percent chance that door was

getting slammed straight in their faces. Margot winced in anticipation, her chances withering like a week-old grocery store bouquet.

It didn't come. Instead, Enzo sidestepped and pushed the door open wide. *"Benvenuto."*

16

La Galleria Bianchi was the stuffed manicotti of antique markets.

Dust clogged the air, thick and musty. Booth after booth had been weighed down with relics. Heaps of trinkets and curios were piled on glass display cases like the ones Margot saw in a Dillard's perfume department, and they reached high above her head. Crates teetered in lopsided stacks. The treasures they held, Margot could only guess.

A few faces glanced up at them as they entered. Sellers, Margot realized. A man wearing a jeweler loupe frowned when she caught his eye. Something a lot like fear twisted in her gut— when Suki said underground market, had she actually meant black market?

Margot stretched onto her tiptoes, but she couldn't see the end of the stalls. This market must have taken up the whole storefront next door to the lingerie shop, hidden from curious eyes. Banners of triangular flags looped across the ceiling, alternating colors with the logo stamped on Enzo's hoodie. Had Margot seen that logo before?

Van inched in behind her, so close that she could feel his chest against her back, and Enzo shut the door behind them with a latching *click*.

"Welcome to La Galleria Bianchi," Enzo said, coming around to face them. His gaze settled on Margot, warming her up like she'd been placed inside a microwave. "I could give you a guided tour."

"No, thanks," Van bristled. He moved to leave, but Enzo stopped him with a hand against Van's chest. Margot could practically sense Van's blood pressure rising.

"Only twenty euros," Enzo said. A smarmy smile glazed his mouth. "Each."

Margot hedged, "How much is it without the tour?"

"Still twenty."

"For this?" Van asked. He swiped his finger across the top of a display case, and it came back coated gray.

Enzo shrugged, but its meaning was clear: either pay or get out.

Margot reached into her pockets. Her leftover tip money budget didn't account for mediocre museum extortion. But if the shard was here, they didn't have another choice. She pathetically smoothed out the wrinkled ball of bills before handing them to Enzo, a detail that made Van's lip twitch.

"*Grazie, bella.*" Enzo finally stepped aside.

They'd barely made it past the first stall—a few dirt-coated coins bearing a weather-worn version of Julius Caesar's face—when Van grumbled, "*Grazie, bella.* Who does he think he is?"

"An employee doing his job, perhaps?" Margot eyed an impossibly preserved fresco tucked back behind a stack of crates. A little red tag had been tacked next to it. Squinting, she asked, "Does that say eighteen *million* euros?"

Van paced forward. "That's not what we're here for."

"Sorry to break it to you," Margot said under her breath, "but if what we're here for is eighteen freaking million euros, then we're out of luck."

Van didn't slow. Margot could barely take in their surroundings—the rusted blades of iron swords, the tattered edges of forgotten scrolls. "If what we're looking for is still here, we won't be buying it."

"What do you mean we won't be—oh, my god, you want to steal it." Margot lowered her voice, trying not to draw the eyes of vendors. Her heart ran rampant in her chest, thumping around in all the wrong places. "We can't. We'll never get away with it."

Van halted so suddenly, Margot breezed several steps past him, lost in her swirling thoughts. She had to backtrack to where he stood, feet planted like old-growth oaks on the checkered tile. At first glance, he was totally expressionless. But Margot had learned to read the topographical lines of his face.

The way his forehead creased and his eyes narrowed. Focused and determined.

The way his lips flattened. Thoughtful, careful.

The way the freckles along his cheekbones perched upward with the tilt of his head.

Margot swallowed thickly. The realization settled in her stomach like fool's gold at the bottom of a river.

If they found the shard, they *had* to steal it.

It wasn't negotiable. What other choice did they have? Margot's flight was mere hours from now. Soon, she'd be shoes-off in the security line, boarding an all-night flight back to Georgia. The thought of her dad's frustrated scowl was as striking as a guardian arrow through the heart: *You're just like your mom sometimes.*

Her mom, who lived in a constant state of romanticizing her life, always searching for the next big thing. Her mom, who gave up on things when they got hard. Her mom, who left them.

Margot had always known it was true. That she and her mom shared more than a few traits. The same brunette curls that streaked with honey gold in the summer sun. The same wrinkles in their nose when they laughed too hard, all scrunched up. The same big smile, all gums and teeth, the same deep well of tears that seemed to never dry up, and the same slingshot between them like there was no middle ground. Highest high or lowest low and no in-between.

"Okay," she heard herself say to Van. "Teach me how."

Van stepped closer. The toes of his boots met her sneakers. A new look painted his features, one Margot didn't recognize, his eyes as sharp as emerald. "You want to learn how to pick pockets?"

Margot straightened her spine, shoulders pressing down as she craned her neck toward him. Defiant energy coursed over her skin, electric. "You don't think I can do it? I can totally do it."

"I'll admit I have a reservation or two."

Margot torqued an eyebrow.

"You don't have a subtle bone in your body." Van's head lowered until his voice was a whisper against her ear. It raised goose bumps over her skin. Suddenly Margot wasn't sure she had *any* bones in her body.

"I do, too."

"You most certainly don't, but I didn't say it was a bad thing. You just have to know how to use it." There was a tilt to his lips that made Margot's breath catch in her throat. His hand grazed down Margot's side, fingers hovering just barely over the dip in her waist. The trail of his touch brushed the back pocket of her jeans, so delicate she was certain she'd imagined it.

Quietly, she asked, "What are you doing?"

"I'm teaching you how to steal. Isn't that what you wanted?" he asked. Margot nodded, wordless, and he added, "So, what do you think?"

Margot checked her pocket: a single slip of paper. No, a receipt. From the thrift shop they'd gone to. "This is literally trash."

His mouth twitched, fighting a grin. "I meant your new bracelet."

When Margot looked down, a roll of jade beads had been slipped over her wrist. Each green jewel wore webs of white and gold. The same greens as Van's eyes. Not that she paid *that* much attention to his eyes. But if she had. They were totally the same color.

"How did that—" Margot glanced toward the stall next to them. The vendor's back was turned, fiddling with the contents of a box. A box she quickly recognized held similar bracelets. She hadn't even noticed him swipe it off the counter and slide it onto her arm. *"Van."*

His shoulders lifted innocently. "Van, what?"

"That's not part of the mission." Margot put the bracelet back on the counter before the seller could whip around with an accusatory glare.

"You *just* said girls liked that sort of thing." A confused wrinkle appeared between his brows but vanished as soon as it came. He swiped the bracelet off the counter and forced it back onto her hand. "Never mind. You can't put it back. That's not how this works. And don't be so obvious."

"How is this bracelet supposed to help me?" Margot said it too quickly. A feeble attempt to squash the fluttering thing taking residence in her belly.

"It's the first rule of thievery," he said casually. "Misdirection. Make them look somewhere else, and then do what you need to do."

Margot ran her fingers over the cool surface of the beads. "Let me guess: there is no second rule."

"No, the second rule is don't get caught."

Margot's phone dinged in her pocket, but she didn't reach for it. Her system jolted like it was a starting gun all the same. A flight reminder, no doubt.

As they rounded the corner to another lane of stalls, apprehension washed over Margot. The shard had been here for nearly a century. It could have been traded a hundred times. Nothing guaranteed it would still be here.

They'd have to search this place from the floor to the rafters, and Margot didn't exactly have the time for that.

"We need to split up," she said. "We'll never find it like this."

Van hesitated. "If you find the shard—"

"I can do it. I'm not some damsel in distress." Margot stood her ground. "Unless there's a third rule of thievery you've neglected to tell me."

"No," Van said, shoving his hands into his pockets. "I was

going to say that if you find the shard but we're still separated, give the signal."

"And the signal is?"

"I'm sure you'll think of something."

With that, Van headed toward a row of figurines and furniture, and Margot slipped down a corridor where neoclassical paintings gave way to Renaissance art that may or may not have been originals. She followed a stream of other shoppers—women with sleek ponytails and crisp blazers, and men in tailored suits. Suddenly, Margot felt supremely underdressed.

She trailed past a display of mirrors with ornate frames and long, thin handles. The seller, a beady-eyed woman with a gold incisor, said, "This one belonged to Helen of Troy. I've heard it was enchanted by the gods to make her the most beautiful woman in the world."

"Is that so?" Margot asked, backtracking toward the counter.

The seller held the mirror toward her, and Margot clasped its silver handle. She peered into its streak-free surface and swiped on another coat of red lipstick, touching up the edge with her pinky finger. Not too shabby, enchanted or not.

"You know," Margot said, "I'm looking for something also rumored to be touched by the gods. Venus, specifically."

"Is that so?" the seller mimicked. She turned her back to rummage through a stack of crates.

While she waited, Margot took one last look in Helen's mirror, and her stomach lurched. Behind her stood Enzo. Not *close*

close, but close enough to make her wonder why exactly he'd abandoned his security post to go full Joe Goldberg.

The seller returned to the counter with a handful of boxes. The first held enough gold to put Midas to shame. She wagged an eyebrow, but Margot shook her head. The next box was equally as disappointing: a collection of bronze rings. Then, she opened a chest of chipped pottery nestled on a bed of velvet. It wasn't just a collection of broken plates and jars. Margot bit her cheek to keep from gasping.

The shard.

Black and webbed with gold. Right there in the box. A tiny price tag sticker next to it read €450,000, which, while not eighteen million, would require Margot to work overtime at the coffee shop for the rest of her mortal life.

To Margot's surprise, the seller lifted out a different clay fragment. A black-and-red sliver that Margot had absolutely no emotional connection to. "This belonged to Venus herself."

Margot nodded, at least trying to look like she believed the woman. But the truth—the real shard—was inches from her fingertips.

Make them look somewhere else. Van's words ricocheted through Margot's head, but there was nowhere else to look. Enzo shifted in her periphery, moving closer, and the seller's unforgiving stare bored straight into Margot's soul.

Maybe Margot couldn't make them look somewhere else. But she could make them look at her. She cut her eyes back at

Enzo, trying to pretend he was someone else. Someone blonder. Grumpier.

"Marie," Enzo said, sidling up to the table, "take your break. I'll cover for you."

The seller smiled, gold tooth gleaming. "*Grazie*, Enzo."

As she slung a woven purse over her shoulder and squeezed out from behind her stall, Enzo planted a hand on the display case, turning toward Margot. "Find something interesting?"

Margot trained her eyes on his, refusing to glance toward the Vase's black and gold. "Marie was just showing me some pottery."

"I haven't seen you here before," Enzo said. She couldn't decide if it sounded like he was flirting with or threatening her.

Margot tried on a loose grin. "I'm just here on a school trip."

"How long are you in Rome?" he asked. His eyes glittered with equal parts mischief and intrigue.

Turning, Margot focused on a sliver of pottery that wasn't the shard in a feeble attempt to throw him off her scent. "A few more hours."

He clicked his tongue. "A few hours is nothing. This city has so many secrets. How did you hear about La Galleria Bianchi?" Margot had to admit, the gallery sounded much cooler in his Italian accent than Margot's southern drawl or Van's transatlantic lilt. Even if it did feel a little bit like he was interrogating her.

"A friend of a friend," Margot said—technically not a lie,

although her heartbeat ticked upward as if it were. There had to be a way for her to distract him enough to grab the shard.

"Enzo Bianchi," he said, extending a hand.

"Bianchi," Margot echoed. His palm was warm against hers. "Like, *the* Bianchis of La Galleria Bianchi."

"The very same." He retracted his hand and drummed his fingertips atop the glass case. "I know this gallery in and out. Any questions, you ask me. I'm your guy."

Margot's thoughts spun like her brain had been replaced with a cotton candy machine. How was she going to manage to extricate herself *and* the shard with Enzo watching her with those big, brown eyes?

She pointed at the piece of clay Marie had shown her. "Did this *really* belong on the gods' kitchen table?"

Enzo smiled, a sly thing. "So the legend says."

"What's that one?" she asked delicately, begging her voice to sound innocent. Maybe being the damsel in distress could work to her advantage. If the glossy look in Enzo's eye was anything to bet on, she'd up her ante.

"This," he said, pulling out the Vase shard, "is something not many people know about."

He fixed her with a stare. Margot's stomach bottomed out.

As fast as it had vanished, his smile returned. "But the ones who do, know it's worth protecting."

In one quick motion, Enzo's hand wrapped around the hilt of a nearby sword, and he wrenched it free from its sheath. The silver blade, broken off at the end with a rough edge, tested the distance between Margot and the Vase shard. She sucked her stomach in, dodging its point.

Every neuron in her brain rapidly fired. She needed three things in quick succession: a weapon; the shard; and to get the hell out of here.

Margot ducked when Enzo brandished his blade—which was still enormously threatening despite basically being half a sword. Was he seriously going to try to attack her? In public?

As if reading her mind, Enzo growled. The other vendors barely looked over.

Today's forecast was evidently cloudy with a chance of stabbing.

Enzo's other hand, the one he wasn't trying to finely mince her with, held tightly to the shard. So tightly his knuckles lost their blood, and Margot imagined the rough edge etching into the skin of his palm.

She swiped the fake shard from the display, barely missing the swing of his blade. Maybe, somehow, she could swap them. If she didn't get shish kebabbed first.

Scanning her immediate surroundings, she searched for something, anything.

There was a leather sack and its accompanying silver coins, a stack of books, presumably in Latin and possibly cursed, and a rusted iron pot. Definitely the pot.

Margot dove for its handle as Enzo lunged forward, and his

blade zinged off the ancient metal. A surprised yelp—of both triumph and fear—tore up her throat.

Enzo doubled down. "Your partner is not here to save you."

She slammed the edge of her makeshift shield into Enzo's forearm, and his hand instinctively opened. The shard clattered to the floorboards. "Lucky for you, I took a quarter of reflexology for my PE credit."

Margot didn't wait for him to respond. She dove to the floor, lifting the pot over her head as Enzo struck down on her, and scooped the Vase piece into her hands. Using the cookware as cover, she stuffed the shard in her back pocket but clutched the decoy in her fist.

Enzo grasped the hem of her shirt, and Margot fumbled. The decoy slipped out of her fingers, launching into the air. He reeled back, reaching for the clay, and caught it like a major-league shortstop. While he relished his catch, she ditched the pot and slid between Enzo's legs.

Margot raced through the market. Her head swiveled, searching for any trace of Van. A signal. She needed a signal.

"Wait!" Enzo shouted. "Thief!"

So much for not getting caught. He must have realized he had the fake.

The stalls blurred around her as she sprinted. She launched herself over the top of a display case and then dove under a clothing rack, tangling herself in a tunic. On the other side was a stall with an assortment of instruments—some Margot recognized and others she didn't. Like the curlicue trumpet perched on a stand.

That would do.

Pinching her mouth tightly, remembering the training of exactly two weeks of band camp, Margot blew into the horn's mouthpiece. Nothing happened, except for the vendor zapping to attention and hollering something Margot didn't catch.

With Margot's next breath, the trumpet let out a brassy cry.

But Enzo cleared the corner. She had no choice but to drop the instrument. Her arms pumped, and her legs pedaled as fast as they could. *Van, where are you?*

17

Enzo had the stamina of a marathon runner. His relentless chase had Margot's lungs searing.

She cut each corner close, desperately trying to add a few feet between them. As she ran, she slid the stolen shard into her backpack, zipping it up safe. Then, she used both hands to launch herself over a display case housing an alarming number of shrunken heads.

(An unalarming number of shrunken heads was probably, like, zero.)

Margot landed on her feet and powered forward. She chanced a glance back at Enzo, several stalls behind, and grinned, which was just long enough to slam into something she quickly recognized as Van's chest. For a minute, electricity pulsed between them. But then, Margot jolted backward, like she couldn't stand the voltage.

He held her by her shoulders. "A cornu. Nice choice for a signal."

"I stole it," she gasped.

"The cornu?"

Margot squinted. "The shard."

"Like I taught you?" Van asked. Something a lot like pride welled in his gaze.

"Not exactly." Margot faltered. "Remember rule number two?"

"Yeah . . ." Van's eyes darted over her shoulder. Presumably toward where a very angry Enzo was running toward them at full speed. "Margot. What did you do?"

They shot off in tandem, zigzagging through the displays. Margot was running out of juice, but Van's hand wrapped around hers, tugging her forward. Enzo wasn't far behind.

"Duck," Van said. Like it was voice-controlled, Margot's body responded.

Enzo's blade zipped overhead, and the momentum of his swing crushed a display case. Glass shattered underfoot. Margot tried not to think about how close he'd gotten and pushed forward.

Van wove through the market until Margot was thoroughly lost. But then she saw it.

Probably the most beautiful thing Margot had ever seen: stairs. Stairs that hopefully led to an emergency exit or even a window. Any semblance of an escape route would do.

Margot took the stairs two at a time to keep up with Van, seriously wishing she hadn't abandoned her borrowed shield. At some point, Enzo had traded his short-range sword for a spear with a sharpened tip. He prodded upward, and Margot lurched left and right to avoid its jabs.

"Give it back!" Enzo yelled and hurled his spear javelin-style.

The tip of his weapon wedged into the wall, separating them. Enzo wrapped two hands around the spear's wooden shaft, but Margot had no intention of waiting around for him to wrestle it free.

"Run faster," she urged.

Van grouched, "You run faster."

At the top of the stairs, a hallway spread out in a *T*. A set of painted-white double doors flanked either end. Apartments, maybe? Offices? Frankly, Margot didn't care as long as they led her somewhere she wouldn't get unceremoniously skewered.

The hall before them was, like the rest of the gallery, crowded with globes and glass-paned displays stuffed with scrolls and parchment, and broken pieces of stone friezes. Off one of the nearby tables, Van grabbed a golden apple from a potpourri cornucopia and lugged one of the doors open.

With one arm, he nudged Margot into the room, placing her protectively behind him. Around the door, he launched the apple down the hallway.

Margot heard the crash but didn't see it. Just like she heard Enzo's pounding footfalls chase after the noise.

Van closed the door and wrapped his arms around her, reeling her in so that her face was pressed flat against his chest, his thundering heart underneath. They stood motionless and silent on the other side of the gallery door.

Margot wriggled out of his grip, blaming the way her own heart stammered on the chase scene and not his proximity. Her eyes adjusted to the light in the room.

This part of the gallery was spacious and airy; arched windows ran the length of the walls. Instead of cluttered stalls, here there was a polished granite floor webbed with silver and onyx, the foundation for statues of great ancient leaders and the women who made them that way. Dozens of sculptures, all still and stone.

For now. But knowing their track record, probably not for long.

"Van . . ." Margot said, refusing to peel her gaze off the emperors, imposing in white marble, towering over their heads. Their plaques named them: Trajan, Nero, Augustus. Was it her imagination, or did Hadrian just blink?

Next to her, Van pressed his ear to the seam in the door. Margot could barely hear anything over her jack-hammering pulse. Her chest burned, lungs weary from all the running and the subsequent panicking. Van had barely broken a sweat.

"He's upstairs still," Van whispered.

Nero's head swiveled on his neck. Oh, god. Margot was going to be sick. There was no other outlet. Just the door against her back, a hallway with an aggravated treasure hunter, and a gallery of soon-to-be murderous emperors.

"Hurry," she urged. "We've got company."

Van made a noise at the back of his throat. Something between disbelief and annoyance.

Margot pinched Van's chin between her thumb and forefinger, turning his head so he had no choice but to reckon with the fact that every statue in this corner of the gallery had gained consciousness. Because apparently that was a totally normal thing that just kept happening.

"Oh no," was all he said.

Nero, holding a marble fiddle, shifted toward them. Every step was an earthquake. If Enzo didn't know where they were before, he knew now. Nero swung his bowstring like a stone blade, entirely too closely for comfort.

Margot wasn't going to wait here to get smashed to smithereens. She hauled the doors open, but waiting on the other side was Enzo.

The boy staggered back a few steps at the sight of the sentient statues. His resolve, however, resolidified the moment his gaze settled on Margot, judging by the way his jaw clenched tight. His hand still clutched the faux shard.

Sandwiched between a small militia of angry statues and Enzo, they didn't have the greatest odds.

"I have a plan," she said quietly. Stumbling backward, her eyes locked on Enzo as he, too, sized up the statues. Margot's back pressed against Van's as their opponents circled. "It's your plan, kind of."

"My plan was don't get caught, and clearly that's no longer viable."

"Fair," Margot leveled. With her voice low enough only Van could hear, she said, "But we could still divide and conquer. Make them look somewhere else. Then, we make a break for it."

"Deal." And, then, he was off.

Van went right, while Margot darted left. The statues split up as well. Half tailed Van, while the rest homed in on Margot. Enzo joined them, his stare bloodthirsty.

Augustus slashed his marble sword, and it made contact with the pedestal Margot crouched behind. Stone crumbled, the dust sifting onto her hair, her cheeks, her hands. She tucked and rolled, narrowly missing another strike.

All she had to do was split them up long enough for her and Van to escape.

Margot wove between two sculptures and jetted across the room, huddling behind a full-body depiction of Juno. At least the stone goddess of marriage wasn't going to maim her. Worst she'd get was turned into a swan. Enzo got roped into a sparring match with one of the later rulers—Hadrian, maybe?—and it gave her just enough time to catch her breath.

A sickening crunch jolted Margot onto her feet. The sound of bone against marble.

By the looks of the way Van cradled his fingers, he'd tried to punch Emperor Trajan. To little avail. Although now didn't seem like the best time for criticism. Scarlet stained his knuckles.

The stern-faced statue didn't care. It raised its sword to strike again.

Margot shouted, "Watch out!"

Her hesitation was all Enzo needed for his hand to latch on to the handle of Margot's backpack. He jerked her back, and her arms slipped through the straps.

"Get off of me!" Margot yelped. She hooked her elbow, catching the strap with her arm. But it didn't matter. Enzo sliced his silver blade through the fabric and tore the backpack out of her grasp.

Slinging the remaining strap over his shoulder, Enzo tried to make a break for it. The operative word being *try*. Van lashed out, wrestling him to the ground before he could get very far.

Enzo landed an elbow to Van's sternum, knocking the air out of his lungs, and Van rolled off, clutching his chest.

Margot couldn't get onto her feet fast enough. Enzo nudged open one of the windows and dove through. The metal grates of the fire escape rattled beneath his feet.

Scrambling after him, Margot hoisted a leg over the windowsill. No way was he getting away with this.

But then, behind her, Van let out a strangled cry. Margot whipped around, panic flooding her system. Blood, deep red, pooled against the cotton-polyester blend of Van's T-shirt, right across his bicep. The statue of Augustus still had his sword extended as Van thudded to his knees.

His name parted her lips. She expected Augustus to take a ruthless swing, but it didn't come. The statue—every statue—froze. Their uncanny movements ceased entirely.

Margot was by Van's side in an instant. "Are you okay?"

Van peeled his hand away from his arm. Gravel slipped through his fingers as he huffed out a shocked breath, his green eyes wide on hers. The sleeve was still stained crimson, but as Margot slid her palm across the dampness, searching for an injury, her hand only met cool, hard marble. Beneath the blood, which crusted into gravel under her fingers, his skin had turned to stone.

The bathroom at Mia Bella's was as pink as the rest of it. Van did not look particularly comfortable on the closed toilet seat, despite the fact it wore a fuzzy shag cover, but there wasn't exactly a better triage room at their disposal.

Margot propped the fossil of a first aid kit she'd found under the sink on a baby-changing table. "You could have told me sooner," she said through clenched teeth as she tore open a plastic-wrapped bottle of antiseptic and placed it next to a brown jug of hydrogen peroxide. How did she even treat something like this?

Where there should have been an open wound, there was a marble-white gash carved into Van's arm beneath the rolled sleeve of his T-shirt.

"Tell you what?" Van eyed her like she'd grown a second head, or maybe a third. "I didn't know the statues were connected to the Vase. At least, not until it was too late."

Right. Because Van had gotten *stabbed*. With a *sword*. And then his blood dried up into rubble. As if it had never existed in the first place.

"Does it still hurt?" she asked.

"I'm fine," Van said, simmering. "It's just a flesh wound."

"Do you even have flesh to wound?" Margot asked. Fear thinly disguised as a laugh bubbled out of her. "I mean, what changed? You're—are you turning back into a statue?"

"Yes, I believe." The words scraped out of him. "The Vase shards. I think they must control the statues. Including me."

An adrenaline-soaked montage flashed through Margot's head. The guardians in Venus's temple. The nymph opening her hand at the Nymphaeum. The legionary at the museum. The statue gallery. The whole time, she had shards in her backpack. Whatever power Venus imbued into that clay, it must have been enough to make even hearts of stone beat.

"So, when Enzo stole the backpack . . ."

"He took the shards too far away for their magic to reach me."

Margot dabbed hydrogen peroxide on a cotton pad. Was she supposed to clean a wound that wasn't there anymore? "I thought a guy like you doesn't believe in magic because it's impractical."

He winced and continued, "I don't."

The end of the word ticked up. Making *don't* sound like *didn't*.

While Margot patted the cotton pad against Van's arm where the seam of marble tore through his skin, Van clenched and unclenched his hands, testing the joints. It sparked something in her memory, him doing that outside Martines Cucine. As if reading her mind, he added, "It happened once before. The night I left you at the ruins. Slow at first. But by the time you found me—"

"It had moved down your arms to your hands," Margot finished. "And you dropped my prized possession in the sewers. I remember."

"Sorry about that." Van flinched against the cotton pad, but Margot held him steady. He was warm beneath her touch. How long would it last? How much time did he have until the stone reclaimed him?

"So, we're going after Enzo," Margot said, tossing the cotton in the trash. "He took my backpack. We find him, we steal the shards back, and you stop turning into stone."

Van stood, rolling his torn sleeve back down over the stripe of stark white. He took up most of the space in the cramped bathroom. "No point. We know where he's going. Those three shards mean nothing to him without the last two. We'll cut him off at the next trial. There's one in Naples and one in Pompeii."

"What if it isn't soon enough?" Margot asked, each word delicate, like cracks might web across Van's skin and render him to dust before her eyes.

The look Van's face held could hardly be called an expression—he was entirely expressionless—but that was how Margot knew there was something eating away at him, termites in a log cabin. Usually he had some vaguely annoyed, presumptuous look about him. This was . . . empty. Lifeless. "I'm not supposed to be here, Margot."

"I know we're missing Dr. Hunt's assignment, but I'm sure we can catch up."

"I'm not supposed to be *now*." Van closed his eyes and rattled his head. "This was always borrowed time. People like me don't get second chances."

And for the first time since he clawed out of that marble slab, Margot saw a version of Van she thought she recognized from his journal. The boy she could imagine chewing on the end of his fountain pen, palms smudged with black ink, who wrote careful, vulnerable words within the folds of his leather journal. A place he thought no one would ever read them.

When she needed to be brave, he'd been there. Not *him*. But his words. Every sentence in his journal made her feel like anything was possible. Like scheming behind her dad's back wouldn't be the end of the world because she'd find the Vase, just like he had.

Not that they even had the Vase shards anymore. Enzo had made sure of that.

This was just another thing Margot did halfway. Another half-written chapter in the story of Margot. The thought of the inescapable disapproving lecture she'd receive from her dad for the laundry list of things she'd screwed up in the last few days stung her chest and left an acrid taste in her mouth. She'd disappointed him. Again.

But Van. Van still needed her, whether he wanted to admit it or not. Maybe Margot had a track record of giving up on hobbies—but she wouldn't give up on him.

18

Margot missed her flight the same way she missed her dad's call: on purpose.

She waited for the little red notification to pop up after he'd left a voicemail to slide her phone out of her pocket. All too chipper, he said, *"Good morning, Gogo. Or afternoon, for you. I hope you've gotten this out of your system. You'll be onto the next thing soon enough anyway. It's closing day for the Goodwin house, but I'll meet you at the airport around midnight."*

His words chafed against her ear. *Onto the next thing soon enough.* Like what? Doing taxes? Cooking Hamburger Helper for dinner? Leaving PTO meetings early for the fourth open house of the week?

What he didn't say was even louder than what he did. She was just another task on his to-do list to take care of. Less a daughter and more an agenda item.

She put her phone on airplane mode anyway. It felt appropriate.

Margot and Van reconvened with the class moments before they filed out of the museum, so she'd used Van's back like a desk, scribbling frenzied sentences into the blank spaces of her copy of the worksheet. She handed it to Rex, who passed it to Topher, who gave it to Calvin, who nudged it into Dr. Hunt's hands as the class joined a walking tour through the city center. With Suki covering for them, it was like they'd never left.

As they walked, Margot could barely focus on the way ancient Rome drifted past, instead preoccupied with how her heart hammered behind her rib cage. Every face in the crowd looked like Enzo. She saw his high cheekbones, his tanned skin, his dark hair everywhere she looked, like a phantom she couldn't shake. But it was never actually him with his hands shoved in his black hoodie, and one strap of her yellow backpack over his shoulder.

By the time they made it back to the hotel, an establishment that had things like complimentary robes and silver-plattered room service, her whole body ached, and her nerves had worked themselves into knots.

"I can't spend all night in my room," she said as she and Van filed into the elevator.

The thought of wasting the whole evening cooped up watching reality show reruns with Suki and fielding evil glares from Astrid made her skin itch. They couldn't just sit around.

She had to do *something* or she was going to lose Van and the Vase in the same fell swoop.

She jabbed the top button on the elevator panel with her thumb. They emerged onto the hotel's rooftop patio, a small square with a handful of umbrellaed bistro tables and overgrown shrubs. A few tables held ice buckets with bottles of wine, the glasses flipped upside down on carefully folded napkins.

Margot walked straight to the patio's railing, gripping onto the swirling metal fence. She could almost taste the city, sparkling like a LaCroix on a hot summer day. The air was rich: thick with gasoline, stale cigarette smoke, and something distinctly floral from bursting red blooms that trailed down the limestone buildings.

"How are the vibes?" Van asked, coming to stand next to her. The words sounded so unnatural leaving his lips that Margot laughed so hard she might've pulled a muscle.

"The vibes are great. I mean, this is . . ." she said, her voice fading out. When she finally found the word, she finished: "Amazing."

There was a reason they called Rome the City Eternal. The metropolis stretched out before them, sprawled beneath the last drips of a sorbet sunset. From here, Margot spotted the skeleton of the Colosseum and evergreens dotting the Roman Forum. Modernity didn't wipe out the history—it molded around it.

"I spent so much time worrying about what we'd find underneath these ancient cities. Sometimes it's nice to get a little perspective." Van's fingers drummed against the iron banister. He turned back to the nearest table and swiped a bottle of red and a wine opener.

"We can't drink that," Margot chastised.

"Who's going to stop us?" Then, Van lifted himself up and over to the other side. "Come on."

"Here is fine," Margot said. "Here has chairs."

"When has Margot Rhodes ever turned down an adventure?" Van asked, extending his hand.

She took it. Every other time they'd touched, it had been for survival. This was something sweeter. When her feet landed on the other side of the fence, his fingers slipped out of hers, and she knew he only flexed his hands because he was slowly turning back to stone, but she wanted to pretend that maybe, just a little bit, he was testing out the feeling of her palm on his.

They followed the curve of the shingles to a quiet corner where the roofline flattened and sank to the clay tiles. Van wound the silver spiral opener into the bottle's cork like a certified sommelier. It released with a *pop*. He swigged straight from the bottle. When he was finished, he wiped the back of his hand over his lips in a way that would make Miss Penelope drop dead.

Holding the wine out to Margot, the bottle slipped from his grasp. Margot caught it with two hands, a splash of red dripping to the tiles. With a laugh, she said, "Thank god for my Spider-Man-like reflexes."

But her eyes didn't move from Van's fingers. When he'd dropped *Relics of the Heart* into the sewer, it had been the same stiff grasp that fumbled it. It was happening faster this time.

Before she could think better of it, she drank down a big gulp. It tasted like spoiled grape juice. It basically *was* spoiled grape juice. Underage drinking was not an extracurricular she'd intended to pursue, but warmth flooded Margot's body. She could make an exception for Italy.

"Are you sure there's nothing else we can be doing right now?" Margot asked. "The Vase is just . . . out there. Shouldn't we be, I don't know, plotting? Planning?"

"I have a plan," Van said. "And the plan doesn't start until the class gets on the train tomorrow."

Margot's words curled inward like night petals shy against the morning sun. "Promise me you'll be okay until then?"

Van nodded once, firm enough for her to believe him.

Quiet settled between them, as heady and indulgent as the red wine they shared.

"Why did you come here?" she asked when the silence grew too thick. "In 1932, I mean."

Van blew out a stiff breath. His gaze slid sidelong but not really focusing, like he was riffling through the indexes of his mind. Finally, he settled on: "Money."

"Noble pursuit," Margot said.

His eyes flicked toward her. "It is when you've spent the last two years selling papers up and down Manhattan making chump change."

"Did you have to wear one of those silly little hats like they do in *Newsies*?"

Van's eyebrows lowered. "Ivy caps are not silly."

Which was code for he totally had.

He took another swig. "I didn't have anyone or anything. I was a ghost, practically invisible. No one knew me. No one would miss me. All I wanted was to be seen."

"Is that how you met Atlas?" Margot asked.

A small laugh lifted Van's lips. "In a way. I stole his compass. He wanted it back. We made a deal—I'd help him on his excavation, and he'd keep a roof over my head."

"And you kept the compass."

"Collateral," Van said, eyes bright.

Margot thought of the grayscale image tucked between the pages of his journal, where his arm looped around Atlas's shoulders and his smile cut through the photo like a knife. "What happened? Between you and Atlas?"

He tensed at the question. A caged look flattened his features.

Margot shifted toward him, a compass toward the north star. "You don't have to tell me. But you don't have to hide either."

Van cleared his throat. "Different ideas of loyalty."

"He betrayed you?" Margot asked. She sipped again from the wine, letting it make her brave. (Vaguely, she wondered if drinking from the same bottle counted as kissing someone. Not that she was thinking about kissing Van. Not at all.)

Van absently touched the crook in his nose where it had clearly been broken, and she wondered how many times Van thought with his fists. Maybe Atlas did, too. Had they fought like brothers or like enemies?

"It's why I don't do partners anymore."

"What am I, chopped liver?" Margot asked, featherlight.

A reluctant grin flashed across his face. "Fair enough, kid. What about you?"

"Oh, I'd look incredibly cute in a newsboy hat."

There was that look again. It was like Van was excavating her—digging into the deepest parts of her, the ones she didn't even want to see.

"You know that's not what I meant. You read my journal, so you already know everything there is to know about me," he said. He leaned closer, closer, closer. Close enough that Margot's nervous system was going to need a hard reboot. Close enough to kiss her. Instead, he plucked the bottle out of her hand. "Maybe I want to know you."

A hopeful thing fluttered in her belly. To be known. But the words settled heavy in her chest, refusing to come out. What was worse: not being understood, or being understood and still not being enough?

"You're different than your writings made you seem," she said.

"You're deflecting."

So, Margot took a deep breath and prayed for courage.

"All my life, I've been defined by things I quit—I quit ballet, I quit tae kwon do, I quit playing guitar. I stopped painting and got bored with field hockey. I got kicked out of etiquette classes—"

Van scoffed and downed another drink. "What'd you do? Forget to tuck your napkin into your shirt? Use the salad fork as the dinner fork?"

Margot winced at the memory. "Worse, I started a food fight in the middle of our afternoon tea because one of the girls called me *a problem child*. So, I decided to show her one."

Van barked out a laugh.

"Shut *up*," Margot said, but she couldn't stop her spill of laughter. "Whatever. The point is that I can't quit this. I—"

Van's fingers found hers resting on the tile roof and squeezed. Patient and prompting. A soft touch that she realized was probably difficult for him.

"My mom left when I was twelve. Decided she didn't want to be with my dad anymore, didn't want to be with me anymore, and definitely didn't want to be in Dogwood Hollow, Georgia, anymore." Predictable tears rimmed her eyes. "Without her, I didn't know who I was supposed to be."

She'd tried everything. She tried to fit into a box—any box she could find. Summer theater, history club, math club. She'd given them her everything . . . until her everything inevitably wasn't good enough. Quitting was easier than admitting she was worthless at something. Being wrong.

She could still hear the way her dad would sigh every time she told him she wanted to try something new. Could feel the heat rising to her cheeks like she was standing in their sage-green living room with the pilled carpet beneath her feet. Could see the frustrated way he wrapped his fingers against his stubbled jaw when she sobbed or shouted, like she was a wild thing he had no idea how to tame.

Eventually, it seemed like every conversation they had was rife with stomping and slammed doors and cold shoulders and, eventually, bleary-eyed apologies after she was done lashing out.

No version of herself had been able to outrun the ache in her chest from the inescapable question: *Why* hadn't she been enough? Enough to hold her family together, enough to make her dad proud, enough for her classmates to like her. Smart enough, nice enough, strong enough.

"It's just been me and my dad since then, but he doesn't get it. Get me. He's always so busy with work, and I kept thinking I'd find the thing that made him understand me, but—if I find the Vase, it'll be enough to make him love me."

Maybe it was the wine in her system. Maybe it was Van watching her, searing and inquisitive at the same time. But saying it out loud, admitting it to someone—even if that someone was Van Keane—made her feel exposed. Like she'd said too much again. Been too much.

She yanked her hand back from his, cradling it instead in

her lap. Even staring at her cuticles, she could feel the way he looked at her. Like she was a riddle to unravel, a problem to solve.

Finally, he cleared his throat. "That's not how that works."

"I know, I know. You think the Vase gives you treasure, but—"

"No, Margot. You're you. That's plenty."

Van's words were a tidal wave crash that left Margot stunned in the wreckage, battering down all her strongest-built walls. She brushed a curl behind her ear, shaking her head. "I thought I was a troublemaking girl with a brain full of bad ideas."

Van's brow crinkled. That same analytical gaze sank into his eyes. "You held your own in the Nymphaeum."

"I had a panic attack."

"And you solved the *Aura* trial."

"After getting thrown forty feet into the air."

"You're brave, Margot." His voice was tender, quiet. It had lost all patented snark. "It takes courage to let people see you for who you really are."

He sounded like Van from the journal. Her Van.

Although lately, all of him felt more and more like her Van. She liked his jagged corners and sharp lines. He was everything she wasn't—logical and precise and detail oriented. They were two sides of a scale, keeping the other in perfect balance.

She wanted to believe what he'd said about her. She might

have let herself, but a figure below pulled on the threads of her attention. More specifically: a backpack with one strap. The person wove through the crowd, his head covered by a hood. But Margot knew her disgraced Fjällräven when she saw it.

"Is that . . . Enzo?" She lurched upright so fast, her foot slipped out from beneath her.

Van rose, steadying her with an arm against her back. "Let's go."

They hopped over the patio railing, and Margot dropped the half-empty bottle of wine back off in the ice bucket on their way out.

The elevator doors wouldn't close fast enough, no matter how many times Margot jammed her finger against the first-floor button. When they did close, trapping a confused-looking businessman in with them, smooth jazz filtered over the speakers. She'd never hated a sound more.

"Come on, come on, come on," she begged.

She and Van squeezed out the doors before they'd even fully opened.

"Is he close?" Margot asked as the lobby's revolving door spat them out onto the street. She lifted onto her toes. Searching, searching. "Do you feel any less statue-y?"

Van shook his head. Even from his six-foot-something perspective, it must have been impossible to spot Enzo in a crowd this thick. "No? Maybe. I can't tell."

"There!" Margot said, spying her yellow backpack in the

fray. She reached for Van's hand, and he threaded his fingers between hers as they ran.

Margot leaped around a street vendor selling single-stem roses to blushing couples. She dodged a painter's wooden easel but accidentally knocked over a cup of brushes, sending them rolling. Someone's arms flew up to defend themselves, but the timing of it meant that Margot got a face full of cannoli. The orange-flavored cream stuck to her eyelashes and slid down her face. Some dripped onto her lips. At least it was delicious.

Ahead, a green door opened, and Enzo darted inside beneath its weathered awning. Margot and Van surged toward him. The door closed behind them, softening the din of the city. Enzo barged between white-clothed tables, knocking over crystal glasses and steaming plates of cacio e pepe.

Margot and Van tailed him through a pair of saloon-style, silver doors into the kitchen. Here, chefs in tall, white toques swung trays in a synchronized dance. Margot ducked beneath a platter of sfogliatella. Someone yelled after them, but Enzo was already sneaking out the windowed back door.

By the time they made it through the door and into the squashed alleyway, Margot had been dashed with powdered sugar, and Van had a linguine noodle sliding down his cheek.

"Did you see where he went?" Van asked.

"No," Margot said, chest heaving. "Did you?"

Van rolled the tension out of his neck. "No."

They could try to get a better vantage point, another bird's-eye view, but by then it would be too late. It already was. Enzo had vanished into the city center, the shards vanishing with him.

19

Margot was going to go full meltdown mode in T minus thirty-
six seconds, whether Astrid left the bathroom or not. Losing
Enzo, and then finding Enzo, and then losing Enzo again really
put Margot's emotions through a Laundromat spin cycle.

In a few hours, her father would realize that she had not gotten on that plane, and Dr. Hunt would probably get an email
back from Radcliffe finally confirming that Chad Vanderson
didn't exist.

Right now, she was ready for a seventeen-step skincare routine and as much sleep as her body would give her. Assuming
she could squash the mass amount of residual adrenaline racing
through her veins and sleep at all.

She banged her fist against the molded paneling three more
times, praying it really was the magic number.

"What are you even doing in there?" she asked. "Do *not*,

under any circumstances, try to give yourself a perm."

The door swung out from beneath Margot's midair fist. A cloud of rosemary-scented steam wafted out of the bathroom. Astrid frowned in the midst of it. "I have a date."

The sentence shocked Margot's system enough to dam the oncoming tears. Margot had daydreamed about dates more than she'd actually been on them, but based on every rom-com in the history of the universe, she could definitively say Astrid was underdressed.

Her white-blonde hair disappeared beneath a terry-cotton towel, presumably and fortunately unpermed. She wore one of the hotel's complimentary robes with a white tank and soft cotton black shorts underneath. Her eyelids had been painted a heinous shade of blue, rimmed with an equally insulting amount of black liner.

If forcing her voice to stay level was an Olympic sport, Margot at least deserved silver. "I didn't know you cared about human emotions. Is this some kind of body snatcher situation?"

"Relationships have their perks," was all Astrid said before she returned to the double vanity with absolutely no regard for why Margot had been so keen on breaking and entering.

At the edge of Astrid's bed, Suki pulled a perfume bottle out of a wad of rose-colored tissue paper. "So, that's why you bought this."

Astrid tilted her chin higher. "My mom said every woman needs a distinct scent."

Suki spritzed the perfume. Sniffed. "And yours has top notes of elderberry and hypocrisy."

Some spiteful part of Margot appreciated Suki's willingness to stand up to Astrid—until now, Margot honestly hadn't been sure if anyone had the guts except Dr. Hunt—but another, louder part of her knew what it felt like to be on the receiving end of those jabs. The kinds of bruises they left.

Margot sighed, sagging against the doorframe. "Do you need help getting ready?"

"All I have with me are cargo pants, and I tried to go shopping today, but I have no idea what color lipstick to wear." Five lip stains rested in her palm, brand-new. Salmon, baby pink, fuchsia, a horribly out-of-season plum, and Margot Red.

Margot softened like butter. Maybe it was that Astrid was so helplessly clueless or the fact that she was looking at Margot without a hint of disdain, but the calcic shell around her heart shattered. Dr. Hunt *did* say she wanted them to figure out how to work together.

Margot smiled at her surly roommate. "I'll take that as a yes."

Inviting herself into the bathroom, Margot examined Astrid's makeup haul—there was a blond eyebrow pencil, a tube of mascara (notably not waterproof; Margot could never), and the notorious nine-shade eye palette, all cool blues and silvers. She'd also scrounged up a mostly empty tube of tinted SPF, which would have been great if it weren't nearing eight p.m, and a cream blush with a healthy amount of shimmer. Margot could work with that.

She ripped open a pack of makeup removers. "First things first, this isn't 1985."

"But I thought—"

Margot shook her head. She nudged a wet wipe into Astrid's hand. "You thought wrong."

While Astrid scrubbed off her makeup and shook her hair out of the towel, Margot called out, "Suki! Will you grab the jumpsuits in my suitcase?"

"Plural?" she heard Suki ask. Moments later, Suki appeared at the doorway with three options piled in her arms. One was linen, one was ruffled, and one could only be described as Plumber Chic.

"Take your pick," Margot said to Astrid.

A hum. "The middle one."

Ruffles it was.

Astrid shimmied into the ivory jumpsuit, wiggling it up and over her narrow hips. The legs ruffled out capri length, and bell-shaped sleeves landed right above her wrists. It hung a bit loose on her—she was all bone where Margot rounded—but with a belt, no one would ever know.

"That'll do, Donkey," Margot said in an admittedly terrible rendition of a Scottish accent.

There was a knock at the door, and Suki hightailed it out of the bathroom. Topher's voice filtered in, saying something about a Ping-Pong championship happening next door, and Suki shouted a quick goodbye along with a "knock 'em dead!"

"I need to tell you something," Astrid said as soon as Suki clicked the door shut. "Suki can't keep a secret to save her life, but you should know."

Margot's curiosity piqued. She loved a juicy secret as much as the next girl. Her raised eyebrows spoke for her.

"I know Chad isn't who you're saying he is." Astrid watched Margot's reflection in the mirror as she coated her lashes in liquid black. And Margot's reflection was trying its absolute darnedest not to look like Astrid had just ripped a very large metaphorical rug out from under its feet.

"What do you—what do you mean?" Margot asked. Her fingers traced the smooth green beads around her wrist.

"A smirk that could knock a lesser woman dead. A shock of sun-bleached hair. A row of freckles arched over his left brow and a smattering of unruly ones across his cheeks. He could only be one man. Van Keane."

Margot gasped. She didn't even try to hide it. The words had been stripped straight from her application essay and used against her.

"How did you do it?" Astrid asked. "Don't tell me Suki's creepy Ouija board is real."

"No, no," Margot said, surprised by the sudden relief coursing through her. Necromancer she was not. Didn't have the stomach for it, for starters. "He . . . well, it's a long story."

Astrid tapped her phone on the counter. The background was a photo of her holding a blue ribbon. Typical. "I've got twenty minutes."

Unfortunately, there was no succinct way to say "Well, I stole a magical artifact and a historical text from the school's archives, which led me to a secret temple I'm *definitely* not telling you the location of, and while I was down there, the cursed statue of Van reanimated."

Astrid watched her think. Waited. "Nineteen minutes."

Margot busied herself with Astrid's eye shadow palette, dusting one of the matte grays onto a brush. "Close."

Obliging, Astrid closed her eyes. It didn't stop her from grimacing. "Fine, don't tell me. But aren't you supposed to be on a flight back to the middle of nowhere by now?"

The brush stilled in Margot's hand. "How do you know about that?"

"I'm observant." Astrid popped one lid open. "And I saw your phone on the sink this morning when we were rushing for the train. Your dad double texts."

"That's a total invasion of privacy." Margot sounded more like Van every day.

"I thought maybe it was an emergency." As if. "All I'm saying is it would be a downright shame for Dr. Hunt to find out your father requested for you to be removed from the program on such short notice."

"You wouldn't."

"Wouldn't I?"

Margot's jaw tensed tight enough to crack a molar. "What do you want?"

"The truth." Astrid wore a winning grin, sly with the upper hand.

As Margot swirled the shadow into the creases of Astrid's lid, she spoke the way she imagined people would share clandestine information: hushed and a bit hurried. "He was cursed. A hundred years ago, when he was searching for the Vase of Venus Aurelia, everyone thought he'd died when his dig site caved in, but he didn't. He'd been turned to stone."

Astrid scoffed. The sudden movement sent a gray streak halfway to her brow bone.

"Quit wiggling," Margot scolded. She dabbed off the errant shadow with a makeup wipe. "You asked for this, remember? The point is: I found him."

"Where?" Astrid asked, a tinge of disbelief to her voice.

Margot moved to the other eye, mimicking each deliberate motion. Her grip on the brush tightened. "In Pompeii. And when I did, he came back to life."

"Please." It was more laugh than word.

Shaking her head, Margot said, "I know what it sounds like, but why would I lie about this?"

"How?" Astrid pestered.

Switching brushes, Margot moved to a softer blue and swiped it onto Astrid's lids. The familiar movements did little to soothe the exposed nerve of her emotions. She knew why Astrid had suddenly regressed to monosyllabic responses. She didn't believe her. Worse, she didn't believe in her ability to do it at all.

"You wanted the truth. That's the truth."

"That's not all I want." Astrid's words sharpened, determined. "Stop looking for the Vase."

Margot groaned. "This again?"

There was something different in the way Astrid looked at her—warning, protective. The way a friend would look at you. "It's going to get you in major trouble."

It already has.

"I can't," Margot said as she dropped the eye shadow palette back into Astrid's pile of drugstore cosmetics. "I told you. Van's cursed. And without the Vase, he'll turn back into a statue."

"That's too bad because you'll never find it." Astrid reached for her mascara tube. All kindness sapped from her face, like maybe it had never been there to begin with. A mirage or a figment of Margot's overactive imagination.

The words were out of Margot before she could stop them. "You don't have to take my word for it. I know it's real. And I have *proof.* Cold, hard, indisputable proof."

"Yeah, right."

Sliding out her phone, Margot tapped to her photos and thumbed through images of palm trees against blue skies, heaping bowls of pasta, and sneaky candids of Van until she found it. A photo of the first two shards after they'd survived the Nymphaeum. Their gilded edges fit together perfectly, and the start of an inscription wove across the clay fragments.

"Look," Margot said, "I had the first *two* shards, and I would've had the third if it weren't for—"

"Had?" Astrid asked.

Margot chewed the inside of her lip. "Have."

"You said *had*."

"Van has them," Margot said. Her pulse quickened with the lie. "That's what I meant."

Astrid peered down at Margot's phone again and cut her off with a cold laugh. It started as a small, biting giggle, but Astrid couldn't contain it.

A sickening sludge formed in Margot's gut. "What's so funny?"

"I'm not saying I believe *you* of all people found the Vase, but if you did . . ." Astrid paused, and Margot had every reason to believe it was for dramatic effect. "Well, I've heard about this inscription. You did translate it, didn't you?"

"Of course he did," Margot argued. He'd found all the shards before. He must have read what they said.

A tilt of Astrid's head. "Van did. Not you? He translated every word? You're sure?"

Margot tried to remember—tried but failed. "I think so, yeah. Why wouldn't he?"

Astrid finished fanning out her lashes with mascara and

sank the wand back in its tube. "Would've been pretty conve-
nient to leave out the part where he needs a human sacrifice to
unlock the treasure of Venus."

Margot hated the way Astrid forced her hand. Manipulated
the conversation so that Margot had to fold. "What are you
talking about?"

"The treasure," Astrid said, like it was perfectly obvious.
"You think Venus would make it easy for someone to waltz off
with her belongings? *If* that's really shards of the Vase—and,
again, I'm not saying I believe you—it's the key to the treasure.
There's only one way to be loved forever. *Lapideum.* To turn to
stone."

The stodgy thing in Margot's stomach somehow thickened.
"How do you know?"

"I'm literally an award-winning linguist."

"Literally *whatever*. It doesn't mean you're right."

"He's using you. When he's done, he'll have all the riches in
the world, and you'll be a statue. You can't trust him."

"But I can trust you?" Margot didn't mean to spit it out like
Astrid had tried to poison her. It just came out that way.

"You can," Astrid said. "Because I am right, and if you
don't know it yet, you will soon. I'm just looking out for you,
Margot."

Margot couldn't believe her—why would she? Astrid had
been nothing but cruel to her all summer. Tonight was no different. She should have never believed it might have been.

It didn't matter that Margot hadn't seen the last two shards. They wouldn't say that. They couldn't. They'd find the last two shards, and then she'd have the full inscription. And Van wouldn't turn her to stone after everything they'd been through.

"Or suit yourself," Astrid added, snide. She dotted the baby-pink lip stain over her lips without even bothering to ask Margot's opinion. "But when I'm right and you can't see it because you're blinded by your feelings, I'm saying I told you so."

Margot would have expected nothing less.

20

Margot jolted awake when the train lurched to a stop, somewhere deep in the hills of Lazio. Her cheek was still warm with the impression of Van's shoulder—where she had apparently dozed off sometime between boarding the train in Rome and now. She could only hope she hadn't drooled.

"Did I miss it?" she asked, frantically brushing wild curls out of her face.

"Not yet," Van said. His scowl carved deeper into his forehead today, and his voice was gravelly. Margot wasn't sure if it was because of their early morning wake-up call or the distance from the shards. "Next stop is us."

While the rest of the class was going to get carted back to their dig plots in Pompeii, Margot and Van needed to make a quick pit stop. And pray that Enzo hadn't made it there first.

Margot kept telling herself that there was no way he had— Enzo would have had to solve the legend's riddles to decode the trial's location and survive the trial with no existing knowledge. It was a fool's errand. But as far as Margot knew about treasure hunters, they didn't really like to *lose* their treasures after they'd hunted them. Enzo had been a dragon watching over his trove, and Margot was quite certain they'd awakened the beast.

"Is everything okay?" she asked.

Van answered with a grunt that sounded kind of, maybe, like he'd said words, but frankly it was so grunty that she could barely tell.

"That doesn't sound okay."

"I said it's fine."

Margot refrained from reminding him he hadn't actually *said* anything at all. He refocused out the window, watching the sun-gold scenery drift past. Across the aisle, Astrid caught Margot's gaze.

Lapideum, she mouthed.

Margot rolled her eyes. It didn't matter what Astrid thought—Margot knew she could trust Van. Even if he was clearly not a morning person.

Astrid, on the other hand, had apparently had the time of her life last night. A few specks of leftover mascara dotted her cheeks like freckles, but she'd popped out of bed like a toaster pastry this morning and buzzed like her blood was made of espresso. *Some date.*

Margot melted deep into the outdated fabric folds of her seat.

The tips of her fingers traced the shape of the jade beads around her wrist, and she was acutely aware of the space Van took up next to her—the way his knee almost rested against hers, the shape of his spine as it curled toward the window, how his head leaned against the pane, tilting toward the light.

Next to her. But also somewhere far away.

As hard as she tried, she couldn't stop thinking about last night on the rooftop. *It takes courage to let people see you for who you really are.* Her whole body thrummed with the memory, electrified by the way he'd looked at her. Like he meant it. Like she could believe him.

In a feeble attempt to make sure he didn't catch her staring at him, she reached into the canvas tote she'd grabbed at a corner gift shop to replace her stolen backpack and wriggled out *Relics of the Heart.* It hadn't bounced back after its trip through the Nymphaeum. Ridges and valleys curled the paper unnaturally, leaving it stiff and cracking, but she opened it anyway. She smoothed her hands over the coarse pages—briefly, she wondered if she really needed the book if she already had every line memorized.

Gingerly, she separated the pages, taking care not to tear them. As she thumbed through the chapters, she caught glimpses of Isla and Reed's journeys as they transitioned from rival archaeologists to begrudging colleagues to soulmates, tangled in the thread that tied their lives together before they even knew it.

Margot paused at the opening of her favorite chapter. Thirty-one. Isla and Reed were so close to finding the Vase of Venus Aurelia, but Reed had just been outed as a double agent working with the evil Edgar Alfred Durham to double his profits. Isla hadn't forgiven him yet, but he had a grand gesture up his sleeve.

Isla's feet led her to the wetlands at the mouth of the Tiber. A boat was coming, and it would take her away from Reed for good. She'd never have to see him or his goofy smirk or his round brown eyes ever again—even if it broke her heart.

Margot turned the page, and Reed arrived in the scene, his back to Isla and dripping with river water. *What are you doing here?* Isla spat. He'd betrayed her when she needed him most. Margot knew what happened next—Reed would turn, get down on one knee, and propose to Isla with an emerald gem. He wasn't a double agent but a triple agent, and he'd only made that deal with Durham to afford the ring Isla had swooned over during their detour in Florence.

But when Reed turned, it was Van instead, green eyes gleaming in the saffron sun.

Snap out of it, Margot. This wasn't helping. He wasn't Reed Silvan, and she wasn't Isla Farrow. No matter how much she might have wanted to be.

For starters, Van's idea of a romantic gesture was petty theft. Never mind the whole turning-back-into-a-statue thing. Even as the train rocked gently around a corner, sunlight caught on a trail of marble that seeped down Van's skin, crawling out of the gash on his arm. Spreading with every second they spent away from the Vase. When he turned to watch the rolling countryside, it peeked out from underneath his sleeve and webbed up the side of his neck.

She couldn't lose him. Not before she had the chance to have him.

"Walk me through the plan again?" she asked, closing her book.

Van pressed a finger into his temple and loosed an irritated breath. "We go to the trial of *Terra*, we solve it, and we leave."

"Okay, why are you acting like you've got a major wedgie?" Margot asked. "Mad I took away your suspenders?"

He didn't look at her. "I couldn't sleep, so I went back to the archives at the museum."

The museum was totally closed by that time of night, but Margot decided it was best not to ask how he'd managed to get back inside. She'd seen him cheat and sneak and steal enough times to know he had his ways. And she'd take plausible deniability while she had it.

"And?" she prompted at the worried slant of his mouth.

He retrieved a sheet of paper from his pocket. It had been crinkled and clenched, indentions of Van's fingers molded into the parchment. "The curse, it's still spreading, and—"

His sentence ended abruptly, but like she had an atlas of his mind, she knew where his thoughts had led him. "And this is the longest you've been without one of the shards nearby, but you don't know exactly how long it takes to turn you all the way back to stone."

Van swallowed, his Adam's apple bobbing. "There's no guarantee that no one else discovered the last two shards in the hundred years I've been gone."

"They'll be there," she said. "And they'll lead us right to Enzo."

"He might not come."

"He will," Margot said.

"You don't know that!"

Margot reeled back, stunned. A few classmates swiveled in their seats to see the commotion. Van gulped down a breath that did little to flush the color that had risen to his cheeks. She wanted to press an affirming hand to his shoulder, but her hand hung halfway there. It wouldn't have done much anyway. Van jerked upright and squeezed past Margot into the aisle.

She rushed after him. "Where are you going?"

Their stop wasn't for another twenty minutes, fifteen at least.

Without glancing back, Van said, "It doesn't matter."

"Yes, it does," Margot pushed.

"No, it doesn't."

"It does because we're partners." Margot reached toward him, this time refusing to shy away. He shook her hand off his arm like she was nothing more than an annoying fruit fly.

Stomping down the aisle, he jiggled the handle on the bathroom, despite the sign clearly indicating it was occupied, and kept marching when it wouldn't open. One shoulder sagged, heavier than the other, and one leg lagged, throwing off his gait.

Van's foot snagged against a man's briefcase, and he stumbled forward. He caught himself against the armrest of the next seat—but not without startling a bottle-blonde twentysomething clearly on vacation. Her coffee-cart cappuccino spilled down the front of her white dress, leaving a brown Rorschach spot on the bodice.

The girl's gasp was a shotgun start. Van muttered an apology before making a break for it down the aisle. Fortunately—or, unfortunately—his legs were slow, laden with stone. Each move he made was rigid.

"Stop, Van." Margot caught up with him quickly, but it did nothing to deter him. "Stop. *Stop.*"

Van turned on his heels. Angry red rimmed his eyes, their usual hardened peridot gone glassy. "I don't want to talk about it."

An older woman and her all-fluff white dog, both wearing matching blue sunglasses, stared up at them. All she was missing was popcorn.

"You don't even know what I want to talk about," Margot said innocently. "Maybe I want to talk about the renaissance of the thirty-minute sitcom or Atlantic gigantism or any number of unrelated things."

"Don't do that," Van seethed.

"Do what?"

"Pity me."

A voice buzzed over the speakers, fuzzy and distorted. *"Arrivo a Napoli, dieci minuti."*

It cut the tension between them but did little to calm Van. He stormed toward the end of the train car.

Down the aisle, Dr. Hunt stood out of her seat and stretched her arms overhead. If she turned around, she'd see the remnants of chaos they'd left in their wake and order Margot and Van thirty rows back to their assigned seats. But here, they had a straight shot off the train at the next platform. By the time anyone noticed they were missing, they'd already be back in Pompeii. All they had to do was not get caught.

Margot and Van made it to the back of the train, but that only meant there was nowhere else for them to go. With Van on the brink of a nuclear meltdown, they needed cover, and they needed it fast.

The woman and her pooch looked up at Margot. Their blue sunglasses.

"I just need to borrow these for a second," Margot said before stripping the eyewear off their faces.

"Fermati!" the woman shrilled.

The dog barked as Margot closed the distance to Van. Wrapping her arms around his torso like a linebacker, she dragged him into the last seats in the aisle.

"What are you *doing?*" He fought against her grasp. A

stone-hardened elbow dug in between her ribs. *Ouch.*

"I'm—trying—to help—you." Each staccato word was interrupted by a thrashing limb as Van tried desperately to eradicate himself from her vise grip. No way. Not when they were this close to Naples, to the next shard.

She wrangled the woman's sunglasses over his face through sheer force of will, and then sat up, triumphant.

The dog's tiny sunglasses barely covered Margot's eyes, making her look like a John Lennon knockoff. She ducked behind the row in front of her, only peeking out far enough to watch as Dr. Hunt glanced toward the woman and her disgruntled Maltese, both now squinting in the sunlight. Decades could have passed by the time Dr. Hunt finally slid into the bathroom stall.

An exhale peeled out of Margot's lungs. Except that the person who left the bathroom was beelining for their seats. He paused before them, clearing his throat.

"We were just, um . . . leaving." Margot scrambled up, dragging Van with her. He wasn't putting in his fair share of effort, basically reducing himself to defiant deadweight.

"Margot, knock it off," he snapped. "I know what you're trying to do but don't. You're just making everything worse."

The jagged edge of his voice ripped through her. Elephant heavy, a weight pressed against her esophagus. But Dr. Hunt could come out of the bathroom at any moment. Margot was too stubborn to stop now. She strong-armed him into the luggage room and slammed the door shut behind them.

The closet was not . . . big. Or even close to being appropriately sized for two people.

Suitcases had been piled on shelves that rose toward the top of the train. A single bulb was plastered on the ceiling, and Margot tugged on the chain dangling between them. Harsh light filled the narrow room.

Van whipped off his sunglasses. Tension strained his neck, tightened his shoulders. "You're relentless."

"Thank you," Margot said, flipping her sunglasses on top of her head.

A hoarse noise emanated from Van's chest. He clearly hadn't meant it as a compliment.

With every breath, her chest rose to meet his. "I know you don't want to talk about it, so we won't."

And they didn't. For a moment, they just stood there. Margot watching Van, and Van watching her right back.

"I wasn't trying to ruin everything." Her voice was annoyingly soggy.

"You didn't. I just feel like . . . like I can't breathe." Each word cracked like chipped marble. He pushed slow, purposeful breaths out through his nose, and Margot recognized it immediately—the way someone tried to hold back tears.

"You're afraid," Margot said, taking his hands in hers. They were colder than she remembered and that scared her, too. "Honestly, I'd be shocked if you weren't. But you don't have to do this alone. I'm right here."

The rest of Van's resolve shattered. His head sank against Margot's shoulder, burying his face in her neck as shallow breaths racked through him, shaking and sputtering. Margot's hands found his back and pressed flat, firm. Her fingers felt each groove of his ribs, every notch of his spine.

"I'm right here," she repeated, a mantra until the train slowed and Van's frantic breathing slowed with it. Even if she wasn't sure she could do anything else right lately, she was right here.

The gold compass around his neck had wrestled itself loose from its usual confines beneath his shirt in all the hubbub, and he clutched it, the movement second nature. She could just see the lines of the etching beneath his grasp. The very familiar lines.

"The emblem," she said. "It's the same one that was on Enzo's hoodie."

"Yes," Van croaked. "The logo for Atlas Exploration Company. A hundred years later, and Atlas is still finding ways to mess with me."

Margot clasped her hand around his. The compass had warmed from his touch. "We'll find this shard and catch Enzo. I promise."

The train halted. Napoli Centrale.

Margot donned her doggy glasses once more as she pried open the luggage room door, and Van tucked his compass back beneath his shirt.

The station was a glass and steel behemoth nestled between the Naples hillsides and a cerulean sea. When the doors slid open, Van stepped onto the platform next to her. Even though she could see the effort it took him, he held his head higher, determined. The train zipped off without them, sending wind through Margot's curls. Next stop: the trial of *Terra*. Whether she was ready or not.

21

Van brought Margot to a freaking tomb. Not exactly dream-
date material.

They stood shoulder to shoulder at the entrance to the
Crypta Neapolitana. Behind them was a dazzling riviera. The
kind of sight Margot expected to see on vintage postcards at the
bottom of a hat box, all rough-edged and stamped with faded
ink. Buildings with painted stucco walls in pastel yellows and
citrus oranges, adorned with copper, were offset by the too-
green leaves of the pines and palms.

Ahead? The Crypta Neapolitana was a tunnel, long and
winding, where shadows slicked the walls and ivy crept through
the crevices. According to Van, it would take them to the Tomb
of Virgil. But that wasn't their biggest issue right now.

"You mean you want us to go through . . . there. The miles-
long tunnel through the mountain that is"—she gestured

toward a white-and-red striped lever like the kind that blocked train tracks and an empty visitor's center kiosk—"clearly super open for guests."

"It takes us straight to the tomb. No other way there."

He shoved his hands in his pockets, hands she knew were turning to stone from the inside out, and something in Margot's chest twinged. If she didn't do something, soon the swirling stone would encase him, closing him off from her forever, just as she'd started to discover what was underneath his cold exterior.

"You do know that you had been allegedly *crushed to death* in an *unsafe ruin*, right?" Margot asked.

Van sighed. "You do know that *didn't actually happen*, right?"

Glad to see he was back to his ordinarily persnickety self.

They ducked beneath the barrier and plunged into the ancient tunnel. Margot curled her arms around herself. Even though the air was still summertime sticky in the shade, she couldn't shake the shiver from her skin.

"Any funny business I should worry about this time? Trapdoors? Snake pits? Mudslides? Do I have to fistfight the ghost of Virgil?" She'd meant for it to sound light, but shadows clawed at every word.

"This trial is a bit different than the first three. More of a test, less of a task." He circled his neck. The strands of marble that stretched toward his ear groaned with the movement.

Weren't they getting closer? Why wasn't the stone retreating? "Also, Virgil isn't actually there."

"What, did his bones just get up and walk out?"

"He was cremated. And then his ashes were lost in the Middle Ages. So, it's basically just a big stone room."

Margot eyed him. "How'd you learn all this stuff anyway?"

"All what stuff?" Van asked. He stared straight ahead, toward the pinprick light at the other side steadily growing larger.

"Like what happened in the Middle Ages to Virgil's ashes, and everything about the Vase. I don't reckon you read it all in the papers during your *Newsies* era."

Van tugged at the collar of his shirt, fingers grazing over the seam where skin met stone. "Honestly, I . . . didn't know much until I met Atlas. He taught me everything I know."

"Oh, god," Margot said. "Sorry, I didn't know. I never would have brought him up."

"I know." Something crossed his face—a flurry of emotions, faint as fresh snow—and then he said, "He underestimated me, Atlas did. Loved to remind me that I was a grifter he picked up off Fifty-Eighth. But I was a quick learner, and even if I had to work twice as hard to convince him I was worth my salt, I wasn't going back empty-handed."

Margot's ribs squeezed too tightly around her chest. She knew the feeling. Knew what it was like to have people peer down their noses at her, scrutinizing her every move. Every snide remark Astrid made had wormed under Margot's skin, eating her away like dry rot. It found the weak joists and threatened to tear down the very foundations of Margot.

And now she was here, in a mess of her own creation, about to lose the one person who finally seemed to understand her to some dumb freaking Roman curse. Thanks a lot, Venus.

"Van, I—" The words clogged her throat. How was she supposed to say sorry for something this big? It was her fault he was here in the first place, and her job to save him.

But her engines were running low on coal. She hated to admit that all her false bravado had lost its shine. She wanted to believe she could pass some silly test. That whatever it took to heal Van, she'd do it, even if she had to do it alone.

Could she? Or had everyone been right to underestimate *her*?

Van slowed to a stop in front of a stone staircase mostly overgrown with weeds. Above, carved into the cliffside, a doorway watched like an open eye. It reminded Margot of a cartoon supervillain's lair, which wasn't exactly the place she wanted to parade inside unprepared.

She could be brave for him. She had to be.

"Ladies first," she insisted as she took the first step up the staircase.

"Margot, wait," Van said, struggling to catch up with her. "I'll find this one. It's a bit tricky."

"Tricky," she echoed with a laugh that didn't quite land. "After the week we've had, I think I can handle tricky."

If anything, her pace accelerated. She'd been prodded forward with a hot iron of fear. Frankly, she wasn't sure if it was her own, or if she'd borrowed Van's and carried it like it was hers. The more he slowed, the faster she ran.

At the top, Margot could see the white-painted houses dotting the Naples hillsides. The roads were veins, connected to the heart of the vibrant city. A short metal fence encircled the historic area, as if to protect it from overly curious onlookers or amateur gravediggers. It was going to take a lot more than that to deter her.

Shirking off the strap of her tote bag, Margot planted her hands on the fence. She kicked a leg up, hooking it around the top, and then launched herself over. This time, she landed on her feet.

Ahead, a statue wept over a stone bench, carved in swaths of pleated drapery, and beyond that, the mouth of the cave opened wide. The statue shifted her head and batted open milk-white eyes. A jolt of energy surged through Margot. Living marble meant the shard had to be close.

"It's here," Van said. He snatched Margot's bag off the ground as he reached the landing. "I can feel it."

Still, he struggled to heave himself over the fence. His hands clawed through the grates, but his feet kept slipping off, heavy as boulders.

"What do I do?" Margot asked, gravitating forward.

"Wait for me," Van grunted. He tumbled over the top of

the fence and landed hard against the earth. As he tried to lift himself upright, his limbs creaked and moaned, the magic not yet seeping through his bones.

The statue watched their every move. Her ivy-wreathed plaque read The Mourning of Virgil, and when she raised her hand, the movement lifted a pedestal out of the earth at the back of the tomb.

Margot squinted. Was she imagining it, or was the shard just . . . sitting there? Could it really be that easy? So much for being tricky.

A magnetic pull dragged her toward the tomb despite the well of emotion already bubbling up. She wouldn't cry. She would *not* cry. Not now. Now, all she needed to do was grab the Vase shard and turn Van back to normal.

An eerie chill lingered inside the cave's walls, and the whole thing smelled like sage smoke and ash. Thankfully, Van had been right about the whole cremation thing. The tomb was blessedly devoid of ivory bones.

It didn't stop another shiver from slithering across her skin. For all her phases, grave robber never really made the list. She just needed to think happy thoughts. Like the silver glisten of pride she'd see in her dad's eyes when she FaceTimed him with the Vase—whole and real and not some foolish girl's day-dream.

Margot paced along the wide perimeter of the room. Something had been written on the walls, singed into the stone in a way that left a permanent soot stain. Her fingers trailed the shape of the letters, familiar enough to be recognizable but not forming any words she knew.

"Whatever you do, don't go—"

Van's sentence was cut off with a deafening crash.

"—inside."

All the light in the tomb vanished in a single instant, plunging Margot into a pool of black. Panic zipped up her throat, tightening until she could barely inhale.

Her body moved without her permission. Hands scraped against the rough walls, desperate for purchase. Her pulse thudded in her ears, her throat, her belly.

"It's all right," Van said on the other side of the rock enclosure. Was he shouting? Each syllable was hoarse, rubbed raw. "You hear me? It's going to be fine."

Which was precisely the kind of thing you told someone midcrisis where the *being fine* part was still vastly uncertain.

It was a dark so deep, her eyes could hardly adjust to it. Margot searched in the shadows for the shard's gilded gleam, letting its presence guide her deeper into the tomb. She'd seen where it rose, centered at the far end of the cave. All she had to do was get there.

Maybe the trial was about . . . echolocation? Using the feel of the earth to see rather than ordinary sight? Hadn't Van said something about Cupid meeting Psyche in the dark?

Her toes hit the pedestal first. Margot felt around, scaling up the column to its flat surface until finally her hand wrapped around the shard.

The walls of the tomb rattled, awakening.

"Van!" she shouted. "What's going on out there?"

"The walls, they're . . ."

She heard it, then. The sound of friction. Limestone against sunbaked earth. The walls of the tomb were moving—toward her. Something told her it wasn't rearranging for better feng shui. The trial of *Terra* had begun.

Ragged, she asked, "What do I have to do?"

"You took Latin in school, right?" Van asked.

"No. I haven't." Now was not the time to dissect the irregularity of her electives.

A curse slipped past his lips, hushed enough that she assumed he hadn't meant for her to hear it beyond the stone wall. "I thought everyone took Latin."

"Did *you* take Latin?" she asked.

No reply.

Her head drooped toward her chest. "You can't be serious."

"Don't sound so disappointed." She could hear the downturn of his lips.

"As the one about to be freshly squeezed, I withhold the right to sound disappointed."

He huffed. "I tried to tell you to let me handle it."

"A lot of good that would have done." Margot's laugh was desert dry. She kept her palm firm against the shifting limestone, but it did little to slow to its movement inward. Already, she could touch both walls with her hands outstretched, and her elbows were beginning to hinge. "I take it Atlas completed this task, too."

His silence was enough of an answer.

"Is that how he survived?" she asked. "He knew Latin?"

"Margot, breathe." His voice sounded like a staticky television, cutting in and out. "We'll figure it out."

But she couldn't breathe. Her mutinous lungs had their own agenda, and that agenda apparently only involved hyperventilating. Neither of them knew Latin, and if that was critical to the success of this mission, how was she expected to survive this? If it hadn't already been pitch-black in the tomb, she was certain darkness would have tunneled her vision.

Van's words came again, sounding more solid than they had before. Like he'd found his footing again. "Count back from one hundred. *Actual* one hundred this time."

"One hundred, ninety-nine, ninety-eight—" The walls inched closer. Not figuratively. Literally. If she didn't pull it together soon, she was going to be crushed. "It's not working."

"You can do this, Margot. You have to believe in yourself."

"I can't. I *can't.*"

"I believe in you." His voice was quieter, gentler.

The words glided over her skin, a balm for the rasped edge of her nerves. Margot would have squared her shoulders if it weren't for the walls' unforgiving advance.

The room grew smaller, pressing in on every side. The grate of stone against stone filled the air, but she barely heard it over the labored sound of her lungs trying to remember how to breathe. She was running out of time.

Every time she tried to formulate a plan her thoughts fizzled out. Rational problem solving had been replaced with vats of adrenaline. *Think, think, think . . .*

"Van! My phone!"

"What?" He returned, sounding farther and farther away.

"The flashlight! It's in my bag. Somewhere south of the mini pretzels and east of *Relics of the Heart*."

She imagined Van on the outside, rustling through the contents of her tote. What felt like eons passed, everything silent except for the steady narrowing of stones. Margot shifted sideways, making as much room for herself as possible.

Finally, he hollered back, "Now what?"

"Press the screen with your finger, and when it lights up, swipe up. It'll ask for my password, which is—"

"Are these buttons? But it's flat."

This was worse than trying to show her grandma how to text.

"The password, Van. It's nine-two-six-four. Just tap each number."

A sound, something like wonder and confusion, filtered in through the wall. "Now what?"

The walls cinched tighter. Margot fought to keep her words

level. "There's something written on the walls in here. I have a translation app we can use to decipher it."

"What's an app?"

She was never going to make it out alive.

"Look for the little red square that says Global Dictionary underneath it and then tap it. Is it on the screen now?"

"Yes?"

"I'm going to spell the words. You just type what I say."

Her hands found the grooves on the far wall, and she traced the shape of the first letter with her fingertips. As she inched around the room, words began to take shape.

"I think I've got it," Van said when she reached the last letter. *"Quiesce. Praebe te fidelem aut redde quod non est tuum."*

Then, a little, tinny robot voice responded, "Be still. Prove to be loyal or return what is not yours."

"That's it?" Margot shrieked. "Loyalty?"

Her palms flattened against the walls, pushing as if she had the strength to stop them. When that didn't work, she heaved a shoulder with all her weight behind it. Wedged a foot against the opposite wall. Pushed, pushed, pushed. Nothing helped.

No way could she just stand here. *Be still.* How was she supposed to sit here and accept that she was mere moments from being rolled as flat as sugar-cookie dough? The walls were far enough apart that she could still take a full breath, but only barely.

She clutched the shard tighter, hard enough she wondered

if she'd drawn blood. "If I put the shard back, do you think they'd stop? *Return what is not yours?*"

"It said *or* return what is not yours. If you do that, I don't think you'll get another chance. Atlas walked in the tomb, and then he walked out with the shard. Wouldn't tell me what happened inside, but I'm guessing it had something to do with . . ."

Losing his shit but trying to be really tough about it? Because that's what Margot was about to do. Her eyes clamped shut, but it wasn't like it made it any darker. It just felt like the right thing to do before getting squished to death. You know, so they wouldn't pop out or whatever.

"It'll be okay, Margot," he said. "I'm right here."

Her words from earlier sounded unnatural on his tongue, but she had to admit that they loosened the knot of dread that had clumped in her chest. Even if she wasn't sure she believed him.

Van sounded distant, just a whisper, when he said, "Think about why you're here."

Being still was not Margot's forte. Her legs itched to run. To toss the shard on the pedestal and be done with this trial—with this whole stupid quest—once and for all. But she couldn't, wouldn't. She knew what was at stake, everything she'd lose if she threw in the towel early.

Limestone bit into her shoulders. She squirmed, flattening herself between the two stones, giving her chest just enough space to rise and fall. The sour tang of fear coated her mouth, and no matter how hard she tried, she couldn't swallow it down.

She pinched her eyelids closed even harder. Imagining Van on the other side of the wall against her back was the only thing keeping her pounding heart from cracking her ribs right open.

Then. Suddenly.

The walls ground to a halt. She opened her eyes. Light seared through the cave's entrance in blinding contrast to the dark. The walls had stopped moving on either side of the pedestal, leaving only a narrow chase through the cave. Her palms felt along the walls as she pulled herself forward. Even as she fought toward the light, tar-black fear stuck to the corners of her mind.

Van's arms found her the moment she stepped out of the tomb. Hot, fat tears spilled down her cheeks. She was alive, but she could still feel the pressure of the walls against her shoulders, their crushing weight around her.

"You're okay," he said, pulling her against his chest. She barely registered his lips as they pressed against her hairline, warm and soft. "You're okay, kid."

The shard's clay had heated against her palms. When she pulled her hand up, the gold was nearly molten, an amber so deep she could have swam in it. But when she looked closer, her heart seized.

Her fingers trailed over the Latin inscription, pausing on the last word. *Lapideum.*

22

"How long have you known?"

Margot was a Molotov cocktail of emotions. Hurt, betrayal, anger. They lashed through her body like an open flame.

Van reared, pulled back only enough to look at her, then down at the shard in her hands. His palms stayed planted on her shoulders, but she wriggled out of his grasp. Frantically, his eyes scanned her face. She wondered what he saw—skin flamed red and nostrils flaring or if he could somehow see straight to the chasm carving through her heart. "Known about what?"

"That you were going to sacrifice me?" The words cut out of Margot with a serrated blade.

"Margot, that isn't . . ."

"Isn't it? The reward for finding all five shards of the Vase— you thought you'd find gold, and I thought I'd *be* golden. Turns out, we were both wrong. It isn't either-or. It's one each. One person turns to stone, and the other runs off with the treasure." A humorless laugh ripped up her throat. Of all the people to be right, it had to be Astrid. "But you figured that out last century, didn't you?"

While he stood there, mouth ajar, scrambling to think of some excuse, Margot slid the shard into her tote bag. She'd earned it.

Even though the marble veins had receded for good, Van's hard exterior returned and wiped away any memory she had of the Van she thought she knew. His steely gaze and vow of solitude were probably the only true things about him. "What are you implying?"

"I don't think I'm *implying* anything." Margot crossed her arms firmly against her chest. "I know you've been lying to me."

"What makes you think that?"

"*Lapideum!*"

Cold, Van said, "I thought we established that neither of us know Latin."

"But you do know what it means, don't you? If not in theory, then certainly in practice. Stone, Van. Someone has to turn to stone. And you were going to let it be me."

"Who told you that?" He reached for her again, but Margot sidestepped out of reach.

"Does it matter?" The wind stirred, whipping her hair around her head. Like the gods themselves were angry right alongside her.

He watched her. Calculating. "It does if it was Astrid."

Margot didn't answer. She mimicked his cocky raised eyebrows, his *I know everything* stare. If he wanted to keep secrets, so could she.

"You'd rather take Astrid's word over mine?" Van shook his head in disbelief. "Go ahead. But my word means something, and I'd rather turn to stone than trust an Ashby."

A flat grin smeared across Margot's face. "I'm sure that can be arranged."

It was almost worth the panic that flared in Van's eyes. "You need to believe me," he said.

"I don't need to do anything for you anymore."

"Margot, you don't understand." He stepped forward, and she moved back, foxtrotting around the tomb entrance. "I would never do anything to hurt you like that. We're partners."

The Mourning of Virgil watched them, her head propped up on her palm and her heavy lids blinking. Bored or bemused—or maybe both. Like she'd seen two thousand years' worth of heartache from her perch, and this was another rerun.

Heat crawled up Margot's neck, staining her cheeks and ears. "I understand perfectly fine. You probably took one look at me in the temple and thought *she'll work*."

"It wasn't like that," Van said, but his mouth had worked into a pinched frown.

"Two looks, then?" she wagered. Bold for a girl who'd just dribbled snot onto Van's shirt. "You know what I think? I think you betrayed Atlas, too."

His eyes narrowed. "You don't know what you're talking about."

"I absolutely do." Margot pushed her curls away from her face. Every word was vitriolic. "Atlas had been the brains behind the operation, and you were just the brawn. Some *kid* from the city with a chip on his shoulder, desperate to prove himself."

The muscle in Van's jaw twinged. "I trusted him, and he betrayed me."

"Like you were going to betray me?" Margot knew, deep in her bones, that every quicksilver word off her tongue would leave a mark. "Maybe Atlas stood right here, the shard in his hands, and realized that only one of you was going to get the treasure. And maybe he tried to warn you, told you not to construct the Vase. But you thought he wanted the treasure for himself. So, you turned on him first."

Van's armor cracked, if only briefly.

So, she hit where it would hurt. "Someday, you're going to realize that if you're so hell-bent on doing everything on your own, that's exactly how you'll stay. Alone."

God, the humiliation of it all. She'd trusted him. Some part of her actually thought she might have even been able to love him—all of him, not just the idea of him.

Van didn't retreat. Didn't cower. The only sign of agitation was a breath pushed out through his nose. "If you'll calm down, I can explain, but you aren't going to like it."

"Most people don't like finding out they've been used, Van.

I don't know what it was like a hundred years ago, but now there's this thing called *basic decency*, and maybe you should think about getting some." Margot started down the stairs, a white-knuckle grip on the strap of her tote in case he'd gotten any bright ideas from Enzo.

Behind her, Van said, "I tried to leave you out of it, but you said you'd do anything."

"And *anything* usually doesn't include voluntary human sacrifice."

His voice trailed after her, saying, "I'd hoped we could find another way."

Her face burned red-hot. Every step raised her blood pressure. *Calm down,* he'd said. *Calm down.* She couldn't. Margot had never been enough to keep anyone around for the right reasons—she should have known Van was only here for the wrong ones.

And despite everything he'd said, he didn't chase after her. Even when she had the one thing he needed most, he was still too stubborn to apologize.

Wait. He wasn't chasing after her.

Margot peered into her tote bag, rustling through the mass of emergency snacks and loose pens, but there was no fragment of hardened clay shoved down at the bottom.

She turned back, fuming. "How *dare* you?"

The shard was clutched in Van's palm. He must have slipped it out of her bag while they were arguing. He said, "You know why I need this."

The tempest inside Margot stirred faster, like a hurricane finding a pocket of warm water. Even if she wanted to stop it, she couldn't. The words spilled out of her, floodwater through an opened dam. "You can't just steal it from me! I'm the one who almost got pancaked for it."

His jaw clenched, lips thinning. "I tried to tell you not to barge in there, but did you listen?"

No. She hadn't.

"You don't deserve the shard," she seethed. "Turning your back on the only person you have left to care about you? If it weren't for me, you'd still be trapped in that temple."

"And what about you?" he asked.

Margot's fists clenched at her side. "What about me?"

"I care about you, and you're still turning your back on me." He paced toward her, the sharp lines of his face softening, but he tucked the shard into his pocket. Did he think she wouldn't notice? "Don't do this, Margot. Don't quit when it gets hard."

But it was the one thing she was best at.

23

Margot lost track of how long she wandered the streets of Naples or how many self-pitying scoops of gelato she ate along the way. Crowds ebbed and flowed around her in a constant stream. Every time she passed a statue, she flinched, expecting it to spring to life to do Venus's bidding, but Van had the shard, and all the statues stayed still.

The aftermath of her emotions always left a throbbing in her chest. An ache, like the dull point of a blade pressing beneath her skin. This was different. It twisted deeper.

Why hadn't Van chased after her? That was what they did in the books. It would rain, someone would cry, but they fought for each other—not against. Not Van. Van had used her. He wasn't just going to steal the treasure. He was going to steal her future.

Napoli Centrale wrapped around her as the sun started its

descent, sending trails of diaphanous gold through the station's glass ceiling. The queue moved quickly, and Margot purchased a one-way ticket back to Pompeii. She'd pack the last of her things, use Hotel Villa Minerva's painfully slow Wi-Fi and her emergency credit card to buy another return flight, and board the next plane heading stateside.

She should have never come to Italy.

Why had she thought she could prove everyone wrong? If anything, she'd handed them crucial evidence in the case against her. Everything she'd tried this summer had crumbled in her hands. Midas's touch, except instead of gold she got cold, hard stone.

Vase? Gone.

Van? Gone.

Her dignity? Gone.

Just when she thought she'd have the back of the train car to herself, a couple walked hand in hand down the aisle. They looked older than Margot, but not by much. It was almost like staring in a fun house mirror from the future—her with dark curls piled on top of her head, and him with suntanned skin and wild green eyes. They dropped into the seats across from Margot, and he immediately looped an arm around the girl's shoulders. Her head nestled in the crook of his neck. Obviously and sickeningly in love.

Margot turned, leaning her forehead against the cool glass of the window. She was never one to shy away from a serendipitous *main-character-in-a-music-video* moment, but she was too upset to romanticize her life. Not even the blur of the Italian country-side past the train's window could quiet the shouting in her skull.

Her fight with Van lingered in every corner of her mind, replaying over and over and over again. All the things she wished she hadn't said. All the things she couldn't believe she'd had to.

He had every intention of letting the curse turn her heart to stone. Of leaving her in the temple for good while he ran off with the treasure.

Her traitorous brain, however, seemed perfectly content to fixate on the way Van's hands had spread against her back this afternoon, holding her close, firm and certain, as solid as rock. The way he'd steadied her when a sprawling black seemed to crawl out from the depths of her, all-consuming. He was daylight to all her shadows. He'd blinded her, and she'd let him.

God, Astrid was going to give her a hell of a lecture when she realized she'd been right about how big of a failure Margot was, about how Van had just been using her—about every-thing.

She didn't even want to think about what her dad was going to say, but she didn't have a choice. His contact info popped up on her phone. It rang only once before she answered. Better to get this over with.

The minute the line connected, he blared, "Margot Helena Rhodes, where are you?"

"Hi, Dad. How are you?" she deflected.

"Don't *hi, Dad* me," he said. "I drove all the way into Atlanta tonight, and you weren't there. And then, you don't answer any of my calls. You ignore all my texts. I almost filed a missing person report."

Margot sank into her seat. "I'd have to be MIA for forty-eight hours to do that, I'm pretty sure."

"That is not the point, Gogo."

"You were right," she said. Her voice crackled, fighting back a fresh surge of tears. She simply had not packed enough Kleenex for the waterworks today.

She could hear the sigh in his words. "How so?"

Margot sighed, too, and leaned her head back against the cloth headrest. "I got it out of my system, okay?" Her throat tightened around the words like she was having an allergic reaction to being just as impulsive and emotional as everyone said she was.

"If only you'd realized that eighteen hours ago," he said. There was an underlying edge to his voice, the tinge of impatience he often took when reprimanding her.

Margot's voice was barely a whisper. "I want to come home."

"I know," her dad said. No hesitation. Like it was *so* obvious to him that she'd buckle under the weight of being alone in another country and come crying back to him.

Because he'd picked her up off the pavement after refusing to learn how to ride a bike with the training wheels on. Because he'd held her when she accidentally sucked salt water up her nose during their first beach vacation. Because she'd always, *always*, jumped first, thought second.

She'd wanted him to fight. To tell her she was brave and tough and capable. That she'd made a mistake but could still fix it, could stick things out for once even though it had been hard.

He didn't.

Margot should have let it go. Instead, she pressed harder. "What do you mean, you know?"

"You've always had quite the overactive imagination." He said it the way someone would say *You always have liked sardines on your pizza for some ungodly reason.* "This was just another phase, but you'll get over it. And I'm trying, Margot, but I swear, you and your mom are so alike."

"How would you know? You barely know me at all," Margot said, her words filed to a point. Could he tell how the pit in her stomach threatened to eat her alive? How suddenly her bones squeezed around her lungs? Did he even care?

Being like her mom wasn't inherently a bad thing. Parker Rhodes was the kind of mom who wouldn't just read bedtime stories—she'd act them out, costumes and all. She always volunteered for bake sales, even if she'd sometimes forget until ten p.m. and turn their galley kitchen into *Iron Chef* stadium overnight. Everything with her was an adventure; they'd pretend to be swashbuckling pirates in the drive-through line or fairies foraging in the grocery store, anything for a little extra magic.

And then, one day, she left. On purpose. And decidedly without Margot.

Love could be cruel and thankless. It could leave when you least expected it. It could haunt your heart like a creaking staircase, the sound of someone coming home but never actually arriving.

He clicked his tongue. "Don't know you? That's hardly fair. I know you went to Italy because of a book."

"How—" Margot stuttered. When had he realized she'd salvaged it from the donation pile? "What do you know about *Relics of the Heart*? You tried to get rid of it."

A quick burst of surprised laughter burbled from the other end of the line. "Who do you think bought it for your mom on our first date? It was beaten-up back then *before* it spent every night crammed inside your pillowcase."

An embarrassed flush rose on Margot's face. Maybe her hiding spot wasn't as clever as she'd always thought.

"She loved that book," she said, and the words came out pinched.

Loved. Past tense. The same way her mom had loved Margot. Enough to leave them behind.

It was like that rift between her parents extended to Margot, too, marooning her on an island between both of them—somehow both theirs and yet not wholly belonging to either.

Not enough and yet somehow too much entirely.

He quieted before, again, saying, "I know."

Those two syllables wormed under Margot's skin, parasitic. They had teeth, leeching venom into her veins. "Then you also know why I'm here."

"She's gone." Her dad raised his voice, saying, "Nothing you do is going to make her come back. Not even some make-believe magic treasure."

"And what about you?" Margot asked. She tried—and honestly failed—to disguise her sniffle as a cough. "What's your excuse? I know you didn't leave, but you aren't there for me either. I'm surprised we've talked this long, honestly. Don't you have an open house to host or something?"

A bloated silence hung between them. As dusk settled outside, Margot's reflection stared back at her in the window. Patchy red painted her face and neck.

"That's enough, Margot. I'm booking another flight," he said with finality. "No more questions."

She hung up on him while a haze of blues swept past the window and didn't bother scrubbing the tears from her cheeks. Coming here and piecing together the Vase was supposed to make everyone love her so that she could finally, *finally*, feel whole again. Instead, she was more broken than ever.

Her dad's exhausted tone filtered through her head—his disappointment like a stake through her heart. Van was somewhere in Naples with a single fragment of painted clay the only thing keeping him alive, and the sting of betrayal every time she thought about him was like lemon juice in a paper cut.

She honestly wasn't sure if she liked herself right now.

Not even the Vase of Venus Aurelia could fix that.

24

By the time Margot made it back to Pompeii, far past curfew, Hotel Villa Minerva was dark and quiet. Giuseppe glared at her as she walked in, but she carved a straight line for the elevator without making eye contact.

He cleared his throat.

Oh no.

Margot backtracked toward his concierge kingdom, the chest-high desk he perched behind, where he rested a lazy chin on his knuckles.

"Hi, Giuseppe," she said, smiling sweetly. It didn't quite reach her eyes, but Margot couldn't make herself care right now. She'd already cried so much on the train home that they'd probably be puffy into the next millennia.

"Margot Rhodes," he said, holding a cardstock sleeve between two fingers the same way someone might brandish a stinky gym sock. "This came for you."

Ordinarily, Margot's heart would have hammered in her chest at the thought of a courtier delivering mail, but tonight? She knew it couldn't be IRL *Bridgerton*.

Margot leaned closer, inspecting the envelope as Giuseppe slid it across the desk. It hadn't been stamped, just addressed to her in a neat penmanship that she'd know anywhere.

"I don't want it," she said. She'd heard everything she needed from Van.

Giuseppe lowered his head, unamused. "I don't care. It is yours."

He pushed the envelope until it rammed into Margot's fingertips, where they rested on the counter. She groaned but grabbed the letter, muttering a "thanks" and turning back toward the elevators.

Margot Rhodes, Van had written on the brown envelope. Underlined once, a little ball of ink at the end like he'd pressed too hard. She dangled the letter over the trash can. Was there anything he could say to repair the trust he'd broken? But if she didn't read it . . . The thought of being plagued by not knowing what he'd said for the rest of her life was worse than knowing and hating him for it.

As she scooted into the elevator, Margot slid her fingernail beneath the envelope's flap.

> *Margot,*
> *If you're reading this, it means you were right and girls do like handwritten letters. Otherwise, I'm certain you would*

be content to ignore me for the rest of your days, but you have proven me wrong time and time again, so perhaps this will be no different.

I originally sought to complete the Vase of Venus Aurelia as I had done everything for as long as I can remember: alone. You made certain I wouldn't. Never have I met someone as brave or tenacious or strong-willed as you. Venus may have cursed my heart to stone only so that you could chisel it out and make it beat again.

Although you may not wish to see me again, please know that my apologies are earnest, and I would like to finish this as we began. Together. You'll know where to find me tomorrow.

> *With all my heart,*
> *Van*

The elevator dinged at the third floor. Margot moved forward without looking up, eyes glued to Van's words. She read and reread it, analyzing every loop, every letter, every mark of punctuation. Her feet led her down the hall, but her mind was busy decoding each sentence and searching for hidden, back-stabbing meanings.

When she walked into her room, the only light came from Suki's laptop, where she lay on her bunk, probably watching another Netflix reality dating show. She pulled out an earbud. "Your aura is blue."

"I'm sure it's fine." Margot deflected whatever conversation *that* was about to be. She couldn't help but notice the obvious lack of icy remark from their third roommate as she slid Van's letter onto her bunk and flipped on the overhead light. "No Astrid?"

Suki shook her head. "She's off running around with her secret admirer. Won't tell me who it is. Keeps harping about how we need to be having *intellectually stimulating conversations*, not gossiping about boys. As if I don't know about the Bechdel Test."

Margot dragged her massive suitcase out from underneath the bed and flopped its lid open. Her carry-on from the Rome trip had been deposited by the door, but that could hardly hold the myriad of outfit changes she'd packed for the summer. Most of which would go unworn. A shame. A new flight confirmation was coming from her dad any minute—she might as well get a head start on packing.

"What are you doing?" Suki asked, dangling off the bed.

Margot held up the wad of laundry in her hands. "Uh, packing?" *Isn't it obvious?*

"You mean unpacking? We basically just got here."

"I'm leaving," Margot said.

"Like, to do another secret mission?"

Margot's mouth opened slightly and then closed. She frowned, trying to decide on the right words. "I haven't been doing secret missions." ·

Suki closed her laptop and ditched her earbuds entirely. "Has anyone ever told you you're a terrible liar? You and Chad have been disappearing left and right. I know a secret mission when I see one. Plus, after you two bailed and missed attendance at the dig site this afternoon, I told Dr. Hunt you'd started your period and Chad went to buy you another pair of shorts from the gift shop."

"Thanks?" Margot said, uncertain whether fictitiously bleeding through her pants was something to be thankful for.

"So, what's the truth?"

She'd quit a hundred things before. Robotics club, badminton, a brief stint where she wanted to join a race car pit crew. This was no different. So, why did the thought of leaving have such a bitter aftertaste? Unwilling to meet Suki's curious eyes, Margot said, "I told you. I'm packing. To go back home."

Suki shot straight up and bumped her head on the top bunk. Cradling what would definitely turn into a sore spot, she squawked, "No way. But we've got so much summer left."

"You don't have to act surprised. It's not like my mom's a world-renowned museum curator like yours or I'm the descendant of a long line of archaeological prodigies like Astrid. Or one of the guys. I'm pretty sure Rex has a constant loop of Tik-Toks in his head instead of a brain, but even he's treated like he belongs here."

"Margot, you heard Dr. Hunt. You totally earned your spot here. I read your essay, and it was amazing." At that, Margot shot her a disbelieving look, but Suki bulldozed on. "I heard Lance Kiebler didn't get in, and Lance's aunt is, like, an Egyptologist who discovered a new tomb or something."

Margot focused on stuffing her socks into a pink packing cube. "But Pasha Manikas—"

"Pasha, Pasha, Pasha," Suki said with a groan. "Pasha's family summers in Naples every year anyway because her dad's a volcanologist. Who cares if she didn't come?"

"Astrid," Margot said with a stiff laugh, "who will be thrilled to learn I'll be out of her hair soon."

Suki rolled off the bed and landed next to Margot's suitcase. Her bottom lip pouted. "You seriously can't leave. You're the only other person here who cares about more than a bunch of old stuff. And your stunt at La Galleria Bianchi landed me another date with Fernanda, so I'm not even jealous that you totally have a crush on Chad."

"First of all," Margot said, "I do not have a crush on Chad."

Suki's eyebrows raised. "Like I said. Terrible liar."

Margot flopped dramatically onto her back, starfished across the floor. "Maybe Astrid was right. I'm just not cut out for this."

Suki laughed, full bellied and bright. When she came up for air, she sobered immediately, realizing Margot hadn't been laughing with her. "Oh," she said, "you weren't joking. Come on, Margot. Astrid's like that with *everyone*. It's not personal."

"It sure seems personal." All week she'd been on the

receiving end of Astrid's jabs, and her defenses were at an all-time low.

Methodically, Suki started unpacking everything Margot had packed. She grabbed the pair of pants Margot had just stuffed into her suitcase. "Okay, fine. You're a little out of your element, but you're not afraid to try anything. You do what you want. That's badass."

But it didn't feel badass. It felt like being on a roller coaster she didn't choose to board. Unbuckled. And there were loops. So, really, she just spent all her time trying to hold on, and now every part of her was tired and sore.

She wiggled the pair of jeans out from Suki's grasp and dropped it back in the suitcase. "I've messed everything up. With Dr. Hunt, with my dad, with everyone."

"Everyone?" Suki asked. "Or Chad?"

Margot gave a small, sad shrug. "What would Alison Bechdel say?"

Suki scooted closer. "I do know what Catherine Avery Hannigan would say."

A mixture of emotions gurgled out of Margot. Two parts laugh, one part sob. She and Suki might have actually turned out to be good friends if she could have stayed the summer. "What would she say?"

"Chapter twenty-seven," Suki said. "Isla and Reed are on the charter boat, just after escaping the Tunnels of Claudius. Do you remember what he said to her?"

It wasn't uncommon for Margot to be brought to tears, but the first time she'd read chapter twenty-seven, she'd needed an hour to recover from emotional damages. She quoted, *"My heart is yours, every beat and every breath between. There are no vestiges of me that have not been transformed by you."*

Even saying the words aloud brought moisture to Margot's eyes. She blinked, leaning her head back like she might convince the tears not to fall.

"I think," Margot said, composing herself, "that Chad and I are in more of a chapter twenty-nine situation."

Suki gasped. "Not chapter twenty-nine."

Margot tried to tell herself that running away was easier than staying, fighting, but the remnants of this afternoon's anger had yellowed into an aching bruise. She felt carved open, like her heart had been torn out and left behind, bleeding dry.

Absentmindedly, her fingers trailed along her bracelet. Jade beads beneath her fingertips. She hadn't taken it off. But it was too late, now.

The thought was a knife, the kind that might have carved her initials next to Van's into the bark of the willow tree in her backyard. She'd wanted the Vase so badly that she never stopped to realize what was right in front of her.

"Yes," Margot whispered. "He's gone because I left him."

25

As the class filed out of the bus, Margot's head moved autonomously, scanning the ruins for a familiar swoop of blond hair or a brooding presence.

What she'd say to Van if she found him, she hadn't figured out yet. All she knew was that the last shard was somewhere in Pompeii, which meant that he was here somewhere, too.

She wasn't sure how long she'd been digging—Minutes? Hours?—when Dr. Hunt cleared her throat behind Margot. It spooked her six inches into the air. "Margot, I'd like to have a word."

She didn't say it like she was in trouble, but Margot's stomach sank like an anchor anyway. "Sure thing."

The rest of the class arched over their dig plots. Had they noticed Van's absence? As she stood, dusting herself off, Astrid shot Margot a tired glare. She'd returned sometime after Margot fell asleep and hadn't made it down in time for breakfast this morning. Margot had slept similarly poorly with her face smashed against the pages of *Relics of the Heart* like she might telepathically assume some of Isla's ingenuity.

Dr. Hunt turned and exited the dig site, leaving Margot to catch up to her as she raced onto the ruins' main thoroughfare.

"Do you care to tell me why I received a one-thousand-word email from your father diagramming the exact steps I'd need to take to escort you to the airport this evening?" Dr. Hunt asked. She kept her eyes focused ahead as they walked.

"I'd rather not," Margot muttered.

Dr. Hunt cracked a grin. "It really wasn't a question."

Overhead, the wide blue sky didn't have a single cloud. The sun burned brightly, a lone interrogation lamp. As they paced down the ancient streets, Margot recounted the week's events—conveniently leaving out any trace of Van and the Vase—until she reached the present day. Her nerves tied themselves into a sailor's knot as she spoke. She barely registered where they'd wandered until the silver turnstiles at the Nola Gate came into view.

"Where are we going?" Margot asked. A solid part of her psyche thought maybe Dr. Hunt would escort her right back to the bus for a fast track to the airport.

Instead, she smiled. "There's someone I think you should meet."

Dr. Hunt took a sharp turn right and guided Margot onto a

colonnaded portico inside the remnants of a sanctuary. Pastel paint stained the limestone walls with rural murals; statues dotted the courtyard. She stopped in front of one so suddenly that Margot almost rammed right into her.

"Who are we meeting?" Margot asked—the sanctuary was empty except for the two of them. And so deathly quiet that Margot heard her heartbeat too loudly in her chest.

The teacher gestured toward a statue. "Meet Venus."

The sculpture stretched at least a yard over Margot's head, so she wasn't meeting Venus so much as she was meeting Venus's stomach. The goddess stood tall, face smooth with confidence, and her lips quirked upward just enough, as if to say, *I'm the goddess of love. You* do *love me, don't you?*

Margot cut her eyes between the marble rendition of Venus, and Dr. Hunt. Was she supposed to introduce herself back? It seemed like overkill for the bit.

Dr. Hunt, thankfully, spoke again before Margot made a fool of herself trying to shake the hand of a statue that had no intention of coming to life. "Obviously you know how important Venus was to Pompeii. Sure, she was known for being brash and impulsive. Some histories said she felt things too wildly, too raw. Some even say she was so angry from being scorned by a lover that she caused Mount Vesuvius to erupt."

That, Margot could relate to. All her emotions felt molten, wreaking devastation in their path.

"The Romans didn't love Venus in spite of those things but

because of them." Dr. Hunt was still looking at the statue, but her words pierced through Margot's ribs. That thick, heavy muck in her chest softened and stretched thin, taffy in the hands of a confectioner.

Staring up at the goddess of love, Margot asked, "If she could come to life, what do you think she'd say?"

"Love requires us to be brave. Love for others, yes. But also love for ourselves." Dr. Hunt pried her eyes away from Venus and donned a knowing smirk. "It takes real strength to follow your heart. Venus knows all about that."

Margot nodded, afraid that speaking would shake something up inside her she wasn't ready to face.

"Do you know why I invited you on this trip, Margot?"

The sudden change in topic nearly gave Margot whiplash.

"Your essay showed real promise," Dr. Hunt continued.

Margot couldn't help but roll her eyes. Her head lolled back with them, sweeping and dramatic. "Don't humor me. I get it. I don't know anything about archaeology, and honestly, Dr. Hunt? It's way different than I thought it'd be. There's so much dirt, and way too many spiderwebs, and don't even get me started on the bones."

Dr. Hunt laughed, cinching the skin at her eyes. "I'll admit I was surprised when I saw your application, since you'd never been on my roster before, but your research was thorough, and your essay was engaging and enthusiastic. You have a real talent for writing."

Margot had to admit she'd enjoyed writing it. She'd lost herself in the paragraphs and pages, only blinking back into herself in the darkest dregs of night, long after everyone else had left the library. But imagining being an archaeologist wasn't the same as *being* one.

"It was just some silly story."

Dr. Hunt clicked her tongue, disproving. "Stories are how we're remembered. They're the very reason we know about Venus and her Vase. Speaking of, have you found it yet?"

Startled, Margot fumbled. "Um, I . . ."

"I assume you wouldn't let all of your research go to waste, and there must be some reason you insist on skipping half of my excursions." Dr. Hunt faced her then, leaving nowhere to hide. Apparently she hadn't been as sly as she thought she'd been.

"I'm sorry," Margot said. Just another person to add to the list of people she'd disappointed this week.

Dr. Hunt, however, said, "I'm not mad."

"You're not?"

"I brought you here to learn, Margot. Nobody learns without making a few mistakes along the way." Dr. Hunt clamped her hand on Margot's shoulder and squeezed.

"But—"

"And, if you want, I'll talk to your dad."

Margot blinked. "Why would you do that?"

When Dr. Hunt shrugged, it wasn't in an *I don't know* kind of way but more of a *I'm a wizard genius who knows everything* way. "I won't make you stay if you really hate it here, but if you truly didn't want to be here, something tells me a headstrong girl like you would've been gone days ago. You've found something worth staying for."

Margot should have thought of the Vase, but all she could think of was a pair of light green eyes, flecked with amber, one lone dimple, and a constellation of freckles over a once-broken nose.

Dr. Hunt turned toward the exit but glanced over her shoulder and nodded up at Venus's watchful posture. "I know you've got what it takes to finish what you started."

Easier said than done. Van could be anywhere in the city. He wouldn't return to the buried Temple of Venus until he had all five shards. And it wasn't like Venus herself was about to tell her where to find the last trial.

Actually.

Maybe Venus *could* tell her. Something Dr. Hunt said tripped a wire in Margot's brain. *Stories are how we're remembered.* Van had told her days ago that he'd puzzled out the trials by using the legend of the Vase of Venus Aurelia as a guidebook.

It wasn't metaphors and imagery with him. She knew how he thought: critically, literally. One by one, she recounted the trials in the myth, and there was only one left—*Mors.* Even the thought of his carved bleeding heart sent gooseflesh down her arms with a crypt-cold shiver.

"That's it," Margot said suddenly. She jolted into motion,

hightailing it out of the sanctuary. "Yes, I—oh, my god. Thank you, Dr. Hunt. You're so right."

Margot ran, arms pumping, toward Via del Vesuvio, sprinting until Pompeii peeled away from her and she stood at the frayed hem of the city. She could almost see the path she'd taken to sneak into the city after dark, like the earth still bore the tire marks from her borrowed scooter.

Chest heaving, she braced her hands on her knees and peered into the darkness below. The catacombs of the necropolis opened into the earth like an entrance to hell.

Each of the guardian's trials had some correlating element, like *Aqua*'s underwater adventure and the way the earth closed around her during *Terra*'s trial. Fire, water, air, earth—and death. If *Mors*'s trial was going to be anywhere, it was going to be here.

She had survived the Nymphaeum, and it was her—not Van—who figured out a way through the trial of *Aura*. She could do this. She knew she could.

Not for Van. Not for her dad. Not to prove Astrid wrong. But for herself.

26

The necropolis wasn't a tourist attraction. There were no gilded plaques or LED lights illuminating Margot's way down the sloped tunnel. Only a damp dark that threatened to crawl under her skin and never let go.

She took one step and then another. Dirt walls rose up around her until the sky was blotted out by dark soil. Already, her heart thumped harder in her chest. Her arms curled protectively around her ribs, but there was a thrum of excited adrenaline intertwined with the rising anxiety.

The catacombs webbed around her, a maze beneath the city. Tunnels had been hollowed out only to be filled back up with ivory bones. Margot shone her actual, double-A-powered flashlight into the corners as she came to her first fork in the road. Left was dark and cold. Right was cold and dark. It was a fifty-fifty chance, honestly.

Vibes, don't fail me now.

Veering left, Margot kept her breathing even, forcing inhales slowly through her nose so that she wouldn't accidentally start hyperventilating. What she was looking for, Margot wasn't exactly sure. Each shard of the Vase had been protected by a trial, each one deadlier than the last. She wasn't naive enough to hope this time would be different.

The air in the catacomb halls was sticky, wet. A sheen of sweat slicked the skin of her neck. As she drove deeper, marble outcroppings jutted out from the edges of the tunnels. Names in Latin letters had been etched into mausoleums.

Once, Margot realized suddenly, this hadn't been underground at all. Her flashlight glanced from memorial to memorial. Beneath her feet, dirt gave way to cobbled streets, matted with deep brown earth, like the ruins were fighting to raise themselves from the dead. Ahead, one of the tombs had been pried open, surely by inquisitive archaeologists searching for answers to an ancient mystery.

Every step forward increased Margot's pulse until she was certain her heart was going to jettison from her body. Of course, it was in this moment that footsteps echoed down the path behind her.

"Van?" she whispered, but her voice rang out too loudly among the dead.

No one answered, but the footsteps grew louder, closer. Had one of the guards seen her sneak down here? She couldn't get caught now—not when so much was on the line. Margot spun, looking for something, anything, to shelter behind, just in case.

There was nothing but sealed stone tombs. Except for one.

"*Ohmygodohmygodohmygodddddd,*" she whispered to herself as she closed her eyes and pressed back into the tomb. Her back crunched against a bone. Her cotton shirt wasn't nearly enough fabric between her skin and the sharp edge of someone's scapula.

She extinguished her flashlight, darkness wrapping around her like a burial shroud. Definitely tried not to think about the super dead guy behind her, the fact that the footsteps had only quickened, or what on earth she would do if it wasn't Van barreling down the hall—or what she'd do if it was. In fact, she tried not to think about anything except counting.

One hundred. Ninety-nine. Ninety-eight.

The catacombs glowed, orange and flickering, like whoever was coming had light burning. Shadows lashed down the hall as they strode nearer. Margot pressed back into the mausoleum.

Ninety-seven. Ninety-six.

A flash of yellow streaked past, taking the lamplight with it. The yellow of *her* backpack. Enzo. He darted around the corner, sprinting at full speed deeper into the catacombs. Running toward something. Or running away.

Margot launched herself forward, following the amber glow through the otherwise shadowed halls. Enzo couldn't run forever—sooner or later, he'd reach a dead end. And then she'd corner him, steal back the shards, and never have to listen to his smarmy flirting again.

From the belly of the catacombs before her, there was a groan of effort. Ordinarily, Margot wasn't one to believe in zombies, but given the sheer amount of mind-boggling magic she'd encountered in the last six days, she couldn't rule it out entirely. Then, something crashed, and Enzo's light extinguished.

That was one way to find the trial.

She was too focused on the commotion and not focused enough on the way the catacomb floor sloped down. Margot lost her footing. Her butt hit the ground with a pathetic *thunk*. Sliding, she careened beneath an archway sewn from skulls, their empty eye sockets watching her tumble.

She landed next to the lantern, its glass cracked. Flashing her light on, she swept the space, the concentrated beam glancing across Enzo's face. He shielded his eyes with a hand.

"Nice backpack. Where'd you get it?" She'd meant for it to sound snarky, thick with the kind of sass that frequently landed her on house arrest for a week, but it came out shaky. It was hard to sound particularly intimidating after eating dirt.

"What are *you* doing here?" he asked.

"Pretty much the same thing you are." She shifted her flashlight beam, and her stomach twisted with fear.

Given the whole *inside a catacomb* thing, Margot really shouldn't have been surprised by the skeletons. But it was, like, an egregious number of skeletons. All littered around a semi-circle composed of six stone goblets.

At the apex, the nose of a boat jutted out of a rock formation, and sitting on its bow was a limestone statue of an elderly man with drawn, sallow cheeks, cloaked in heavy garments. His fist clenched the rod of a ferryman's pole.

Margot pushed herself upright only to fumble a few steps backward, blanching. The way the ferryman's eyes watched her . . . She knew it wasn't a trick of the shadows. The shards' magic was working.

"You need to leave," Enzo said. Either he hadn't noticed the giant, potentially evil statue man behind him yet, or he was choosing to ignore it.

"There's something I need to do first." Margot's voice wavered. Who could really blame her?

Enzo stepped forward. "You aren't getting the shards back, thief."

Answering for her, the statue slammed his rod against the ground. Enzo's mouth clamped shut. He dared a look over his shoulder and flinched when he saw who had been eavesdropping.

Margot recognized him then. Charon. Ferryman of the dead. Suki had written her application essay about him. She raked through her memory, trying to think of anything she'd absorbed from Suki's essay. What had it been called? Charon's oboe? Charon's oolong?

As she thought, she pulled her lipstick from her pocket, fidgeting with the lid. Opened, closed. It clicked, again and again.

Enzo ogled her like a circus spectacle. "Lipstick? In a time like this?"

Margot frowned at him and quickly swiped it over her lips to disguise the nervous gesture. "So. Do we . . . drink from them?" she asked, pointing at the chalices.

Stalking toward the goblet in the middle, she tried not to pay attention to the giant statue of death watching her every move. With two hands, she lifted the goblet to her lips. A little liquid sloshed around the bottom. Tipping the goblet back, she drained the dregs, but spat them out just as quickly.

Nope, nope, nope.

"Oh, god. Never mind," she said, tongue sticking out. It tasted like dirt water. It probably *was* dirt water, just moisture that had collected underground for the last gazillion years.

Was she imagining it, or did Charon look annoyed as she set the goblet back down?

The statue's palm opened, and he flicked something silver into the air, its surface glinting in Margot's flashlight beam. It landed with a metallic zing, swirling on its edges until it finally rested flat.

Charon's obol. Which Margot was pretty sure was, like, a fancy ancient Roman quarter that people had been buried with, payment for the ferryman to charter them across the River Styx into the underworld.

She really hoped *that* wouldn't be her fate tonight. Imminent death had not been on her summer bucket list.

Enzo recovered from his shock, kneeling forward like a squire to be knighted. "Please find me worthy of the shard."

A laugh rustled out of Margot. "Nice try, but it definitely doesn't work like that."

"How would you know?" Enzo asked, words daggered.

Margot's smile was equally bladelike. "Just a hunch."

With any luck, he'd fail miserably, and she'd use his disappointment as a distraction to steal the one-strapped backpack off his shoulder *and* solve the trial herself.

She propped her flashlight up on a rocky ledge. Its too-white light spilled through the alcove. Charon grabbed the nearest goblet and flipped it upside down, slamming it over the top of the obol. Then, he turned over the rest of the cups with nothing underneath.

Ramming his rod back into the earth, Charon bade the goblets forward as if on an invisible track, spinning and circling. They swapped forward and backward, in and out of each other's paths in a dizzying dance. Finally, they stilled once more in a semicircle.

Margot's head spun. She'd played games like this before. Guess the goblet that had the obol underneath it. Except when she'd played, there'd been three options, not six. And now, with twice as many, she'd completely lost track of where it could be—the last on the left, maybe?

Instead, Charon raised the second cup on the right, revealing the obol underneath it. A knot cinched behind Margot's sternum. She'd been way off. He nodded at them—and Margot understood. Their turn.

She didn't want to think about what might happen if she guessed incorrectly.

Her thoughts wandered, without her permission, to Van. He must have found a way to win this trial a hundred years ago, a way to outwit death itself. Margot's 83 percent chance of guessing the wrong cup wasn't exactly reassuring. But if she had some way to mark which goblet was which . . .

As Charon waited for them to choose which cup to put the obol under, Margot's eyes caught on the faint red smudge on the lip of one of the goblets. The perfect red tint she'd spent months searching for. The goblet she'd tried to drink from.

"Place it here," she said, staring up into the courier's blank stone eyes.

Startling, Enzo bleated, "What?"

"You snooze. You lose." *Literally*, she hoped.

Once more, Charon slammed his ferryman pole into the earth. Margot trained her eyes on the goblet with the obol, struggling to keep track of it as the cups gained speed. It wouldn't matter. When they stilled, she'd know which one was right.

Enzo's head was too busy swiveling back and forth to pay any attention to the lipstick stain. He looked like he'd tried to do a triple pirouette without finding his spot. Dizzy and completely clueless.

As the cups slowed, he turned to Margot as if trying to read her mind. Time to channel her best Van-patented bluff. She kept her mouth neutral, eyes half-lidded like she had a hundred better things to be doing, and bit the inside of her cheek to keep from saying something she'd regret.

Charon tapped his stone fingers against his chin, impatient, although it wasn't like he had much else better to do.

Enzo stepped forward noncommittally. At first, he favored the far-right goblet. Then, he backtracked toward the middle. He glanced back at Margot, but she refused to acknowledge the red-smudged chalice on the left.

After what felt like eons of deliberation, Enzo stalled in front of the goblet second from the right. Only then did Margot make her selection. She planted her hand on the base of the red-stained cup, squaring her shoulders. No hesitation needed.

"*That's* the one you're choosing?" Enzo asked.

Margot quirked an eyebrow.

Charon noted their decisions by reaching forward with his staff and toppling Enzo's goblet. Predictably, nothing was underneath. Shock flickered through his system—disbelief turning quickly into crestfallen disappointment, but shifting again into rage as he was struck with the realization that him being wrong meant Margot might be right.

Reaching once more, Charon tipped her goblet. Gold

glimmered underneath—not the obol, but the shard. Triumph like liquid sunlight poured through her veins as she lifted it into her hands.

Before she had a chance to celebrate, Charon swiped his rod, trying to drag Enzo toward the mounds of bones in punishment, but missed, and Enzo plowed into Margot's middle. The force slammed against her, knocking the air out of her lungs. Enzo's arms wrapped around her as he wrestled her to the ground.

Her fingers tightened around the shard, even if she couldn't quite remember how to breathe. Instead of *in, out, in, out,* her lungs malfunctioned: *in, in, out, out.* Her fists pounded recklessly, anywhere she could land them. Shoulders, arms, back.

It did little to discourage Enzo. He threw her around like a rag doll. The second she landed on solid ground, Margot hooked her foot around the back of Enzo's leg. She planted her hands against his chest and shoved.

Enzo tripped and toppled back into the wall. He knocked over the flashlight, and when it crashed to the ground, the bulb flickered off, plunging them back into darkness.

Everything was ink black. Too dark to see anything but shadows. Still, Margot darted in the general direction of the flashlight. One of Enzo's various limbs snagged against her foot, and she landed face-first in the dirt. Rough stones and uneven earth bit into her forearms.

"Has anyone ever told you you're the *worst?*" Margot asked.

Sputtering, she rolled right as Enzo's fist grazed her shoulder blade. The impact struck through every tendon, and she lost her grasp on the shard. It sank into the soil. Even stretching, it was just out of reach.

She dragged herself upright, one allover bruise. In the shadows, Enzo rustled—ready to pummel her again, no doubt.

Okay, light first, then shard.

Margot dipped right and reached for the flashlight. Grasping in the darkness, her fingers grazed its cool metal hilt, and the bulb zapped back to life with a click.

Just in time for Enzo to set his sights on the exit.

Margot dove for one of the goblets. Hoisting it like a club, she whacked Enzo's middle with it when he tried to run.

Enzo wobbled and then crumpled, palms to his stomach. Margot winced—fighting had never been her forte. She could almost feel the radiating pain as if she'd been the one hit. But a girl had to do what a girl had to do.

With both hands, Margot grabbed her backpack, ripping it upward, but it snagged on Enzo's elbow. "Give it back," she said through gritted teeth.

With another tug, she tore the backpack off his arm. Desperate fingers clasped onto her wrist. Too quickly, Enzo jumped to his feet and pulled her back toward Charon, her spine ramming into his boat's pointed bow.

The stone ferryman hadn't gone entirely motionless, magic still humming through the alcove, emanating from the shards.

His empty stare was focused on Enzo—determined, almost. Waiting to strike again. The look sparked an idea that just might work.

Enzo reared, a bull charging a matador.

This time, Margot held her ground carefully. A deep breath filled her lungs. Emotion swirled through her veins, but she kept it leashed. She let Enzo make the first move. Kicking dust up with his feet as he sprinted, Enzo charged.

Margot waited until the last moment to dodge. A sickening crack rang through the catacombs when his shoulder slammed against the stone ship, and Enzo wailed. The ferryman of the dead shifted. His rod pounded against the earth, trapping Enzo next to his boat.

Sprinting, Margot scrambled toward the far end of the alcove. No matter how hard Enzo thrashed, Charon didn't budge. The shards and their magic were just out of reach.

But when Margot unzipped the backpack to drop in the new fragment of the Vase, her fingers found fabric and little else. Empty. The backpack was empty.

No gel pens, no extra pair of socks in case someone wanted to go bowling, no emotional-support notebook, and definitely no shards. *Where are the rest of them?*

She flew through the pockets on the outside—nothing. Then, unzipping the front pocket, she gulped down a relieved breath. Thank god. Three black chunks of pottery sat at the bottom of the pocket.

"But this isn't . . ." Margot trailed off.

The fragments in her hands were glossy, painted smooth. The chipped edges were porcelain white. She tugged the shard from the trial out of her pocket to compare. Totally different textures, colors. Flipping a fragment from the backpack in her hand, the words Hotel Vil had been stamped onto one side.

As in, Hotel Villa Minerva?

The pieces couldn't fit together fast enough in her brain. The shattered coffee mug on the dresser. The shards—missing in action. Black porcelain in Enzo's backpack. Why would *he* have a broken coffee mug from *her* hotel?

Margot didn't notice the slope of the catacombs until it was too late. Her feet slid out from underneath her. As her skull cracked against the ground, the shards, both real and fake, flew out of her grasp.

She scrambled toward the fragments, hands reaching. Her fingers latched onto the shard, lacing around its sharp angles, as someone's boots stepped into view.

27

Holding a lit torch, Van wore a familiar pair of leather boots, a tool belt strapped around his waist, and an ill-fitting graphic T-shirt that said From Naples with Love.

Van was here. Van was *here?*

A lick of hot embarrassment lashed up Margot's neck—of all the ways she thought they'd find each other again, sprawled out on the floor of the necropolis hadn't topped the list. Margot was fairly certain she wasn't concussed, which meant Van probably wasn't a hallucination, but his sudden appearance stunned her into such complete shock that she almost forgot she had a face full of dirt and absolutely no dignity left. You know, almost.

The way he stood, posture rigid and eyes narrowed, Margot knew he was on guard.

Behind her, Enzo asked, "A little help, *per favore?*"

Margot lifted her eyes toward Van, letting her gaze turn sharp. Were they . . . working together?

In response, Van tilted his head, almost imperceptibly. Not a nod, a gesture. His hand slipped into his pocket, retrieving the shard from the trial of *Terra*. His grip on it tightened—protective, almost.

Maybe, Margot thought with a jab of discomfort, *he'd planned on turning Enzo to stone instead of me*.

Only Enzo wasn't talking to Van.

Astrid emerged from the shadows, her gold-plated shovel in one hand and her backpack strapped over her shoulders. "Why would I help you?" she asked Enzo. "You couldn't even handle one puny trial."

Clearly Margot was missing something. Astrid knew Enzo?

It clicked, then. Astrid staying out past curfew. The blue eye shadow debacle. The coffee mug pieces at the bottom of Margot's stolen backpack. Astrid had been sneaking around with Enzo all week. He must have asked to use the coffee mug shards as a decoy—heck, she'd probably handed them to him herself.

"Astrid," Margot groaned, "you've got horrible taste in secret admirers."

"Who do you think you are, my fairy godmother?" Astrid laughed, thin and airy. She waved her shovel like a magic wand. "I didn't come here for love advice, genius."

The movement raised a red flag in Margot's brain. Her eyes darted to the compass around Van's neck, and her chest squeezed tighter, making it harder to breathe. The emblem on Van's compass was the same as the one on Enzo's hoodie, but they *both* matched the engraving on Astrid's gold-plated shovel. She could just make out the outline of it in the flickering orange of Van's torch—an off-kilter globe wrapped in a satin ribbon.

The Atlas Exploration Company logo. That was where she'd seen it before.

A wave of nausea crashed over Margot. She prayed she didn't already know the answer to the question she needed to ask. "Van, what did you say Atlas's last name was?"

His lips flattened. "I didn't."

"And if you had?"

Van wasn't the one to answer.

"He would have said Ashby." Astrid beamed like she was in a toothpaste commercial. She produced a linen pouch from her backpack. The contents of it clinked together—clay against clay. The other shards. Astrid had them. "Atlas Oswald Ashby. My great-grandfather."

A breath rushed out of Margot as if she'd taken a fist to the breastbone. It was a setup. She should have seen the web they'd been weaving a hundred miles away. Should have realized that Astrid had known the inscription on the Vase before it was even complete. Should have noticed Astrid's resemblance to Atlas in the photo of him and Van—she'd been so enamored with Van that she'd hardly given Atlas a second thought.

But she saw it now. Astrid's white-blonde hair, her slender features, even the pompous way she carried herself, like the Vase was her birthright—of course she felt like that. She'd crafted her own plan to get what she believed was rightfully hers. Exactly like an Ashby would.

Margot steadied herself against an outcropping, but then realized her hand was fully resting on someone's cranium. She shook the feeling of skull out of her fingers and swallowed down a tide of bile. This was all too much. With a temper white-hot, Margot refocused on Astrid, saying, "I helped you get ready for a *date*, and you were just . . ."

"Gathering intel before rendezvousing about the shards?" Astrid said, all too happily finishing Margot's thought. She weighed the pottery in her palm, and Margot imagined what it would look like when they'd slotted together on the altar, a gold seam welding the pieces together in a perfect fit. "Yeah, you'll get over it. Because the Vase is my legacy, not yours. You should have heard the stories I was told growing up. About how Van Keane cheated my family out of what is *rightfully* ours. My great-grandfather put Pompeii on the map. Funded every dig. Was the *only* reason Van ever even made it here. And somehow everyone remembers Van instead, when he couldn't even turn to stone at the right time."

"At the right—he knew?" Margot cut in, a chill creeping over her. Atlas had planned to sacrifice Van?

"Of course he knew!" Astrid said, breaking off to laugh.

"Ashbys actually do the *real* hard work. Translating, researching. Realizing he needed a sacrifice. Always said Van was perfect for the job. Strong arms and a hard head. Marble must have suited him."

Margot gasped, her eyes burning. "Do you even hear yourself?"

"He's the one with the heart of stone—with or without some curse. He's a thief, a cheat, a nobody who faked his way here. He's—"

"Standing right here," Van said, irritation coating each word.

Astrid disregarded the peanut gallery. "And then he stole our family legacy. Well, now he's going to make it up to me by getting me the treasure and getting rid of you."

Margot had been completely taken advantage of and she hadn't even realized. She'd tried to extend an olive branch—tried to make Astrid like her, tried to win her approval. It never mattered. Astrid was as conniving and manipulative as her ancestor. She'd been pulling Enzo's marionette strings the whole time, just so that they could end up right here.

"Funny," Astrid mused. "I had planned to sacrifice Enzo, so you have Van to thank—it was his idea to send you that letter." She smirked when Margot flinched like she'd been backhanded. "He told me you'd come running, and he wasn't wrong. It was going to be such a hassle otherwise."

Margot turned to Van—Van, who needed to be where the Vase was. Instead of searching aimlessly for Enzo, he'd gone straight to the puppet master, not caring that Margot was the one who got tangled in her strings.

"How could you?" Margot asked Van. Fury coiled in her lungs, a viper in a basket, ready to strike.

"You can have your lover's spat later," Astrid said. She paced the alcove's archway, blocking Margot's exit. "Let's go."

"What about me?" Enzo balked. Without the shards close enough to reanimate him, Charon didn't seem inclined to let him go . . . ever.

Astrid pinched the bridge of her nose. "After you botched your one job? I don't think so."

"Someone still has to turn to stone," Margot argued.

Enzo blanched. "Never mind. I'm good."

Margot's mouth opened to retaliate, but Astrid held up a shushing finger. "Van, it's time to take me to the temple," she said.

The muscle of his jaw twinged, teeth clenching.

"Oh, my god," Margot said. "You're seriously going to help her."

"I don't have a choice." Each word was serrated. He shook his head, a statement in a single movement, and Margot's heart sank like a skipping stone after its last splash.

Astrid's smug smile returned. "No, he doesn't. I know I was right about the inscription—*Aureus, amor aeternus et cor lapideum*. Golden, eternal love with a heart of stone. But you finally figured that out, didn't you?"

Margot glanced toward Van, toward the death grip he had

on his single shard. One piece of the Vase would keep him from succumbing to the curse. He could run, right now, and never look back.

For a fraction of a second, she let herself imagine what it might have been like—walking out of the ruins together, him cramming into the seat next to her on the gazillion-hour flight back to Georgia and carrying her suitcases up the front porch steps: coming home with her, fitting into her life like a long-missing piece.

As long as he had that sliver of clay, he could be there with her, anywhere. Whole and human and hers. But the curse Venus placed on the Vase wouldn't just evaporate. They'd be haunted by it. Always triple-checking, worried that someday she'd look over her shoulder and he'd be stone. If they re-formed the Vase in the temple, maybe he could break the curse for good.

And even if they didn't, even if another Ashby turned him to stone in search of treasure, even if he literally had a chance to do it all over again, Margot knew he wouldn't have it any other way.

Walking away wasn't an option for him.

With a grimace, Van said, "Follow me."

Margot had given up on him once before. She wouldn't do it again. Dr. Hunt was right: she had to finish what she started.

"If you're really going to do this, then I'm coming, too," Margot said.

Van, not Astrid, objected. "No, you aren't. It's too dangerous."

It was cute, the way he was trying to be protective. Cute and useless. He'd forfeited his right to cuteness the minute he started working with Astrid.

This was like one of the trials, a puzzle she could solve. Astrid's white-knuckle clutch on the linen bag holding the first three shards wasn't going to loosen, so coaxing her into the temple was the only way to take them from her. Still, negotiating with Astrid felt like striking a deal with the very blonde devil.

"I've got the last shard," Margot said. "And I'm coming with it."

Astrid tugged her eyebrows in tightly as she thought. Then, she yanked open her linen bag and said, "Only if you hand it over. Now." She glanced between Margot and Van. "Both of you."

"What?" Van croaked. If anything, his grip on the shard tightened.

"I'm not letting you sabotage my plan any more than you already have." Astrid shook the bag, the clay shards jangling inside. "So, either give me your shards, or I'll release Enzo and let Charon add you to his collection."

Enzo whimpered behind them, "Can't you let me out anyway?"

All it had taken was a tube of Mac lipstick to outwit Enzo, but Margot had no intention of saying that part out loud. What she needed was all five shards in one place, and if handing them over to Astrid was the only way to do it, it was a risk she was willing to take.

Margot dropped her shard in first, trying to ignore the way Van watched her every move. The way it made her skin feel electrified. Astrid held the open pouch to him. Waiting. His shoulders sagged with a sigh. Reluctant fingers released his shard, and it clanged down with the rest.

Astrid rolled her eyes. "I hate group projects. Let's just get this over with."

She turned to exit, and Margot moved to follow, vaguely wondering if Van was right about it being dangerous—with all five shards in the temple, would the guardians have a heyday? Not to mention, there was that whole risk of her classmate trying to turn her to stone.

"Margot, wait. *Wait*." Van caught her by the arm, holding her back as Astrid raced ahead. "Fraternizing with an Ashby? Not a good idea. Trust me."

She spun to meet his chest. "Me? What about you?"

His jaw tightened. "I'm only doing what I have to. You know that."

Margot ground her heels, staking herself to the spot. "If you're going with her, so am I. Don't try to tell me to stay behind because it's not going to convince me. We're partners, and partners don't give up on each other."

Fear flashed through Van's gaze. She knew it was a Herculean task for him. Trust was a language Van hadn't spoken in a long time.

A hand swiped through his hair as his stare drilled into her. "I can't let you do that."

"You don't get to choose for me," she said.

During their staring match, a million unspoken things were said. Things like *I give up on a lot of things, but I won't give up on you* (her) and *You're the most unbelievably troubling girl I've ever met* (him).

Finally, a gauzy look glazed his eyes. Pliable and yielding. His grip on her arm loosened. "Okay. Okay, fine." Van's hand found hers, their fingers slotting together whether it was a good idea or not. "Honestly, I don't know why I was surprised to find you here."

For once, Margot was grateful to the catacombs for hiding the way she flushed beneath his touch. To be seen and known, she was still getting used to it. "I read your letter. The one that Astrid delivered. Was any of it even true? Or did you just lure me down here as bait?"

"Both." He stepped closer, voice dropping. "You were right. I lied to you, and I shouldn't have. I should have told you about the curse, about Astrid, about everything that night on the roof. I needed Astrid to believe I was only writing it as a trap so she could turn you into the statue, but every word I wrote was true, Margot. It was selfish to put you in harm's way, but I needed you to know how I felt. In case everything went wrong."

Margot breathed out through her nose. At the memory of his neat penmanship, a whirlpool of emotions swirled through her mind, a current she couldn't fight and didn't want to. The dark made her braver. "I'm sorry, too. I shouldn't have left you."

Van tilted her chin up. "But you came back. A part of me

really hoped you wouldn't. That you'd be a thousand miles away from here, away from all this. Safe. But then when I saw you . . ."

His thumb traced the plum of her cheek. *Oh, my god.* Was Van Keane going to kiss her?

Trying to hold back what she felt was pointless. There was more nervous adrenaline pumping through her veins now than at any of the previous trials. She felt everything at once. Wildfire and a whiff of smoke, something both scorching and smoldering, so bright it might burn her up.

His fingers curled around the back of her neck, and he tipped his forehead to meet hers. Everything smelled like salt and cypress, sandalwood and cinders. Orange light danced around them, flickering and flaring. This. *This* was what the romance novels had, what Isla and Reed must have felt deep in the ruins, what Margot had been dreaming of—

Astrid cleared her throat ahead of them. "Enough with the PDA," she said. "I've got history to make."

28

In the temple below the surface, everything was dust and stone, with the faint scent of long-cooled smoke lingering in the thin air. Margot's flashlight sliced through the darkness as she led Van and Astrid past the mural of Venus. The goddess's watchful eyes seemed to cry, *Do you know what you're getting yourself into?*

They'd left Charon to babysit Enzo, but Margot tipped off a guard on their way out. While security was occupied with his search-and-rescue mission, it was that much easier to slip into Venus's sanctuary unseen. Margot's pulse had leapfrogged as the temple's hidden door slammed shut behind them.

Now, all five pieces of the Vase were back in the Temple of Venus for the first time in nearly a century.

Reaching into his tool belt for a box of matches, Van touched the flame to the sill halfway up the temple wall. The familiar blaze twined around the nave, dripping the stones in dancing flamelight. The temple was crypt quiet, so much like the first time she'd entered, but Margot knew it wouldn't last long.

The guardians stood sentry by the door, frozen in various forms of fight—*Terra* strung his bow, *Aqua* took careful aim, *Ignis* held an arrow over his shoulder like a spear, and *Aura* leaned around the corner, preparing to strike. *Mors*'s empty stone eye sockets bored into Margot, like he'd been waiting for them to return.

Astrid shoved Margot aside, sprinting deeper into the temple on her own. The look of wonder that streaked across Astrid's face, Margot knew she'd worn it, too. It was impossible not to revel in it—a temple worthy of the goddess of beauty.

Frescoes danced overhead: nymphs weaving through greenery; soldiers with their swords; poets writing on tablets; and a widow, mourning. Margot followed the paintings like an atlas, letting them lead her deeper into the temple. She tried to appreciate it because as soon as this was over, she never wanted to come back to this place ever again.

Dashing forward, Astrid said, "You can decide amongst yourselves who's getting turned to stone because frankly, I don't think I care."

"Astrid, slow down," Margot said.

"Well, it's not like you didn't know *someone* was getting sacrificed," she huffed. "And we left Enzo back there."

Margot laughed because otherwise she was going to cry.

"Yeah, because it's not nice to sacrifice people on the third date."

"Suit yourself," she heard Astrid grumble.

As she drove toward the altar at the far end, Astrid missed the way the shadows shifted in the corner of the temple, but Margot didn't. Marble bones creaked behind her. She didn't need to look to know that each sharpened arrowhead was aimed straight for their hearts.

Van froze next to Margot. "Ashby, stop moving."

She turned on her heels, already annoyed. "If you're getting cold feet, don't blame—"

Terra loosed his arrow, and it pierced the air next to Astrid. Paling, she let out a mouselike squeak.

The guardians' stone bodies had awoken quicker than they had the first time Margot had entered this temple. With all five shards here, the magic was more potent, more dangerous.

"They don't want you," Margot said as calmly as someone about to get Boromired could. "They want the shards."

"Okay, and? What do you want me to do? Fight them? I'm not an idiot." Astrid bolted, shooting toward the staircase to the second-floor balcony. She took the stairs two at a time, but it wasn't going to be fast enough. *Terra* nocked another arrow, and it split the wall behind her, only narrowly missing her thigh.

Then the statue jolted forward, following Astrid. *Ignis* joined him up the stairs, cutting Margot and Van off. Their stone bodies moved unnaturally, too stiff in the knees, too rigid in the elbows.

Margot pressed her back flush with Van's. She grabbed one of the tools from Van's belt, a pointed shovel. As if that was going to be enough to fend the statues off. They rotated, trying to keep eyes on the rest of the guardians at once.

Aqua, Aura, and *Mors* surrounded them. Not to fight, she realized. The guardians were herding them, keeping Van and Margot away from Astrid and her shards.

"She's right. We can't win against them," Margot gasped. A plan formulated in her head—something Astrid said locking into place. "But they can fight each other. We split up, make them aim at each other, and let them destroy themselves."

"Genius," Van said between breaths.

Margot counted down from three—starting with three, of course—and then she and Van darted opposite directions. *Mors* followed him, and *Aqua* tailed her, while *Aura* planted himself firmly in the center of the temple, releasing stone arrows toward both sides.

Ahead, Astrid rounded the balcony, bobbing and weaving between pillars as she tried to outrun the guardians. Margot surged closer, trying to position herself in line with *Ignis*. *Aqua* took aim, and Margot steadied herself. Heart pounding against her ribs, she waited, waited, waited.

The moment his carved fingers released the bow, she ducked. The arrow *whooshed* overhead. It struck stone with a crack. Looking back, the arrow had wedged itself in *Ignis's* arm. Crevices formed on the surface of the guardian's skin, the way Magic Shell cracked on top of vanilla ice cream. His arm crumbled to dust, landing in a heap by his feet.

"Yes!" Margot whooped, but her cheer was short-lived. *Terra* refocused on Margot, sandwiching her very literally between a rock and a hard place. "Never mind. Too soon."

On the other side of the temple, *Mors* lurched toward Van. He dragged an arrow out of his sheath, and pulled his bowstring back. Van dodged left, and the arrow zipped across the temple, grazing *Aqua*'s leg.

Margot dove toward the nearest pillar. *Terra* and *Aqua* paced toward her from either side. An arrow slammed into the column, chipping marble off the side, and she hunkered down lower. Panic writhed in her chest, but she breathed it out through her nose. *You can do this.*

A scream interrupted Margot's pep talk.

Across the balcony, *Ignis*, with his one arm, had Astrid cornered. Margot couldn't sit here and do nothing—she wasn't like Astrid. She'd never be able to sleep at night if she knew someone had gotten hurt because she'd done nothing. Even if that someone was Astrid Ashby.

"Please don't make me regret this," Margot muttered.

She raced toward Astrid, sliding between *Terra*'s legs like a softball shortstop. She watched over her shoulder as the guardians couldn't course correct fast enough, and *Aqua* barreled into *Terra*. They ricocheted off each other, *Terra* crashing into the wall and *Aqua* into one of the pillars.

Ahead, *Ignis* held an arrow in his fist, poised over his shoulder. It happened too fast, a scene from a movie: *Ignis* slammed his hand down, Astrid skirted left, and the arrow's dagger-sharp point skimmed her cheek, drawing a scrape of blood to the surface. She clutched the linen bag with the shards to her chest, shrinking herself into the corner. There was nowhere else for her to go.

Checking over her shoulder, Margot confirmed that Van was still sparring with *Mors*, but by the looks of it, he wasn't winning. His white shirt had been stained in russet stripes with dried blood, and his skin wore a coat of sweat and grime. They couldn't fend them off much longer.

She had to do something.

God, she hoped this worked. On the ground, *Aura* traced Margot's path with a nocked arrow. Perfect. Margot ran faster, her backpack bouncing with each step and her knuckles aching around the hilt of her borrowed shovel. She only had one chance.

She heard the snap of *Aura*'s bowstring first, then the zip of his arrow as she tucked and rolled. The arrow sank into Astrid's linen bag, splitting the fabric, and the shards scattered against the stone floors. A necessary casualty.

"No!" Astrid hollered, which was a weird way to pronounce, *Thank you so much for making sure I didn't get impaled!*

Pushing Astrid behind her, Margot wedged herself between her dig partner and *Ignis*, holding her tool like a sword.

Astrid scowled. "You think a spade is going to stop him?"

"Actually," Margot yelled, "it's a trowel!"

Putting all her force into her swing, the trowel-that-was-maybe-a-spade smacked into *Ignis*'s chest. The hit threw her off-balance, and Margot skidded backward across the floor. Her head slammed against the ground. Black swam through her vision. Each breath came heavy, hurting.

Ignis wasn't in much better shape. Her shovel had lodged itself in his chest, and now hairline fractures etched over his marble skin. He staggered backward into a pillar, and the impact cracked the stone column. All the way through. It severed in the middle, the top half sliding off the bottom. The pillar toppled over the balcony edge and landed with a crash over *Aura*.

Margot watched, flat on her back, as the rubble scattered into the far reaches of the temple. That was four guardians down. The only one left was *Mors*.

She twisted her head back to center. Blinking. Was that . . .

The ceiling splintered. Cracks webbed across its surface. Evidently, the pillar had been pivotal to the structural integrity of the temple. Load bearing.

"Oh no," she whispered.

Fissures spread, and a chunk of stone shook itself loose. Margot rolled, barely avoiding blunt force trauma as the ceiling rained down around her. *A dig site collapse.* That was what they said had killed Van. Suddenly, she seriously hoped it hadn't been a self-fulfilling prophecy.

Next to her, Astrid coughed and sputtered. She'd not been as quick on her feet, and a coat of white dust painted her from head to toe. On hands and knees, she searched the wreckage for the shards.

"Where are they?" Astrid asked as she dug through the rubble.

With the temple in this condition, they couldn't stay down here much longer, and Margot wasn't about to let Astrid eeny-meeny-miny-mo to see which one of them would become the sacrifice.

Margot stood, straightening the straps of her backpack. Her head throbbed where she'd smacked it against the limestone tiles, but she helped Astrid parse through the debris. Five gloss-black slivers of clay, that was all they needed, and she'd find a way for her and Van to survive this.

The ground beneath her feet quivered—the whole foundation of the temple had been jeopardized, struggling to withstand the pressure from thousands of years of compacted dirt over their heads. Margot dug faster. When her hand clasped around a black fragment, she couldn't stop herself from gasping.

Astrid rushed to her side and forced the shard from Margot's fingers. "Give me that." She gathered the rest of the shards into her arms, half-feral like a raccoon hoarding grapes. Then

Astrid sped back downstairs, leaping over *Ignis*'s fallen body.

Margot weaved between *Aura* and *Terra* as she chased after Astrid and the shards. "Astrid," she warned, "whatever you're doing, you're going to have to live with it for the rest of your life."

Astrid barked out a cold laugh, still hurtling down the stairs like she wasn't about to curse someone to an eternal purgatory by way of metamorphic rock. Or not caring that she was. "I don't need advice from you. Believe me."

On the balcony, Van let out a warrior's shout. Margot looked up in time to see him sever *Mors*'s skull from his skeletal frame with a chisel. He dropped the makeshift blade and fell to his knees, catching Margot's eye.

They did it. They defeated the guardians.

Van's lips curled into a smile, grin gleaming in the temple's tawny light. He leaned over the balcony ledge and let out a triumphant holler. With his hair disheveled and his shirt blood-stained, the sight left Margot breathless. An invisible string drew her toward him.

But it wasn't over.

Two hands shoved Margot sideways. Astrid pushed her onto the spot where she'd found Van that first night, encircled by wilted myrtles. It all happened too fast. Margot, stunned, stood paralyzed as Astrid slid all five shards onto the alabaster altar.

Their broken edges aligned. Reunited at last.

A strangled cry left Van's mouth—a wounded sound Margot

was certain she'd never be able to forget. She closed her eyes, wondering what it had felt like for him all those years ago as the stone crawled up his legs, through his chest, and into his heart.

There was no rush of cold over her skin like the marble had claimed her. No vibration of cruel magic in her bones. Her throat didn't tighten, and her lungs didn't squeeze out their last breath.

She peeled one eye open. "Did it work?"

"No, it didn't work, or else you wouldn't be asking that, you buffoon," Astrid wailed.

Van flew down the stairs three at a time and leaped off the edge before making it to the platform. An expression Margot had never seen him wear before twisted his face as he slammed up against her. His hands surveyed Margot, roaming from her cheeks to her shoulders to her hips and back up again.

"You're all right," he said. Less like a question and more like a statement he was trying to convince himself was true.

The ceiling quaked above them. She craned her neck upward, and the color drained from her face. Margot didn't need a bunch of credit hours in architecture to know that the roof wasn't going to hold much longer.

Astrid seemed to know it, too. "Forget it," she said to herself more than anyone. She shoveled the clay fragments into her backpack. "I'm not dying down here! The shards are better than nothing!"

Van moved to stop her. Gravel in his voice, he said, "We had a deal."

Margot knew what he was thinking. How he'd handed his shard, his one tether to humanity, to Astrid—to an Ashby. That the second Astrid got out of his sight, the stone would seep straight back into his heart.

It didn't matter because it was too late. The cracked ceiling caved beneath the weight of earth that had buried it. Astrid charged toward the exit, but when Van tried to sprint after her, Margot grabbed his hand and pulled him beneath the altar, holding on as the world fell down around them.

29

All Margot knew and may ever know again was dirt. Thick, dark, suffocating. Sheets of rock crashed through the center of the temple—hundreds, if not thousands, of years' worth of history sliding with it. A wall of sediment separated Margot and Van from the staircase back to the surface. They'd only barely made it far enough away to avoid getting crushed, and Van's arms folded around Margot's shoulders and head, shielding her.

She slithered back, just enough for his face to come into focus. Van batted his eyes open, bits of dust and debris clinging to his lashes. One, two breaths. They lay nose to nose, chest to chest. Together.

"It's okay," she whispered. "We're okay."

Van sat up so quickly that he banged his skull against the underside of the marble altar. He didn't even bother to rub the sore spot. "No, we're not. Astrid's gone."

His voice took that robotic timbre it always did when he was stressed—even-keeled but clipped. Margot wanted to smooth out the tense fold between his brows.

"Astrid's gone," Margot repeated. "*And* we're okay."

Van hauled himself fully upright just so that he could start to pace in front of the altar. His eyes lingered on its smooth surface, like he could still see the shards on it. "She took them."

The corner of Margot's mouth lifted. "Did she?"

Van pressed the heels of his palms against his forehead. "Yes. You saw her. She took the shards and ran, and now we're here with—"

"With the shards?" Margot unzipped her backpack and reached down to the bottom. She cradled five black-and-gold fragments in her hands. The Vase of Venus Aurelia was all right here.

The sight was enough to stop Van cold. "What did you do?"

A smile flared across her face, impossible to snuff out. "What any good partner would. I made her look somewhere else."

The guardians had helped, whether they knew it or not. Slicing Astrid's bag, letting the shards scatter across the floor. Astrid hadn't even noticed that the clay fragments she picked up were the cracked pieces of a coffee mug while the real shards had been stuffed way down at the bottom of Margot's one-strap backpack. Too preoccupied with gloating as she offered them up to Venus that she hadn't paid any attention to the little white letters of Hotel Villa Minerva's logo on the backs of the shards.

It was exhilarating, the way Van looked at her. Margot's stomach bottomed out—not in a bad way.

Van swept Margot into his arms. Her feet lifted off the ground as he twirled her. She looped her arms around his shoulders, burying her face in the hollow of his neck.

Murmuring into her curls, he said, "There is no one like you, Margot Rhodes."

She laughed, weightless. When she finally found her footing again, she felt like a can of shaken-up soda. Her heart was trying to burst out of her chest. A sheen of silver lined her eyes, blurring Van's edges. "So, now we just have to find a way out."

Her hand trailed down Van's arm until it latched around his fingers and squeezed. He didn't reciprocate. His eyes focused on something over her head.

Margot lifted onto her toes, forcing herself into his line of sight. "What is it?"

"There is only one way left." When he finally dragged his gaze to meet hers, it had hardened.

The set of his jaw. The firmness of his gaze. Whatever it was, she wasn't going to like it.

"When I put the shards on the altar, there was a door that opened, I remember. Presumably to the treasure room. I never got to see inside, but when they built this temple, they would've made sure there was a second exit." His palm was warm against her cheek, but it didn't change the cold precision of his tone.

That voice was a surgical knife cleaving them apart.

Margot shook her head. "But we can't open that door without remaking the Vase."

Van's lips thinned, smiling although it was hardly the time. "I know."

"I can't," she said. "I *won't*."

Van looped his arms back around her shoulders, pressing her against her chest. Quiet enough she thought maybe she'd imagined it, she heard him say, "You get the Vase, and I get the treasure, remember?"

"If we do this, you won't get the treasure." Margot pulled back—how was she being the rational one right now?

He brushed a loose curl behind her ear. It did little to quell the dread weighing down her bones, an ache that permeated all the way down to the marrow. "But you will, and what's that thing Dr. Hunt is always harping on? The buddy system. A win for you is a win for me."

Margot's voice cracked with emotion. "You're the one who said there's always another way. There has to be something else we could do."

Every muscle in his body coiled tight. His shoulders rose, fell. He looked her square in the eye, spine straightening. "Not this time."

"But I—"

The ceiling shuddered, threatening to send more soil cascading down.

"Margot, you can't stay here. It isn't safe," he said. His words slowed with intention. A dam holding back the river. "All you have to do is put the shards on the pedestal. When the door opens, look for a staircase. Put your name on the discovery. You did it. You earned it."

"What about you?" she asked. "It's yours as much as mine."

He scanned her face. Cataloging, remembering. But he didn't waver. "I was never meant to leave this temple. You were my one last adventure. Go. Before it's too late."

Van backed himself into the circle of wilted myrtle blossoms, but determination staked Margot to the ground. Her arm stretched, holding onto his hand as long as possible. Until, finally, their fingertips fell.

No. *No.*

Margot's heart shattered into five jagged pieces she'd bury at the bottom of her ribs like the Vase itself. She knew, even if she didn't want to believe it, that Van was right, and what it meant for him to be.

The curse had a price that demanded to be paid.

One by one, she set the shards on the altar until the Latin inscription stared back, taunting her. *Aureus, amor aeternus et cor lapideum.* Everything she thought she wanted. Useless to her now.

Behind her, Van said, "You never needed the Vase, you know. Anyone would be a fool not to love you."

A sob rattled through Margot, but he gave a reassuring nod.

Hands shaking, she added the last shard to the altar.

With one last desperate breath, he said, "I'm so in love with you, Margot Rhodes."

She didn't get the chance to say it back.

On the altar, the shards lifted on invisible hands. Suspended midair, the Vase sewed itself back together with a golden thread of light. When their jagged edges met, a hot, bright light flashed through the temple, and Margot winced, covering her eyes.

When she opened them, Van was still standing there, the remnants of a smile carved onto his lips. But he was completely still. White marble dripped down his jaw, his neck, his shoulders. It clawed down his arms, hungry. Ivory stone encased him before she could reach him.

Her hand rested against his blanched cheek. All the warmth had seeped out of him. Her lips pressed to the tilt of his marble grin, leaving a red stain behind. Nothing like how her first kiss was supposed to be.

"I love you, too," Margot wept. "Isn't that enough?"

In the quiet that followed, floodwaters poured through her, furious and unyielding. Strong enough to carve out canyons. A mudslide she wouldn't withstand.

Please, please, her heart begged, heavy in her ribs. *Come back to me.*

It did nothing. Van was gone.

How could the goddess of love do this to her?

"Are you happy now?" she asked the empty temple, hoarse.

Hopefully her voice lifted straight to Olympus. She wanted Venus to hear her. "Because I totally don't get it. I did *everything* you asked. Everything!"

Margot might not have received the Pliny Junior Scholastic Award of Linguistic Achievement in Latin, but she understood the inscription. Some part of her knew the Vase would never have granted her Venus's mystical power. The only way to be revered and adored forever was to be carved by a sculptor's hand. Frozen in marble to be admired from afar—distant and lifeless. A blank canvas for everyone to paint upon, forcing yourself to become what they wanted to see.

But to be loved—to let yourself be known, every soft, scared part of you? It couldn't be defined by a cinematic moment or a picturesque snapshot—it required flesh and blood, scars and blemishes. A once-broken nose and an unbalanced dimple. A broken heart, healed again.

The Vase, sparkling and whole, floated back down to the altar. As if that could replace the boy she'd turned her back on to rebuild it. On the far side of the temple, an archway lifted. Light shone from within, reflecting streaks of gold across the temple walls. Treasure. Margot barely registered it. The sight twisted a blade of guilt in her stomach.

"Take your treasure! I don't want it," she screamed.

Margot was hardly a girl anymore. She was a storm, forty-seven different emotions all hurtling into each other. They writhed around Margot's torso with hurricane-force winds.

Her ears burned, her blood boiling. A cry ripped up her throat.

She didn't think, just moved. The Vase was in her hands, the clay now cooled. Distantly, Margot heard the treasure room door slam shut beneath the howl of heartbreak in her ears. Who cared? The amphora hummed with enclosed magic—magic that was supposed to fix things for Margot, not make them worse.

With a single downward pike, she shattered the Vase against the stone floors.

30

In the aftermath, the temple was deathly silent.

What had she done?

Margot fell to her knees. She couldn't cry anymore, and her throat had gone hoarse with rage. She'd been hollowed out, emptied entirely. A husk of who she was supposed to be.

The door to the treasure was gone. It had mercilessly closed, booming as it hit the floor. She'd be sealed into the temple—into her own mausoleum.

A cold sweat whipped across Margot's forehead. The bitter aftertaste of an emotional outbreak clogged her mouth. She couldn't swallow it down. Behind her, Van was still as stone as he had been. She'd ruined her only chance for escape—the chance he'd given up everything for her to have—because she'd been too emotional.

Margot plucked one of the pieces off the ground—the shards

had fractured, five turning into fifty. This one had the remnants of the word *aeternus* stamped into it. Ridiculing her. The filigreed gold shimmered.

No, the whole fragment shimmered. Faint yellow at first, then brighter until nearly molten.

She dropped the shard as it burned, hissing against her palm. It clanged against the floor, an edge chipping off. Next to it, another sliver of clay gleamed. One by one, the shards ignited until the floor glowed; each speck of dust was a map of stars against a night-black sky.

Then, a piercing light strobed through the dark temple.

Beaming out from one of the shards, a stripe of gold slashed the shadows. Another lanced out from a second chipped piece. And another, another, another. Light filled the room until everything was saturated. Margot nearly had to cover her eyes as warmth poured into every corner, daylight yellow.

One sharp spear aimed straight at the broad plane of Van's chest. The beam sank into his marble shell. Margot lurched, her body reacting on sheer instinct, throwing herself in front of the beam, but it was too late.

And then the light was gone. A wind rushed through the temple, surprisingly brisk in contrast. It whipped through the torch flames, and shadows swelled again across the ceiling. When the gust settled, the room grew dim, only a single ribbon of light remaining.

The glimmering strand wrapped around the mosaic's tiles,

winding through the delicate paintings, the flowers blooming and then wilting, until it traced up Van's legs. Margot stepped closer to him as the drop of sunlight expanded. Rivers of gold flowed through his marble casing and etched into the grooves.

A hopeful thrum rang through Margot like the first note of a symphony as the gilded cord wove around Van's chest, arms, hands. The air shifted again, sweet smelling—like sandalwood and cypress and saltwater foam.

The marble cracked, tectonic plates shifting over Van's skin. And then shattered.

Like breaking off a plaster cast, stone crumbled to the floor. A stark white mask gave way to the suntanned, freckled expanse of Van's face. Margot grasped at his hand, and his cold marble palm grew warm in hers. His eyes blinked open. Alive, alive, alive.

"Margot?" Van asked, dazed as if he'd stepped out of a dream.

She sprung onto her tiptoes, her arms latching around his neck. Her lips found his.

He startled back in surprise only momentarily, and then, Van's hand wound around the back of her head, threading his fingers through her curls. He leaned into her. Firm but patient. Like he'd been waiting for this, and he didn't want to rush it.

The rest of the universe dimmed around them. Margot forgot to care about whether or not her lipstick had smudged. She pulled Van closer, and his hands grazed down her sides, landing at her hips. Stars spun behind Margot's closed lids as Van toyed with the hem of her shirt, his fingers pressing against the smooth skin of her waist.

When she finally pulled away, out of breath and beaming, Margot cupped Van's face with both hands. She whispered, "I love you, too. You didn't let me say it back."

His lips dipped against her forehead. A laugh filtered from them—the kind of sound Margot hoped she never had to miss again. "But Margot, what did you do?"

"Oh, I, um—" A rush of hot embarrassment flushed Margot's cheeks. That familiar sting of leftover emotion prickled beneath her skin. Her head hung low. She couldn't even look at him. "I smashed it."

Van's eyebrows raised so high, they nearly got lost beneath his hairline. "When I said you could have the Vase, that wasn't exactly what I anticipated."

"I didn't want it anymore," she said. "I just wanted you."

Around them, the shards on the floor had dissolved into dust motes that sifted through the air. Every trace of the Vase of Venus Aurelia had vanished. She braced herself, but Van didn't look at her like she'd overreacted. No chastising huff, no pinching the bridge of his nose.

He stretched his fingers behind his back and then his elbows over his head, testing his joints for stiffness. A slow smile overtook his face. "You got me."

He wrapped his arms back around her, lifting her off her feet as his lips pressed to hers once more.

When her feet hit the ground again, she said, "I don't under-stand." Although if it meant he'd keep kissing her, she wasn't going to complain.

"Don't you see?" he asked, eyes gleaming. "Without the Vase, there's no curse."

It was as if, then, the glow from the shards radiated through her chest, lighting up the deepest parts of her. Her emotions hadn't ruined anything—they had saved him.

There was only one problem. "I think no more Vase also means no more treasure. The minute I grabbed the Vase, the door closed. We're super trapped."

His eyes trailed toward the door. He considered this new input as he shook the dust out of his blond hair. "There has to be a way out. Think of it like another trial."

Above them, the ceiling quaked again. If they didn't find a way out soon, they might never have the chance.

Van paced the room, palms shifting over the stones in search of some kind of trapdoor, but Margot couldn't bring herself to move. Whatever he was looking for, she was almost certain he wouldn't find it. Venus hadn't crafted the Vase for nothing—it was the key to the treasure, and it was gone. The inscription had said gold *and* a heart of stone. Not *or*. This wasn't a choose-your-own-adventure.

She sagged against the altar. Her hand depressed the center of the stone pedestal, and she yipped in surprise. The farther

her hand sank, the more the opposite wall shifted with the groan of an archway opening.

"Is that . . . ?" Van trailed off with a question mark of disbelief tacked on the end.

The door to the treasure room—a stone plate that slid beneath a carved frieze of tides and moons and myrtle blooms—stood wide open. Margot raised her palm slowly, stopping halfway. The door followed, sinking low but refusing to close.

Again and again, she tested the door's response. A thought percolated, bubbling closer to the surface with each rise and fall of the stone slab. Without the Vase, it was like whatever magic tie had protected the gold had severed. Now, it was a simple pulley system.

Van and Margot pivoted toward each other and, in unison, said, "The House of Olea!"

The door operated with a pressure plate—they didn't have the Vase of Venus Aurelia, but all they needed was *something* to keep it triggered. Just like they had with the stones in the House of Olea, operating the pendulums.

She could practically see the light bulb go off in Van's head. He said, "Wait right there!"

But when Van dashed toward the staircase, half-submerged beneath a thousand tons of soil, the door to the treasure slammed shut so forcefully, it kicked up a cloud of dust.

"Was that you?" he asked.

"Definitely not." Even leaning all her body weight against

the altar, the door wouldn't budge. Margot slumped against the cool stone with a groan. They were never getting out of here alive.

Van backtracked toward her. Halfway, the door shifted again.

Margot propped herself up on her elbow. Her gaze sliced between Van and the door and back again. It didn't make sense. Was *he* controlling the treasure room? One more step, and the doorway closed, leaving Van bobbing in the center of the temple, hands outstretched warily.

Then, Margot saw it. He'd stepped inside the ring of mosaic myrtles, the same place he'd turned to stone. Of course. It wasn't enough to have the Vase of Venus Aurelia—just like the inscription said.

"I need to stand here, don't I?" Van asked. "We can't both leave."

There was supposed to be a statue *and* something needed to be placed on the altar to trigger the door. Which meant that someone would get left behind. Unless . . .

"No. Let me," Margot said. His face contorted in a pained expression, but before he could get any more heroic ideas and try to sacrifice himself again, she added, "You said it yourself. It's like the House of Olea. If we put something on the altar, and I stand here, the door opens. Then, I can run off, and you can hold it open until I make it through."

"I know what we need." Van jumped into action, hoisting

himself onto the staircase, and trekked back to where *Mors*'s skeletal frame laid in severed pieces. He lifted up the guardian's skull and trudged back toward the altar.

Even—or maybe especially—decapitated, *Mors* gave Margot the heebie-jeebies.

The stone skull was nearly the size of Van's chest, and he wobbled down the steps, cradling it with both arms. With the scraping sound of a column splintering, the temple trembled. A layer of debris collapsed behind Van.

A scream clawed up Margot's throat as Van teetered on even feet. The weight of *Mors*'s head dragged him downward, just as a sheet of sediment blocked the upper half of the staircase.

"Hurry!" Margot yelled.

Van righted himself with a groan and a grimace. As he situated the guardian's head on the altar, Margot scooted into position. Like she'd hoped, the door across the hall scrolled open.

She knew what it would mean to stand here—that Van could turn his back on her, decide she wasn't worth as much as the treasure, and abandon her in the temple. Maybe love was just trusting and being trusted in return.

As Van approached the doorway, she wondered what he saw. What that first glimpse of gold looked like, what the first promise of notoriety felt like for the boy who had nothing to lose.

Then, he shifted, turning back to face her. There was no

hesitation in his gaze, only glittering determination. He planted his feet, grounding his heels into the stone floors. With his arms primed to catch the door, he asked, "Ready?"

She sucked down a steadying breath. There wouldn't be a second chance. "Can I get a countdown?"

Van's forehead creased. "One hundred, ninety-nine, ninety-eight—"

"Three, two, one, go!" Margot shot toward the archway, and the rock wall released.

Sisyphus beneath his boulder, Van's arms trembled with immediate effort. Margot pumped her arms at her side. The closer she got, the more she could see Van's struggle—the bulging vein in his forehead, the sinew of his biceps.

Van fell to his knees, bracing his shoulders against the wall. With one hand, he reached toward her. "Faster!"

Margot slid onto her belly, diving toward the gap and sincerely hoping she wouldn't get cut in half like an amateur magician's assistant. Arms outstretched, Van caught her by the bracelet as his fingers snagged against the band of jade beads.

The cord inside snapped, beads scattering, but it gave him enough time to get a better grip on her wrist. He tugged her through to the other side milliseconds before the door banged against the tiles. Closed for good.

Lungs heaving, Margot pushed herself upright. Next to her, Van slung his arm around her shoulders, reeling her in. He murmured a single syllable: "Wow."

It wasn't a treasure room so much as it was an entire treasure *wing*. Mounds of gold lined a hall so long, Margot couldn't see the end of it. Shelves striped the walls, holding rolled parchments, the kinds of ancient histories that academic archaeologists like Isla and Reed would have salivated over. Empirical busts and statues of Pompeii's patron goddess were surrounded by gilded weapons and sparkling gems.

But Margot's gaze caught on maybe the best treasure of all.

"I know," she breathed, leaning her cheek against his chest. "A staircase."

31

The staircase led them to a hatch that opened to a wholly unmemorable alleyway, a place where no one would consider prying up the cobblestones to find what waited underneath. When they resurfaced, the ground shook beneath Margot's feet as if the guardians' pounding footsteps were chasing them.

Van closed the hatch behind them. "What is that?"

The ground continued to rumble, rattling through Margot's joints. They were a block or so from the grassy knoll, and the guardians . . . the guardians had all been buried, no magic left in their rubble bones.

Then, a stampede of cross traffic rushed down the main road toward the temple.

"Where is everyone going?" Margot asked a passing woman with a number-two pencil holding up her French twist.

The woman smiled. "You haven't heard? Someone found the Vase of Venus Aurelia!"

Margot grabbed Van's hand, and they joined the stream of white-sneakered tourists and archaeologists in loose linens and khaki cargo pants. Ahead, the far half of the lawn had caved in. The sunken temple was barely visible, a few marble columns protruding from the earth in bone-white shards. A crowd had gathered on the hilltop: TV crews, bespectacled journalists, photographers with cameras flashing. Overhead, a helicopter buzzed, and if Margot squinted she could see an eagle-eyed airborne reporter, peering down at the city.

Everyone wanted a peek at the treasure.

Wading through elbows and shoulders, Margot and Van tightened their grip on each other's hands. Who knew a mythological treasure trove resulted in so much press coverage?

Of course, Astrid stood at the epicenter, red-faced and sniveling. But she was intact, barring a few purpling bruises and patchy scrapes. A shock blanket had been wrapped around her shoulders, and she clutched it at the nape as she spoke to a huddle of other Radcliffe students, saying who knew what.

Next to her, Enzo chatted with a reporter, a wired microphone tilted beneath his jaw. He wasn't the only one being interviewed. There must have been four or five different news sources present. All hoping to break the news of the person who discovered Pompeii's oldest mystery.

"There they are!" Suki shouted, jumping and pointing.

Dr. Hunt rushed forward. She planted protective hands on both of their shoulders. "Margot, Chad, is it true? You found the Vase?"

Margot's smile beamed, bright as a flashbulb. "It's true."

Suddenly, about six different men in stuffy-looking blazers appeared out of thin air with voice recorders at the ready. A barrage of questions hit them with tropical-force winds. What were their names, how did they find it, where is it located, what kind of treasure is it?

Van shuffled forward, stuffing a hand in his pocket. She heard him say, "Chad's just a nickname. I usually go by Van. Van Keane."

Dr. Hunt hovered next to him as they fielded questions, but Margot sank backward. She let the tides of people flow around her. A sea of faces looked back. Proud, gleaming eyes watched them, admired them.

She expected a swell of emotion, the sunny glow of achievement. After all, she'd found the Vase of Venus Aurelia, discovered its treasure, and suddenly she had the adoration of the world. So, why did it feel like she was missing something?

Her phone dinged in her pocket. She yanked it out, tapping to the notification. A text from her dad.

Is this international data plan working? Look left

Look left? What, did his text send before he was ready? Like it was supposed to say, *Looks like you left your phone on silent and missed the new boarding pass I forwarded you.*

Then, she spotted a familiar face in the fray.

"Dad?" Margot called, voice tinged with disbelief.

Rupert Rhodes belonged beneath the Main Street magnolia

trees, taking calls in his AirPods with one hand holding a brief-case full of mortgage paperwork and the other a triple-shot latte. Not in the middle of the ancient ruins wearing a wrin-kled, salmon-colored polo shirt, clearly fresh off a flight.

Margot was vaguely aware of Van explaining how they'd solved the trials to reporters from the freaking BBC and AP News, but her dad was here. *Here.* Her brain couldn't hardly believe it until his arms wrapped around her, tugging her into the tightest hug she'd ever endured.

He said, "Oh, thank god. You're okay."

Every muscle in Margot's body clenched. Wasn't she sup-posed to be grounded for the rest of her life? She forced out the question: "What are you doing here?"

Her dad held her at arm's length, scanning her head to toe for bumps and bruises, and, let's be honest, her body felt like it had been squeezed through a pasta maker in the last week, so she wasn't sure what he'd see. She expected the pinched frown he always wore when she jumped headfirst into something and ended up crash-landing, but instead his face smoothed with relief.

"You skipped your flight. You stopped answering my calls. I thought you might have fallen into the Mediterranean or something," he said.

Still stunned, Margot shook her head like it might rattle things into place. "Did Dr. Hunt talk to you?"

"Only once I landed," he said. "After our last conversation,

I did buy a plane ticket—for me, not for you. I thought I was going to have to pick you up and bring you home myself. But, somewhere over the Atlantic, I started thinking. I know we haven't seen eye to eye this past week."

"So, I'm not in trouble?" Margot asked, rolling onto the balls of her feet and innocently batting her lashes.

"Oh no. You're going to spend the rest of the summer with an eight p.m. curfew, so don't think I'm letting you off the hook." Well, it was worth a shot. "But I love you. Always have, always will."

Something in Margot's chest cracked wide open. She choked out, "But you said I'm just like Mom, and she wasn't good enough."

"I love your mom," he said tenderly, a sound like honey straight from the comb. "Still would if she were around to let me. But that's the thing, Gogo. Sometimes loving someone best means letting them go and . . ."

His voice chipped at the end like ice in a glass of lemonade on a sweltering day, a nostalgic sound from the summers before her mom left. Before Margot lost days, weeks, months constantly trying to win his attention and approval.

"I only came here without telling you because I knew you'd be too busy with work to actually listen, and you'd say no, and we'd end up in a big fight," Margot said, her bottom lip quivering.

Her dad brushed her wild curls away from her face, gentle

and caring. "You're right. I haven't always been there for you the way I needed to be. I held on too tightly when I should have let you spread your wings." He laughed, then, a wet sound like he might tear up, too. "I just knew one day you'd grow up to be this brilliant, adventurous young woman, and I was going to lose you, too."

"*Daaaad*," Margot said. She swiped at the tears leaking out the sides of her eyes, totally about to smear her mascara. "I thought I was losing you because . . . Sometimes I feel like I have to stop being me to make you happy."

He shook his head. "I'm sorry. I want you to do what makes *you* happy. Not what you think will make other people happy."

Well, she'd followed her heart, and it led her here.

And here was . . . not exactly like she'd imagined it. Somehow, it was better.

Across the meadow, Margot found Van, still engaged in a conversation with eager reporters (and Suki, who had taken it upon herself to produce a notepad and a novelty pen and was now certainly asking the hardest-hitting questions). His chin rose like he felt her eyes on him, and when his gaze met hers, she winked.

"Margot! Come with me. Let me get a photo of you and Van!" a journalist with a hefty DSLR strapped around his chest said.

She let herself be corralled through the crowd until Van was back at her side, his arm fitting comfortably around her waist.

The journalist pressed the camera's viewfinder to his eye and swiveled the lens, shifting them into focus.

"How does it feel? Finding the treasure of Venus?" the journalist asked.

"I'm never letting go," Van said.

Margot leaned in closer, a sappy smile spreading wide, but Van tilted her chin up toward him. As the camera flashed, he kissed her, like they were the only two people in the world. The kind of kiss that would rival Isla and Reed's. Windswept and sunlit and lipstick stained.

32

Fictional adventurer Wren Cahill had just wrangled the jewel thief into a headlock when Van plopped a filthy trowel-spade at Margot's feet.

Margot peeked over the screen of her laptop, her attention snapping away from her Word document and back to reality, as Van swiped the back of his arm across his forehead, leaving a streak of dirt behind in the afternoon sweat. "How's it going down there?"

They'd abandoned their old dig site and migrated to the grassy knoll and its mounds of freshly upturned dirt to excavate Venus's temple. Which was fine by Margot. She didn't mind if she never saw Plot D again in her life.

"Topher and Rex just discovered a first-century spatha, so Suki's taking bets on who loses an eye first," Van said as he sank into the pastel-colored folding chair next to her, beneath Dr. Hunt's white tent.

Margot laughed. "My money's on Rex."

The boys' underhanded comments at Margot's beginner's luck had ceased immediately when they realized that her name would be added to their textbooks someday. Even Astrid had surprised her by turning delightfully tepid, too excited by the prospect of new documents she'd get to translate to keep up the charade of annoyance. Neither of them would ever admit it, but now that they were partners, Van and Astrid managed to get along—her academic prowess paired well with Van's hands-on know-how, and a century-old feud fizzled out with every studied scroll.

The Campania sun had sprinkled new freckles across Van's cheeks, and his face had a pink tinge, newly sunburned. His steps had grown lighter with every day since the curse had broken. The divot of his single dimple appeared as he said, "I've also got something I want to show you."

"It's not Rex's eye, is it?" she asked.

Van leveled her with a look.

"Okay, great, because as soon as Wren finishes kicking this guy's butt, she's going to realize she's totally lost." Her nails tapped against her laptop keyboard as Margot pressed the save button before closing out of her half-written manuscript.

Wren was the kind of archaeologist Margot had wanted to be. She didn't care if she got dirt in her nail beds and wasn't squeamish around bones and wouldn't take no for an answer, even if it meant leaving her comfort zone behind. And while

Wren was stuck in Ariadne's labyrinth trying to save the crown of King Minos from a masked thief (who was obviously secretly super hunky and going to be forced into working with her), Margot had never been more certain of her own footing.

On the page, Margot could become anyone, but every word somehow brought her closer to herself. There was something magic in every sentence, every finished chapter. Writing was the one place where she didn't have to try to stop herself from getting carried away, from diving in too deep, too fast. All her daydreams and every one of her wildest ideas—they weren't just allowed. They were encouraged.

While the rest of the class unearthed and analyzed every golden artifact from the buried temple, Margot had spent the last few weeks dreaming up Wren's story, every emotional arc and unexpected plot twist. Van helped, fielding any world-building snags she ran into along the way.

Margot could hardly believe Dr. Hunt managed to convince her dad to let her stay the rest of the summer under the guise of auditing the class for research. And next quarter, she'd sign up for a creative writing elective. This one, she was certain, would stick.

"Don't suspect you've found a Cretan treasure map down there, have you?" Margot asked, still ruminating on her looming plot hole.

Just then, a trio of other students came up carrying big plastic bins of sorted discoveries. They quieted when they noticed the two of them. One of the boys whispered something that made another one laugh. Van stiffened, standing, and extended a hand to Margot.

She took it and slid her computer into her chair in her place. Wordlessly, Van led her to the other side of the tent, behind a stack of crates that shielded them from their classmates' prying eyes.

"We don't have to hide. Everyone knows we're dating, Van," she laughed. "It's not a secret."

He reached into his pocket. "No, but this is."

She didn't know what she expected—an actual piece of Cretan gold from Minos himself?—but it wasn't a bouquet of delicate white myrtles. Nestled in the blooms was a wax-sealed envelope with a familiar school crest.

"What is this?" The cardstock envelope was heavy, a thick ivory. Margot recognized the spilling maroon seal from her own Radcliffe acceptance letter. "*How* is this?"

Van rocked his weight between his feet. Nervous, almost. "Dr. Hunt wrote one hell of a recommendation letter since I'd never actually finished high school. And tuition's covered, all things considered."

Margot threw her arms around his neck, lifting onto her toes to reach. "You're seriously coming?" When he nodded, she squealed, squeezing tighter.

"Oh," he said casually as he pulled out a scroll and started walking down the alley between the ruins, "and there's this."

Margot ran, shaking her flowers and shouting after him, "You had a treasure map, and you didn't lead with that?"

"What?" Van asked, and she could hear the smile on his lips. "I thought you said girls like flowers."

"Girls are not a monolith!" she said, her feet pounding the cobbled pavement.

"I'm sure you'll keep on surprising me." Van sped up, even if he kept a hand in his pocket, pretending to be unbothered. But when he darted a glance over his shoulder, Margot saw the way he grinned.

Framed by the gauzy afternoon sunlight with laughter bubbling out of her as she chased Van through the ruins, a breathless kind of happiness took Margot by surprise—and it wasn't just the unexpected cardio. She was enough to be loved, exactly as she was.

And as Van caught her hand and twirled her into his arms, pressing a kiss to her lips, she knew that their happy ending was only the beginning.

ACKNOWLEDGMENTS

First and foremost, I'd like to thank Brendan Fraser. Obviously. The very first inkling of this book was an *Encino Man*-meets-*The Mummy* mash-up. So, thank you for helping Margot and Van find their footing.

To my editor, Sara Schonfeld, you are a guiding light I would be lost without. Thank you for your trust in me and for your unrivaled ability to know what I'm trying to say before I've found the words to say it. To everyone on the team at HarperTeen, thank you for working your transformative magic yet again. Turning sentences into books is a feat of wizardry I will always marvel at.

To Claire Friedman, superstar agent and constant voice of reason, I'm so grateful to have you by my side every step of the way. And to the entire team at InkWell Management, you have made my dreams come true again and again. I will never be able to say thank you enough for that.

To my critique-partners-turned-besties: Kara Kennedy, thank you for listening to every one of my waking thoughts and for being so psychically linked that I don't always have to say them out loud. Mackenzie Reed, there's no one else I'd rather navigate publishing with. From first pitch to finished manuscript, I'm so thankful we're on this ride together. Kahlan Strop, thank you for always being my extra set of eyes and a shoulder to cry on. (Sometimes literally.) I am a better writer and friend for knowing you all.

To Abby, Alex, Barb, Brit, Cassie, Crystal, Darcy, Helena, Holly, Juju, Kalla, Kat, Lindsey, Maria, Marina, Morgan, Olivia, Phoebe, Sam, Shay, Skyla, and Wajudah: Thank you, thank you, thank you. I'd never hoped that the writing group we started in 2020 would become home to me, but I'm so glad it did.

To Olivia Nash, this book might not have survived past the first draft if it weren't for your endless cheerleading and steadfast belief that Margot's story was worth writing. Thank you for excavating it with me. And to Abbey, Liz, Sarah, and Taylor—this book wouldn't have been finished or half as much fun without you (and Fido potatoes). I'm forever thankful that your friendship found me when I needed it most.

To Kaleigh, thank you for loving every version of me for the last twenty years. Your friendship is a wellspring of joy that never runs dry.

To Tyler and Alex, thank you for being my brothers. I know we didn't really have the choice, but given the chance, I'd choose you every time.

Thank you to my parents, Trey and Linda, for letting my imagination run wild, for wiping every tear, for every inside joke and every belly laugh, for introducing me to all my favorite movies, for every road trip sing-along—for every piece of you that makes me *me*.

And to Christopher, I'm grateful every day that I get to do this adventure with you. Thank you for your unfailing belief in me and for listening to (and somehow always solving) every plot hole. I love you *especially when*. You are my happily ever after.